PRAISE FOR *WELCOME TO NIGHT VALE: A NOVEL*

"This is a splendid, weird, moving novel about families, the difficulties of growing up, and the deep-seated vulnerabilities involved in raising children. It manages beautifully that trick of embracing the surreal in order to underscore and emphasize the real—not as allegory, but as affirmation of emotional truths that don't conform to the neat and tidy boxes in which we're encouraged to house them."
—NPR.org

"*Welcome to Night Vale* lives up to the podcast hype in every way. It is a singularly inventive visit to an otherworldly town that's the stuff of nightmares and daydreams." —*BookPage*

"Fink and Cranor's prose hints there's an empathetic humanity underscoring their well of darkly fantastic situations. . . . The book builds toward a satisfyingly strange exploration of the strange town's intersection with an unsuspecting real world." —*Los Angeles Times*

"The charms of *Welcome to Night Vale* are nearly impossible to quantify. That applies to the podcast, structured as community radio dispatches from a particularly surreal desert town, as well as this novel." —*Star Tribune (Minneapolis)*

"The book is charming and absurd—think *This American Life* meets *Alice in Wonderland*." —*Washington Post*

PRAISE FOR *IT DEVOURS!: A WELCOME TO NIGHT VALE NOVEL*

"Different from other mystery novels . . . as captivating and light as any mystery novel can be but explores one of the most complex issues: the conflict between science and reason on the one hand and, on the other hand, religion and cult."

—*Washington BookReview*

"Compelling. . . . A confident supernatural comedy from writers who can turn from laughter to tears on a dime."

—*Kirkus Reviews* (starred review)

"(A) smart exploration of the divide—and overlap—of science and religion. . . . A thrilling adventure and a fascinating argument that science and belief aren't necessarily mutually exclusive."

—Tor.com

"Very clever. . . . With a gripping mystery, a very smartly built world (a place similar to our own world but at the same time distinctly other), and a cast of offbeat characters, the novel is a welcome addition."

—*Booklist*

"A mysterious, must-read exploration of the Great Unknowns, with a touch of Carl Sagan and Agatha Christie."

—Marisha Pessl, *New York Times*–bestselling author of *Night Film* and *Special Topics in Calamity Physics*

WHO'S A GOOD BOY?

WHO'S A GOOD BOY?

Welcome to Night Vale
Episodes, Volume 4

JOSEPH FINK AND
JEFFREY CRANOR

HARPER PERENNIAL

NEW YORK • LONDON • TORONTO • SYDNEY • NEW DELHI • AUCKLAND

To Bandit, Bear, Brown, Bubbles, Emmy, Madison, Mariel, Miriam, Pepper, Webster, and all the future dogs in our lives

HARPER ● PERENNIAL

Illustrations by Jessica Hayworth.

HarperCollins books may be purchased for educational, business, or sales promotional use. For information, please email the Special Markets Department at SPsales@harpercollins.com.

FIRST EDITION

Library of Congress Cataloging-in-Publication Data has been applied for.

ISBN 978-0-06-279811-4

19 20 21 22 23   LSC   10 9 8 7 6 5 4 3 2 1

CONTENTS

FOREWORD

WELCOME TO *WELCOME TO NIGHT VALE*: A WELCOME

I.

MY FIRST ENCOUNTER WITH *WELCOME TO NIGHT VALE* WAS NOT through the podcast itself, but instead through their Twitter account. This was in the tail end of 2012, around the time I got interested in Twitter as a creative medium, and the *Welcome to Night Vale* Twitter account (@NightValeRadio) was one of the first ones that I fell in love with because it made me realize just how many different ways a medium like Twitter could be played with. Joseph and Jeffrey (or, whoever runs the Twitter account—I still don't know, to be honest!) were doing something really interesting with different recognizable formats—they were taking something familiar and turning it on its side and into another dimension.

Here's the first tweet of theirs I ever retweeted:

Today is a day to appreciate your family, to think about what you are grateful for, & to ignore that new shape in the sky & what it implies. (November 22, 2012)

Here's another favorite of mine, tweeted on New Year's Eve of 2012, which makes it even more strange, yet, somehow, also even more *accurate*:

Ask your doctor what all these deer are doing here.

They played with formats:

Knock knock. / Who's there? / [*hollow scraping sounds*] / [*hollow scraping sounds*]
Who? / [*hollow scraping sounds followed by shrieking*] (January 8, 2013)

Congratulations! You have won one (1) death. Please allow 1-100 years for delivery.
(July 16, 2013)

They tweeted things that made me pause and made me cry:

"Nobody knows what that thing is, or why it's there," says the scientist, pointing at
everything. (July 12, 2013)

When a person dies and no one will miss them, the mourning is assigned to a random human. This is why you sometimes just feel sad. (November 12, 2012)

Among everything that Night Vale is, there is this constant tension, this eternal play between the everyday and the never-have-I-
ever-in-my-life. It is this game of taking something wholly familiar
and quotidian and commonplace, mining it for its strangeness, and
then, once you are taken through to the other side of it and into an entirely foreign dimension, you see yourself in all the strangeness of the
ordinary and all the ordinariness of the strange. This is at the heart of
Night Vale. You can see this, as I did, even through their tweets.

Later (an embarrassingly long amount of time later), I found out
that this Twitter account was actually the companion to the podcast,
the first episode of which was released in early 2012. (Night Vale's
Twitter account's first tweet, on the other hand, came late in the
summer of 2012, and reads: "It is afternoon in America. It is double-noon in
Night Vale. Eat your oranges!" This was followed shortly after by: "To clarify:
you should only eat the light orange oranges. DO NOT EAT THE MEDIUM-LIGHT-ORANGE
oranges. Consequences. #psa.")

If their tweets contained the DNA of the game at play, then
the podcast is the expansive expression of that DNA. It's the shadowy and shapeless and slimy creature that DNA was taken from:
a community radio show, familiar in format, then flipped inward
and outward and through-ward, arriving at a place completely unfa-
miliar and uncanny and strange but still incredibly and deeply and

unsettlingly . . . human. To me that's always been the heart of Night Vale. It's easy to do strange; to do human is the real challenge.

II.

As the *Welcome to Night Vale* project grew, gathering momentum and size, first through the podcast, through the tweets, then, through the novels, the podcasting network, these script books, and more, my relationship to the people behind the podcast grew too. Through the Twitter account, I found out that Jeffrey and Joseph both had their own personal accounts. As I became more and more entranced by the work, I found out that, wow, so many of my favorite people were working within the Night Vale world: Mara Wilson! Dylan Marron! Maureen Johnson! Cecil Baldwin! Jessica Hayworth! Meg Bashwiner! And more and more! The more time I spent with Night Vale, the more I saw the community of artists and conspirators and contributors that made up the project, and who became the project, and who give life to the project. At its heart, *Welcome to Night Vale* is a community of people who want to make a thing together. That's what makes it so magical.

As I reflect on what Night Vale means to me, I realize the reason why it works. Why, for all of its potentially cold and alienating strangeness, there is instead a sweet and genuine and human strangeness to it is because of how sweet and genuine and human the people within it are. A few personal highlights of spending time with Joseph and Jeffrey and other Night Vale crew:

- Meeting Joseph and Jeffrey and Dylan and Mara and the rest of the live show group for the first time after a show in Toronto, where I found them at a poutine place, and we mainly talked about our favorite joke formats on Twitter.
- Joseph insisting I take his tickets to go see the Neo-Futurists (the New York off-Broadway theater group where Jeffrey and

Joseph first met) when I was passing through New York for the evening a few years ago. It was watching that show and seeing, like Night Vale, a delightful and human and strange thing put on by a bunch of artists, who loved it and believed in it, that I understood where that spirit within Night Vale came from.

- Jeffrey coming to a book talk of mine when we were both co-incidentally in Seattle at the same time, and seeing his face in the crowd and feeling instantly supported and seen and no longer nervous to do the book talk.

- When I was worried about how to go about doing my own first book, I called Joseph and Jeffrey for advice and they told me everything they had learned, on preparing submissions, submitting to agents, talking to publishers, choosing a pub-lisher (hello, Harper Perennial, aka mom to both myself and Night Vale!), and more. It seems like whatever my next cre-ative step is, Joseph and Jeffrey are a few steps in front of me, and wholly excited about sharing what they've learned. I'm ex-tremely grateful for that generosity.

- When I hosted Dylan Marron for a conversation at the MIT Humor Series at the Media Lab in the spring of 2016, a direc-tor of one of the groups at the Media Lab was so excited that Dylan was coming and we added him to the event so we could all be in conversation with Dylan—Night Vale has fans even among the directors at the MIT Media Lab, it turns out!

- Moderating a book talk with them for *It Devours!*, and focusing the discussion around the follies of religion—the event was held inside a church.

- Hanging out with other Night Vale folks, like Maureen and Mara and Dylan, around the world, during chance encounters and finding out we were at the same events—New York, Van-couver, Melbourne, and all over! It feels like there is always someone in the Night Vale family around.

I see all these people as my friends now, and I have to remember that my relationship to them all started from *Welcome to Night Vale* first. And all this comes down to Joseph and Jeffrey, who had the idea to make the thing in the first place. I admire them as artists who made a thing, and through it built a community: of artists, of friends, of listeners and readers.

III.

WHAT YOU ARE HOLDING IS JUST WORDS. WORDS ON A PAGE. BUT WITHout them, none of this would exist. These are the words that everything gets built from, and builds upon.

These words are the starting point, and I hope that by reading them, they illustrate the difference between just the words and the entirety of the world and community built around the words. This is in no way to disparage or discount the words at all—rather, I hope this collection shows just how a community of artists and listeners and readers rallies around the words to make Night Vale real. This collection is a testament to the words, as the utmost necessary foundation to all of this, and all the things that grow and are built from the foundation.

I owe a great deal to the community they've grown. I suspect that you may, or perhaps one day *might*, owe a great deal to their words as well. In one of my comparative media studies classes at MIT, I saw the teaching assistant wearing a Night Vale shirt and instantly felt a sense of belonging and kinship to them. This is just another very small example out of a sea of examples of the power of the community of listeners, readers, admirers that they've built through their work.

Every time I go to a Night Vale event in person (whether it's a live show, a reading, or a book talk that I get to moderate), I am in awe of that feeling of community among strangers, united by their love of a thing together. And every time I come across that community online, there is something powerful about it that you can feel through the screen.

And maybe that's even more important. While the live events are discrete expressions of the community around Night Vale, the real everyday community exists on the internet, and grew from the internet. It's where the work of Night Vale lives and where it came from. I think it's important and exciting to recognize that Night Vale is, at its heart, an independent project, one that was born into this Wild West of the internet, and one that has found its home among its online denizens. And every time I come across that community online, I feel just as connected to the work, and the artists, and to the community, as I do at those live events.

That's special, and delightful, and wonderful, and rare. And even rarer, it's a community that's inclusive and diverse, something that is reflected in their characters, stories, and words.

Despite its absurdity, or maybe because of, what shines through are the very human relationships, the sense of community, the importance of people. Jeffrey and Joseph center and respect characters who are rarely centered and respected in stories like this. That's what has always grounded this and made it special. Complementing all the strangeness, they are dedicated to our relationships to ourselves and to others. *Welcome to Night Vale* illuminates that, and shines a light on the most important things in our worlds that we hold dear and close to our hearts within our hearts.

Spending time with what Joseph and Jeffrey have made and continue to make makes me realize something else, too. Perhaps the most important part of *Welcome to Night Vale* isn't the "Night Vale" part at all. Rather, it's the first word that means the world to me.

Welcome.

> —Jonny Sun, over the course of being
> on a number of different planes traveling
> between a number of different cities, 2018

INTRODUCTION

THIS BOOK COVERS THE EPISODES AND LIVE SHOWS THAT *WELCOME TO Night Vale* performed from June 2015 to June 2016. Those twelve months were an eventful time for both the show and for me personally. I will present that year to you not as a narrative, which our lives so rarely are, but as what it felt like: a series of events, one right after another, without necessarily any connection other than the people they were all happening to.

In June 2015, I got married. Meg is the tour manager and emcee of the *Welcome to Night Vale* live show, and the voice of the credits at the end of every episode. She's also the love of my life, and by the time we got married, we had been together for six years. We got married on our anniversary, so we wouldn't have to switch anniversary dates. We're efficient people. The ceremony itself was simple, done in the living room of our Brooklyn apartment, with only our immediate family in attendance and officiated by Dylan Marron, voice of Carlos the scientist. We have a taxidermy goat head on our wall, and because a Brooklyn apartment doesn't have a great deal of room, we ended up getting married under the goat head. From then on, we started referring to the goat head as "the goat of our love."

In September, we did our second ever UK live tour. We played shows in Leeds and Cardiff, and ended with a three-night run at a centuries-old church in London. Meg, after a brutally long year of touring, earned Hilton Diamond status at a DoubleTree near the venue.

Also in September, we released the first *Night Vale* novel. Stepping away from the list for a moment, to expand on this:

I have wanted to be a writer since I was four years old. Before that, I wanted to be a storyteller, the kind who shows up at children's fairs and assemblies at elementary school. Once I learned that there was a very similar kind of job called a writer, and that they wrote something called novels, I decided, *Sure, I'll do that*, and started planning out the novels I would write. The first I came up with was called *The Traveler*, a series of brick-size epics I was planning about a purple-caped hero going about a vaguely Medieval world, righting wrongs and being cool as heck. Later, when I was twelve, after abandoning *The Traveler* series as childish, I planned out a story about a culture of people who had lived on old-timey wooden sailing ships for centuries, never touching land, and who made a living by seizing and looting modern cruise ships. There was to be a touching romance between a young woman who grew up on the sailing ships and a young man who was a passenger on one of the cruises. I think I got about five pages of that one done.

Through all of this though, the basic goal never wavered: write novels.

A few decades later, *Welcome to Night Vale* blew up and we suddenly had a "popular internet thing." What happens when you have a "popular internet thing" is that you get a lot of emails from companies asking if they can please cash in on your "popular internet thing." Most of those emails didn't interest us much, but the emails from publishers absolutely did. Jeffrey and I decided we wanted to write a novel, a new story, never told in the podcasts. In Harper

Perennial we found a lovely group of people who understood and shared our excitement.

Of course, we then had to write a novel. Jeffrey and I get asked a lot about the difference between writing a podcast and a novel, and the answer sounds flippant but isn't: a novel is a whole lot longer. A novel is so long. Think of a long thing to write. A novel is longer than that. Thinking out a story on that scale, and then the sheer daily drudgery of hitting the word goals week after week, these were new challenges. But they were exciting challenges, even in their occasional tedium. We were getting to make something we had both always wanted to make.

The release of the novel was a series of surreal experiences. Opening a box of finished books and realizing that this story we told was actually going to be printed and sold in stores. Seeing the book in a store. Being interviewed on Stephen Colbert's show (I was completely calm until the commercial break before our segment as I waited in the wings, at which point I suddenly was more nervous than I've ever been in my life). Seeing our names on the *New York Times* bestseller list (we received the news while eating at a delicious Chinese food truck in Portland; I still go back to that truck when I find myself in the city, and eat my bestseller lunch).

In December of that year, Meg and I moved to a house in the woods of upstate New York. The closest neighbor is a half mile away. There is no better ballast to the chaos of touring than a house where the nights are utterly silent and the Catskill Mountains are visible without having to get out of bed.

In January 2016, we toured the live show to New Zealand and Australia for the first time ever, flying some twenty hours from northern hemisphere winter to southern hemisphere summer. I remember one night, before the Perth show, we ate a barbecue picnic prepared for us by our booking agent on the beach at sunset as a pod of dolphins swam by. And we all had to ask each other: *How had a podcast gotten us here?* I'm still not sure. I only know what happened, not why.

In March, we did a book tour to Germany, as an actor read the translation of our novel to audiences while we politely nodded along to say, "No, we don't understand, but we believe this is probably close to what we wrote." The actor, we were told many times in these specific words, was "the German Ed Norton."

And in June, Meg and I celebrated our first wedding anniversary, and seven years together. We didn't go anywhere special. We didn't take a big trip. For once, for once, we stayed home. It was wonderful.

The twelve months covered by this book were busy and often stressful. But it was the busy and stressful I had always wanted. What do you do when you achieve your dreams? I guess you put your head down and get to work making more dreams.

—Joseph Fink

EPISODE 71:
"THE REGISTRY OF MIDDLE SCHOOL CRUSHES"

AUGUST 1, 2015

BOY AM I GLAD TO BE STARTING THE BOOK WITH THIS EPISODE. THIS IS one of my absolute favorites. Many of our favorite episodes are memorable to us because they have some kind of specific concept that made the writing of them tricky. Or they often have unusual structures, cool guest voices, multiple parts. But this episode is none of that. The only voice in it is our central narrator. There is no other file you need to download to get the story. The structure follows our usual Night Vale format, with the narrative scattered among other town news and bits of radio business, then coming to a head after the weather. So this episode remains a favorite for a simple reason: I think it's a really good story and I'm glad we told it.

If you haven't heard or read the episode, please do that first. Because I don't know how to talk about this episode without spoiling it.

There are few story formats more tempting to the writer than the heist. It's like a mystery, but even better because instead of working to discover a culprit, the culprit is introduced from the start as our hero and the problem we are trying to piece together is the most interesting part: just how are they planning to pull off this crime.

So I knew that I wanted to start this year of Night Vale off with a heist. But of course in order to have a heist, you need a clever plan. And those are tricky to come up with. I don't have a natural thriller writer's mind, and so finding a way to have all the pieces come together wasn't easy for me. And the format of a monologue makes the whole thing even trickier. There's a reason that there are many classic heist movies but not so many classic heist novels. To make things worse, by the very premise of our show, everything that Cecil is saying is being broadcast live to everyone in town. How do you set up a heist of a heavily protected vault when all the information is being given out in real time to the people guarding that vault?

The breakthrough came when I realized that the key to the heist needed to be in its weakest element. The fact that the information was open to everyone needed to be the central part of the plan. And so the entire heist became a lie hidden under a familiar narrative of heist ingenuity. Which essentially meant I needed to write two heists: an outer one that seemed busy enough to be plausible, and an inner one in which the actual heist would take place.

In this way it becomes not just a heist, but a heist of storytelling. For a show that has always ultimately been about a single voice telling you a story, it seemed very fitting that the beating heart of this crime would be the story that Cecil was telling.

And of course this episode also starts to develop Janice as her own character. She had been there before, but we really wanted her to start having her own problems, her own motivations, and her own endings. Why did she need to steal the Registry of Middle School Crushes? I might have a few guesses, but ultimately her reasons are her own, and I respect her privacy.

—Joseph Fink

I trip the light fantastic. And then I offer to help it up, and when the light fantastic is halfway up, I let go and it falls again. Me and the light fantastic do not get along at all.

WELCOME TO NIGHT VALE

To start us off, a follow-up on a recent story. Local ne'er-do-well and five-headed dragon Hiram McDaniels will be brought to trial for his attempts to assassinate Mayor Cardinal and take over Night Vale city government.

This trial is already being referred to as the Trial of the Century, and indeed could be referred to as the Trial of All Time, because Night Vale has never had a trial before. Judicial matters are usually handled directly by the Secret Police, whose judgment is above question, even when it's really bad and obviously wrong. Or, in some extreme cases, handled by the City Council itself, who might relegate the wrongdoer to detention in the Abandoned Mine Shaft outside of town, or might just eat the wrongdoer. It depends on whether the City Council has had a heavy lunch.

But Hiram McDaniels is huge, and a dragon, so the City Council and the Secret Police are both declining to get too close to him. As a result, for the first time ever, we will have a fair and open trial here in Night Vale in front of a jury of Hiram's peers. Speaking of which, Night Vale invites any dragons to come down to the

courthouse to serve as his peers. Failing that, any multiheaded beings are welcome, although I can't immediately think of any of those
except obviously deer, and deer can't take part in juries because of
their profound belief in egalitarian anarchism.

Pamela Winchell, former Night Vale mayor and current director
of Emergency Press Conferences, will serve as the prosecuting attorney, and Hiram's gold head will be acting in his own defense, as well
as the defense of the other three heads accused. His fifth head, the
violet one, who had secretly been working to stop the other heads,
is not charged and is expected to take the witness stand against his
same-bodied brethren.

Updates on this exciting legal story will continue, as we all try
to figure out what law means outside of the context of the despotic
control of shadowy government forces.

And now, listeners, from matters of news to matters of personal
urgency, I present to you a heist. Here is the mission: to retrieve a
top secret document. Here are the players: myself, of course, mind-
ful speaker in the mindless night; Carlos, scientist extraordinaire,
extraordinary scientist, great hair; Steve Carlsberg, jerk, good father
maybe, don't tell him that; Abby, my sister, whom I have not spoken
with in quite a while but whom I am hoping to speak with more;
Old Woman Josie, opera aficionada and friends with powerful and
forbidden beings who are handy with a lockpick and who claim to
know a thing or two about hacking.

Finally and foremost, of course, little Janice, my niece, and the
second most important person in my life. She is the leader of our
mission. She is the reason we are all involved.

This then is the team. Here then is the target. City Hall, specifically the Hall of Public Records. One of the most secure and
dangerous places in Night Vale, where all public information is kept
hidden from a public that might misuse it. Few have gone in and

survived. No one has ever managed to remove or even view a single document from it.

So why are we trying? Why risk our lives to do what is, by all accounts, impossible? Because within that Hall of Records is the Registry of Middle School Crushes, a ledger that documents every slight swoon of our young citizens' lovesick hearts. This registry, like all municipal documents, is constantly updated via invasive satellite mind-scanning.

Janice wants us to retrieve the Registry of Middle School Crushes and destroy it. I will not ask why. We don't have to ask why. We know that a family member is in need, and we act accordingly. The plan? Ah, ah, but that would give it away. More soon, whether the powers that be like it or not.

First, a word from our sponsors.

Today's sponsor is VenomBox, the subscription service that sends you a box of venomous creatures every month. Last month's theme was Hidden But Deadly, and those who survived that will love this month's theme, Fanged and Impossibly Quick.

VenomBox has been sending me samples and boy, have I almost died.

I have almost died a lot. They are very dangerous, these boxes. Each individually curated VenomBox is literally a box of toxic and aggressive creatures. That's what they are.

It's not even a secure box. It's a hastily constructed cardboard box. Often the creatures escape before you can open the VenomBox. The only thing worse than opening a box to find venomous creatures inside is opening a box that is supposed to have venomous creatures inside and instead finding nothing. Then looking around your home, feeling . . . is that a tickle on your toe? You were imagining that, right?

To get a free sample, just do nothing. Or try to prevent it. Actively try to keep the VenomBox out. It doesn't matter. Whatever you do, you are subscribed to VenomBox every month from here on out. Good luck.

This has been a word from our sponsors.

And now traffic.

A woman walks into a bar. Presumably she did not just appear there. Presumably she opened the door from the outside and entered it. Presumably she drove to the bar. Presumably she had obtained the car she used to drive to the bar somewhere, presumably with money. Presumably she had received that money somehow. She presumably had spent days, months, even years before this moment. Presumably she was born at some point, to a mother, presumably. Presumably she was a child once. There had been years spent in which she could not completely feed herself. There were years in which she was smaller, and stayed all day in rooms where adults taught her to be similar adults to the adults they were. There was a first kiss. Nights spent in terror of the nights to come. The first vestiges of independence. Moving out. Finding a job. A decision, at some point to go the bar. Presumably.

"Can I have a drink?" she said to the bartender.

"Oh, I'm sorry," said the bartender. "This is the end of my shift.

Ed will be out in a moment and he'll be able to help you." The bartender left the bar.

Presumably he opened the door. Presumably he got into a car. Presumably he drove home, the radio on and playing him through the soft focus darkness of the hot night. Presumably he had a bed somewhere, got into it, slept, and, presumably, dreamed. Presumably he grew older, day by day, and looked at each day as a missed opportunity to live a life that was in no way better than the life he was living, but just different. Presumably he edged toward death, fearing losing what he had, regretting ever attaining it. There was a last kiss. Everything was forgotten, but in pieces, and in the most painful order. New things were learned, slowly, and in the least helpful order. A basket of fruit, indicating a sentiment too weak, communicated too late, to a person who was already gone. Presumably.

This has been traffic.

Back to the main event. Plans run apace for our heist from the City Hall Public Records room. The obstacles are grave and myriad. First, there is simply getting past the guard at the door of City Hall. The guard doesn't stop anyone, so as I said, getting past is simple.

Then there is avoiding the City Council, who lurk within City Hall, a manyform municipal entity, waiting for citizens to civically devour. We will have to tread carefully to avoid it.

Then, there are the stairs to the basement, where the records are kept. These are very dangerous. Thousands of people die falling down stairs every year. So we will have to take care not to trip.

Beyond that is the thick vault door, combination unknown, immune to detonation or heat. Rumor has it that the door to the Records room could survive a nuclear explosion. Rumor has it that it already has.

Past the door, information becomes more piecemeal. Rumor becomes our only guide. There is apparently a grid of lasers, carefully calibrated so as to look mesmerizing and cause an intruder to stop and watch them, thus failing to complete her mission. There are pressure sensors in the floor, heat sensors in the wall, thought sensors in all of our brains. The security is diabolical. But we have devised a plan past all of it. Which, again, I can't tell you. I'm sorry. Saying the plan on the radio would make it tricky to successfully perform it without being caught. But it's really good, I promise.

We will make sure Janice gets the Registry of Middle School Crushes so she can destroy it. We just will never be able to tell you how.

And now the answer to last week's audio "Spot the Differences" Quiz.

Of course, the two audio scenes we set for you were quite similar, perhaps even, at an aural glance, identical, but there were eight specific differences. Did you spot them all?

Let's find out. Here were the differences:

1. The shadow of the howling man is smiling in one scene but missing in the other.
2. There are shrouded figures in the grass in both scenes, and they look identical, but in the first scene they are watching while in the second scene they are listening.
3. Only the first scene scares me.
4. The cow has one extra spot in the first scene.
5. The cow has all of its blood in the first scene.
6. The howling man is howling in both scenes.
7. We don't know why he is howling.
8. Maybe it's because of his shadow.
9. What does the second man have to do with anything?
10. The child is absent from both scenes.

How did you do? If you missed any, don't worry. The Secret Police will be arriving soon to take you to a reeducation camp, and after that you definitely won't be messing up any more puzzles or messing up anything or even doing anything ever again.

Oh, I just can't resist. Our brilliant plan is too brilliant not to share. I mean, it doesn't even matter that much I guess because the plan is already in motion. What could the powers that be possibly do?

So first Old Woman Josie had her beings who cannot legally be called angels hack the thought sensors and the mind-scanning satellites so that instead of playing our current thoughts, they play a loop of thoughts about which sandwich place is our favorite (obviously the Mario's Very Authentic Italian Ice Cream Sub Sandwich place at the mall. Obviously).

Then Abby, Steve, and Carlos all simply walked past the guard. Again, the guard doesn't stop anyone. Simple.

Abby used a series of mirrors and clip-lights in the doorway to City Council chambers to create the illusion of an empty hallway for the monstrous municipal members within, thus allowing the wonderful Carlos and the foolish . . . ly brave Steve to go down the stairs, carefully and without tripping.

Those two and those two alone entered the basement. There Carlos used a mathematical formula that he had arrived at scientifically to deduce the combination of the great vault door. Once inside, of course, Carlos would become instantly fascinated by the laser grid, determined to understand it, which was why it was Steve's important job to keep him focused and moving.

They then put on harnesses which Janice had spent the last several weeks making from a home cat burglar kit she got as a prize in a box of Honey Nut Flakey O's, and which she had lined with bags of frozen peas to throw off the heat sensors.

And that is where they are now, dear listeners, creeping ever closer to the Registry of Middle School Crushes and to a triumphant end to a triumphant plan. Nothing can . . . oh no. Somehow it seems that the City Council has discovered the plan. I don't know how that could have happened. Steve and Carlos are still in the basement, still in danger. Still right behind the closed vault door. Where can they run? How can they hide? I will try to sort out what to do, and in the meantime, I must take you to the weather.

WEATHER: "My Postcard" by Toys and Tiny Instruments

We have returned, listeners, to a heist complete. This was not a heist of action at all. It was not a heist of diamond-tipped drills or advanced electronics.

No, this was a heist of words. A heist of fiction. It was a heist of storytelling, and it was magnificent.

For there was no hacking by Josie and her friends. No mirror held by Abby. No absurd mathematical formula devised by Carlos. And no Steve. Thank God. No Steve. There was none of that.

Carlos, Old Woman Josie, Abby, and Steve are safe at home, never having left their beds in this warm, still night.

I created their action, I created their danger with my words, and I delivered that danger to you. That was the entire plan, all of it. It was me, here at this microphone, telling you a story. A story about a successful entrance to the well-protected vault of the Hall of Public Records. And in response to my story, the City Council rushed to the records hall, flung open that vault door, deactivated the sensors and alarms, and charged in to capture Steve and Carlos. But those two were, of course, not there to be captured.

The only person who was there, having avoiding the danger of stairs by safely taking the ADA-compliant elevator down and having waited patiently in the shadows for the City Council to rush by, enraged, and open the door of the vault for her, was a very clever eleven-year-old in a stealth wheelchair of her own design. She waited, and when they had passed, she followed quietly after them. And while they searched, roaring, for intruders that weren't there, she slipped the

Registry of Middle School Crushes from its shelf, rolled herself back to the elevator, and was gone before the council had even an inkling that they were chasing only figments of my imagination.

It was, despite all of my misleading words, a two-person heist. An uncle, who can tell one hell of a story. And a niece, who can come up with one hell of a plan.

Janice took the registry out into the scrublands, and there, in an arroyo that has not seen water in many years, she lit it on fire and watched the smoke pass up through the evergreen leaves of the Joshua trees.

I don't need to know why she wanted it destroyed, although perhaps I could guess. But I won't guess. I only know that she needed my help, and so I helped her.

Before everything, before even humans, there were stories. A creature at a fire, conjuring a world with nothing but its voice and the listener's imagination. And now me, and thousands like me, in little booths and rooms, at mics and screens, all over the world, doing the same for a family of listeners, connected, as all families are, primarily by the stories we tell each other. And after: after fire and death or whatever else next, after the wiping clean or the gradual decay, after the after, when there are only a few creatures left, there will be one at a fire, telling a story, to what family it has left.

It was the first thing and it will be the last.

Stay tuned next for more stories being told to you, all of the time, whether you are aware of them or not.

And from whatever fiction it is that we happen to be living together tonight, Good night, Night Vale, Good night.

PROVERB: I had a dream in which cow-sized pugs existed. I was on a train, and one loped along outside my window. I'm sorry your dreams aren't as good.

EPISODE 72:
"WELL OF NIGHT"

AUGUST 15, 2015

GUEST VOICE: MEG BASHWINER (DEB)

I REMEMBER JOSEPH TALKING ABOUT HIS IDEA BEHIND WRITING EPISODE 13: "Wheat and Wheat By-Products." He had that title first—just a phrase stuck in his head—and then he began to write something that used that phrase.

That's what "Well of Night" was for me. It's rhythmic and a touch mysterious. I played it on repeat in my head, like a verbal GIF file. Well of night. Well of night. Well of night. Sometimes it was a constant whisper. Sometimes a distant chant. Sometimes it crescendoed like an atonal *Bolero*.

So in an effort to exterminate the earworm, I wrote an episode about it.

Also, there's a joke in this episode about David Mamet's *Oleanna*. I don't recommend reading or viewing or (please, god, no) staging this play. If you enjoy reading or listening to *Welcome to Night Vale*, I'll tell you that *Oleanna* is the opposite of that.

It's fast-paced, dialogue-heavy, and it never savors the funny, the divine, or the gentle.

I watched a touring production of that play in college in the late 1990s. It's about sexual harassment, abuse of power, and the whole he-said/she-said approach to storytelling. It's a two-hander featuring only a female university student and a middle-aged male professor.

Spoiler alert, it doesn't really hold up to 2019 criticism. I didn't think it held up to 1997 examination well either, to be honest. Anyway, in this episode, I describe a much better version of the play, because I can do that. I don't mean to be flippant about our conversations around consent, power, and sexual assault. I do, however, mean to be flippant about David Mamet's conversations around those issues.

Anyway, let's all enjoy a bit more juggling and a lot less shouty, interrupted dialogue between wholly unlikable characters.

—Jeffrey Cranor

Kill it with kindness. And if that fails,
kill it with sharp sticks or knives.

WELCOME TO NIGHT VALE

I didn't sleep well last night. I imagine none of you slept well last night, what with all the chanting and stomping. I could see from my window a stark white V opening skyward just to the south of our apartment. Within its inverted cone, long shadows cutting in and out, a vertical static. I could hear a distant, repeated chant. Bum bum BUM. Bum bum BUM. Something like that.

Again, that's not so unusual. When you live in a city long enough, you get used to the nighttime noise of car alarms, or howls of stray cats, or the occasional carolers crouching by your front door singing about some new god they invented in a nightclub. It's basic urban life.

But this chant was different. I first heard only the shouts of one or two people. Bah dah BAH. Bah dah BAH. Whatever the chant was. I figured they were simply college kids who discovered some dinosaur bones, which I understand is a thing college kids are all into these days.

Carlos was able to sleep through the sounds. (He can sleep through anything—alarm clocks, heavy construction, even that godawful screeching the sunrise makes.) But I was in and out of light sleep all night. By just before dawn the handful of chanters had grown to a large crowd. What was that chant? Wah wah WAH. Wah wah WAH. I couldn't tell, but there must have been dozens of them.

Well, hopefully they keep it down tonight. Let's have a look now at the community calendar.

Wednesday night, the staff of Dark Owl Records will be holding a séance to try to reach the ghost of Taylor Swift. They'll be lighting candles and holding hands and playing Swift's newest album, *1879*, which was named after the year she was born into a human body for the fifteenth time.

Record shop owner Michelle Nguyen said it's important that they get hold of Swift's ghost so they can ask her detailed questions about what kind of music she was into back then because the Dark Owl staff is running out of music that no one else has heard of. They want to find music that no longer exists so they can get into that.

Nguyen also wants to trash-talk Emile Berliner, who was Swift's ex-boyfriend and who totally stole Swift's idea to invent the gramophone. "He hated music," Nguyen said. "He had some pretty fly ties, so, like, I could see him inventing a pocket square. But not a turntable. Ugh. Did I just use the word *fly*?" Nguyen added.

The séance will be from 10:00 P.M. to 2:00 A.M. and there will be a live DJ, snacks, whispering, and darkness.

Thursday afternoon, the Night Vale Community Players will hold auditions for their fall production of David Mamet's *Oleanna*. Director Shaundra Richardson wants to take a fresh approach to this controversial play, stating that she plans on removing all of the words and stage directions, instead simply presenting a stage full of actors juggling and/or eating things like candles and fruit and rodents.

Richardson says that the original 1992 play took a literal approach to the broad topics of gender and power, and she wants to find a more challenging, metaphorical approach to this difficult material. "Talking in English directly about a subject is a very 1990s thing to do. I think we can update this story by stripping it of language and narrative and just juggling and eating things," Richardson said.

Hopeful actors should meet at 2:00 P.M. at the Rec Center and bring their own candles and rodents. Fruit will be provided. No previous acting experience or understanding of any specific language is necessary.

Friday night is the Night Vale Alive! Fireworks Spectacular put on each month by a vague yet menacing government agency. Representatives for the event, speaking through other representatives who we met in disguise using code names in an undisclosed location, said this month's Fireworks Spectacular promises to be the largest and most exciting of the year. You won't want to miss it, the representative whispered from behind a granite-colored Dodge Grand Caravan. But unfortunately, the representative added, you will have to miss it because it is a covert and secret fireworks show. Everyone must stay inside and close all doors and window coverings.

So prepare a picnic and gather the family into the panic room this Friday night.

Saturday is already over before it's even begun. Where does the time go? That's not even a metaphor. This coming Saturday ended weeks ago, and no one knows where it went or why.

An update on last evening's weird lights and chanting, I'm getting word that the gathering of chanters was down by the old well in the south of town. Of course, we all know the old well. It's that well that inexplicably appeared a few days ago. We call it the old well, because it's been a really long week this week, what with getting back from vacation and returning to work and school. Plus it's been superhot here this August. We're all just kind of over it. So, like two or three days, feels like ages. That well's been there basically *forever*.

Apparently a couple of people noticed that after sunset, the well emanates a bright light. As they approached the well, their eyes and hair disappeared and they began whispering "Well of Night" to passersby. They kept repeating the whisper "Well of Night" to anyone who would listen, but given that it is bad luck to acknowledge a stranger, most people hurried by without paying too close attention.

Eventually, someone pulled their car over near the well and asked the whisperers for directions to Chipotle. The whisperers replied "Well of Night," and in a blink, the car was gone and the driver was standing next to the two whisperers, equally eyeless, equally hairless. All three of them shouting "Well of Life! Well of Life!" The three of them then did a series of moderate calisthenics, where they took large skipping steps, bringing their knees up to their chests and twirling their arms as straight sticks in conflicting circles above their heads.

Or maybe this wasn't calisthenics but ritual dancing. I'm not sure. Both are important parts of a solid daily health regimen.

More on this as it develops but first a look at today's traffic.

There's an accident on Galloway Road beneath the overpass of Route 800. Everyone is very sorry about what happened. They didn't mean for it to turn out like this. They didn't mean for anything to turn out like it did. It was totally an accident and everyone apologizes profusely. Can you try to understand how something like this could happen to anyone? Can you try to forgive them? Can you?

Emergency crews are on hand to help clear debris and to offer hugs and empathy to all those affected, directly and indirectly.

Moving on, there's congestion in downtown right now because of construction, narrowing Somerset down to a single lane. The Sheriff's Secret Police has sent traffic cops down there to shout and scowl and point, which has helped considerably. It's actually made the traffic worse, but everyone in the traffic feels stronger, more emotionally prepared to deal with adversity than they were before getting in their cars.

Tunnels and bridges are completely clear this hour, as they are most hours, because they're either totally secret or off-limits to

public use. But today they're especially clear of even the black se-
dans, armored vehicles, and windowless vans that normally clog
those roadways.

Listeners, the Night Vale Highway Department would like to
remind you to buckle up. Then to hunker down. Then to forget everything. Then to remember everything. Then to open your eyes to
what's really going on. Don't you see what's really going on? The
Highway Department would like to call you all sheeple. Sheeple,
they scowl as they roll their eyes. This has been a public service announcement from the Night Vale Highway Department.

Here now with a message from today's sponsor is Deb, a sentient patch of haze. Hi, Deb.

DEB: Hi, human broadcaster. Hello, mortal listeners. It's back-to-
school time again, and the kids still need new clothes, bags, lunches,
falconry gear, rappelling equipment, and other basic school supplies.
So much stuff. Where will you find time to go to all of those stores?
Well you don't have to go to a bunch of different stores. You only
need one store: Joann Fabrics.
CECIL: Cool, I thought Joann Fabrics only sold fabrics.
DEB: That's simply untrue. Why would you even say that?
CECIL: Well, I just assumed from the name that Joann Fab——
DEB: Stop talking.

   [*pause*]

Joann Fabrics welcomes any parent too overwhelmed by school
or life or parenthood or whatever. Anything. Maybe you're afraid of
flying and you have to get on a plane soon. The threat is real, you
know.
CECIL: I think planes are actually much safer—
DEB: Oh my god, Cecil. Can we have a conversation for once?
CECIL: You're right. I'm sorry, Deb. I mean the thing is Joann Fabrics

does fabrics better than anyone. So a creative person could make clothes and bags and all kinds of stuff for their kids.

DEB: You're obsessed with fabrics.

CECIL: Well—

DEB: Fine. Go on about your fabrics. What do I care about petty human concerns?

CECIL: Carlos bought a nice batik at Joann recently. It's got . . . um.

DEB: You don't know what a batik is.

CECIL: I don't.

BOOMING VOICE: Joann Fabrics.

DEB: Aah! Who the heck is that?

CECIL: I don't know. I've never heard that voice before.

BOOMING VOICE: For all your back-to-school needs.

DEB: Oh my god. That's really weird.

CECIL: It is.

BOOMING VOICE: Jooooaaaaannnnnn

DEB: I'm outta here.

BOOMING VOICE: Faaaaaabrrriiiiics

CECIL: Bye, Deb.

Listeners, I'm just getting word that right this moment the old well has begun to cast a ray of darkness upward. As the sun reached its apex, darkness cut across the bright day in a thin long V. The chanters, whose numbers have apparently grown into the high hundreds, are doing their strange dance or exercise around the well and chanting.

More and more are joining this throng. I'm being told that all of their eyes are completely overgrown with skin and that their hair doesn't actually fall out. Apparently each hair retreats rapidly back into their heads like a scared worm.

I can see from my studio that tall funnel of black against the blue sky. I can faintly hear the chanting. There it is. Wah wah WAH. Wah wah WAH. That's it. That is the chanting I heard last night. Well of Night. Well of Life. Well of Night. Well of Life.

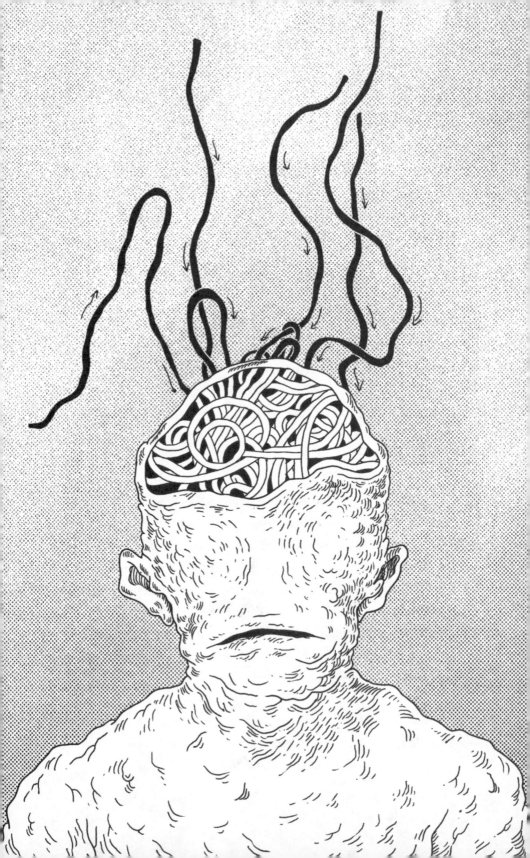

Listeners, I can feel the power of the chant. I can feel my hair shortening, reentering my scalp. Oh that feels so . . . ugh . . . so . . . rewarding. Well of Night. Well of Life. My eyes are being covered in skin but suddenly I can see so much. More than I ever thought was possible. I must go to this well. With the well, I will see everything! [*growing more and more off mic*] Well of Night. Well of Life. Well of Night. Well of Life. Well of Night. Well of Life. Well of Night. Well of Life. Well of Night. Well of Life. [*door slams*]

[*long-ish silence; door opens; Cecil returns to the mic*]

I almost forgot. Here's today's weather. [*shouting and leaving again*] Well of Night. Well of Life. Well of Ni——

WEATHER: "Children of God" by AJJ

Oh wow. What fun that was, Night Vale. Those Well of Life people are wild but so sweet.

I was a bit nervous at first because it's been years since I've been unwillingly inducted into a cult or chanting circle. I kind of thought I'd get there and everyone would see how out of practice I was. And boy, if you saw my kick steps, you'd know I hadn't done a jumping jack or prayer dance in forever.

But here comes old Cecil with his hair withdrawn and eyes covered in flesh, ripe for the teasing, and they welcomed me without judgment or hesitations. I wasn't two steps into their circle before someone drew blood from my neck and everyone cheered. What fun! Then someone else turned into a birdlike animal (a little furrier than a normal bird) and we all followed it into the well.

And down in that well, we all chanted until the bird person touched each of our foreheads with its bird hoof or whatever birds call their feet. And some of us joined hands and droned for a little

bit. A few others were watching baseball highlights. And a few more were enjoying the hummus someone had made.

Then I was back here, skin covering gone from my eyes, hair returned to my scalp. The only thing different is that I'm now wearing a black plastic poncho, cat ears, and yellow galoshes. This was definitely not what I wore to work, as I do not own yellow galoshes. They're orange. Well, I dunno. These are kind of orangeish. The lighting in my studio is weird. Maybe these boots are mine. I'm wearing exactly what I was wearing before, I think.

Anyway, I met some amazing people today. People I don't remember anything about except the feeling of love and acceptance I felt when I was with them. Their faces and bodies are blurs. But for a short time we all chanted and did aerobics as one. We all mattered to each other even though we knew we didn't matter at all. That seems wrong, I know, but two conflicting things can exist simultaneously. And they did. And it was a great moment. One I will cherish. And one I hope to never have again, because it would be ruined by the unattainable perfection of nostalgia.

The old well is gone now. In its place a barely noticeable bulge in the earth, slightly pink, and soft to the touch. The Parks Department has already erected a historic plaque to commemorate the well. The plaque reads: "Nothing unusual happened here or will happen here. You have been photographed reading this plaque. What were you hoping to learn?"

Stay tuned next for less of what you once were but more of what you think you are.

Good night, Night Vale. Good night.

PROVERB: When someone says, "I'm a dog person," I always reply, "Yeah? Well, I'm a lizard person." And then I peel off my face.

EPISODE 73:
"TRIPTYCH"

SEPTEMBER 1, 2015

GUEST VOICE: KEVIN R. FREE (KEVIN)

I RAN INTO A DUDE ON EAST 4TH STREET IN MANHATTAN WHO TOLD me that he didn't like "Triptych" because he didn't like for Kevin to have any human qualities. He likes his Kevin straight villainous, no frailties or feelings or fleshed-out whys or wherefores. I disagreed with that dude, but that was way back in 2015, a lifetime ago, when I didn't have the words to be able to describe exactly why Kevin is a villain. So I will do that here. Please indulge me:

1. Kevin was just a dude. Sure, he had an important job as radio host, but he was just a regular guy. Like, say, for example, Senator Lindsey Graham of South Carolina. A dude with an important job.

2. StrexCorp moved into Desert Bluffs, and Kevin resisted them. He was part of the RESISTANCE. Like, say, for example, Lindsey Graham was in 2015, when he said that Donald J. Trump was ". . . a race-baiting, xenophobic religious bigot. He doesn't represent my party. He doesn't

represent the values that the men and women who wear the uniform are fighting for."

3. StrexCorp then takes over Desert Bluffs, and Kevin gets brainwashed. He defends StrexCorp, even praises it. Like Lindsey Graham, who said about President Trump in 2018: "He's not, in my view, a racist by any stretch of the imagination. I have never heard him make a single racist statement. Not even close."

4. Then we find out that Kevin is depressed and regretful about what happened to him and Desert Bluffs, as a result of capitulating to StrexCorp.

Does Kevin's regret make him any less a villain? Will Senator Lindsey Graham one day regret the way he's ingratiated himself with the president and supported his racist, xenophobic, and, might I add, sexist and transphobic policies, let's say—for the sake of argument—probably? But—like Kevin—he's still a villain.

I hope that dude from East 4th Street reads this.

—Kevin R. Free

What's past is prologue. What's future is epilogue.
This right here is maybe chapter 4 or 5.

WELCOME TO NIGHT VALE

Today's top news is the Screaming Vortex that opened up in the Night Vale Mall food court, completely obliterating Ice Cream on a Stick, Lucy Tropic's Fried Ice Cream, and Mario's Very Authentic Italian Ice Cream Sub Sandwiches, while doing significant damage to American Teddy's Ice Cream and Falafel. American Teddy's owner, Teddy Rahal, said that this is the worst case of food court vortex that Night Vale has seen in decades, and then he started hollering about the figures he could see approaching from within the depths of the vortex, and I'm sorry but . . . I'm getting some weird feedback in my headphones. Just some slight technical difficulties. Let me see if any of these wires are loose and we'll get right back to this important story. Okay, this one looks a little loose, I'll just wiggle it a bit . . .

[*static*]

[*Kevin here is a little younger, less soullessly chipper, more actual-humanly happy.*]

KEVIN: . . . started hopping up and down joyously about the figures he could see approaching from within the depths of . . .

CECIL: Oh no.

KEVIN: Hello? Is there a new friend on the air with me? This is Kevin in Desert Bluffs.

CECIL: We know who you are, Kevin. And another thing. Just because you have decided to name the other desert world that you are living in Desert Bluffs doesn't make it the town of Desert Bluffs. That's not how names work. You couldn't just start calling me Cecil [*British pronunciation*] and have that suddenly be my name.

KEVIN: Wow, you have so much passion. What a passionate individual you are. Cecil [*British pronunciation*] is it?

CECIL: Cecil!

KEVIN: Delightful. But to your . . . um . . . point, while where I live is definitely a desert, I don't know what would make it other than your world. And I didn't call this town Desert Bluffs. Someone much older and smarter than me, I'm sure, did that. And I'm glad they did. Because you couldn't ask for a better hometown than the Bluffs.

CECIL: Ugh, what a stupid name. Night Vale is a way better name by any measure. For instance, I like it more. By any measure.

KEVIN: That's disappointing news. But I've never heard of any place called Night Vale. I can't imagine anyone disliking us here in Desert Bluffs.

CECIL: What do you mean you've never heard of Night Vale? You and that evil corporation StrexCorp tried to take over Night Vale very recently.

KEVIN: StrexCorp? That faux-friendly big-business corporate monster? Don't talk to me about them. StrexCorp is the worst. Strex has been buying up a few of the businesses here in Desert Bluffs and I am not happy about it. It makes me very unhappy to be unhappy. I'm much happier being happy.

No, Strex is against everything I believe in: community, radio, community radio, government intervention in the world, World

Government intervention, Secret Police, and, of course, adorable cats.

CECIL: I love cats!

KEVIN: Who doesn't love cats? Heartless people, that's who. Monsters without the capacity for love. Without the capacity for love, Cecil. That's who doesn't love cats.

CECIL: Wow, you're way nicer than I remembered.

KEVIN: I want to represent my town well. We're decent people here. Good people, sharing what we have. A watchful and oppressive government keeping us safe from ourselves and others. Children playing in the schools, working hard in paramilitary clubs, and marching with crisp, clean uniforms in parades.

CECIL: Your marching band has crisp, clean uniforms? But that hasn't been true since the . . . Is it possible that somehow I am getting a radio signal from Desert Bluffs all the way back from before the incident?

KEVIN: I have no idea what any of that meant, but it sounded terrifying.

CECIL: You don't like Strex?

KEVIN: Of course not. But don't worry. We won't let them get too powerful. Not here in the Bluffs.

CECIL: Please stop calling it that.

KEVIN: Sure. We're all united on keeping StrexCorp just a small local business here in the Bluffs.

CECIL: It's so strange to hear this version of you. I don't know how this stray signal ended up in this where and when, but here it is. This you before everything that happens that makes you . . . whatever you become.

KEVIN: Wow, sounds like I have some fun stuff to look forward to once I kick StrexCorp out of town. You know they've been trying to buy the radio station? Can you imagine how awful that would be? They'd probably try to take me off the air and replace me with someone else. Or worse, try to change my personality completely. Ugh. I would never let that happen. I would never—

[*beat*]

CECIL: Kevin? Kevin? I don't think he can hear me anymore.

[*static*]

[*Kevin here is normal, Strex-influenced Kevin.*]

KEVIN: You don't think who can hear you anymore?
CECIL: Oh thank the lights in the sky, Kevin, you're still there. I need to warn you about Strex . . .
KEVIN: Warn me about Strex? Why would you ever need to warn me about an honest family business like Strex? Why, ever since they bought the radio station years ago, I've learned so much about good business practices and the value of hard work, and individual responsibility and smiling and destroying the weak and eliminating the lazy and smiling and smiling and smiling.
CECIL: Oh no, I must be getting a radio signal from the much more recent past.
KEVIN: The warping of linear time is exactly why I don't trust radio, Cecil, especially community radio.
CECIL: Kevin, what did you become?
KEVIN: I'm just a happy-go-lucky guy. It's like they say. Work hard, play hard, then work hard again, work hard more, work harder, keep working hard, have you been working hard enough?, work harder if you want to live. And then, *and then*, play. Play very, very, very, very hard.
CECIL: Do you remember nothing of the you that was? The you that believed in good healthy things like family and a caring, totalitarian government?
KEVIN: I . . . oh, that's a good question, what do I remember? I remember being a real grumpster, just a grouch and a half about

everything. Mr. Frowny Face I'd call myself now if I were talking to myself then. But Strex bought out my radio station and everything changed for the better. Ha! Can you believe it? I actually tried to stop them from buying it. I tried very hard. I put my own body, this fragile thing, in between the Strex representatives and the entrance to the building but they forced their way past me using ethically brutal methods that left me forever physically changed. What a silly old hen I was about all that.

Once Strex entered my life and showed me the power of the Smiling God, why nothing was the same for me ever again. I felt so much happier. I did terrible things. I felt so much happier. I tore and bit and growled. I felt so incredibly happy. My skin rent. Blood drops on the ceiling. Someone's throat—whose?—in my hand, so deliriously happy. You know what, thank you Cecil for bringing back such good memories to me.

CECIL: I am so, so glad that we drove StrexCorp out of Night Vale.

KEVIN: Oh, but that's not true, Cecil. We only just started moving into Night Vale. Why, I believe we bought your radio station only a couple weeks ago?

CECIL: That's because you're talking to me from my past. The radio signal got temporally misplaced, as sometimes happens, obviously. In the time you're speaking from, we haven't led the secret revolution against Strex yet.

KEVIN: So you're saying that there will be a secret revolution against Strex? Hang on. I'm jotting down a few things.

CECIL: Oh, um. Nope. Doesn't sound right at all. I think Strex has nothing to be worried about and should just be relaxed and complacent.

KEVIN: Cecil, your jokes delight me! Just in case, though, I'm going to send a new supervisor over to Night Vale. Daniel is fresh off the line and one of our most efficient radio content manufacturers. You'll love him. Or not you now. You then. I guess. Time is weird, isn't it?

CECIL: So weird.

KEVIN: Right? Anyway, Daniel will keep a close eye and if anything seems wrong, well, me and some StrexCorp executive or another will head right over to set things right.

CECIL: Well . . . Ah . . .

KEVIN: Oh, don't sound down about yourself. We all make mistakes, Cecil. Except wonderfully productive StrexCorp, bursting at the seams with the power of our awesome Smiling God. They don't make mistakes. And that is why we are all grains of sand beneath their feet, the bended neck at their throne. Isn't language fun?

CECIL: Kevin, I already kicked you off my station once. I'm not just going to sit back while some errant radio waves from the past somehow put you right back on here. Maybe if I wiggled the wire this way?

KEVIN: Lauren! Lauren! I've just heard some interesting ideas about the future on the—

[*clunk, buzz*]

CECIL: He seems to be gone. Well, I have some feelings about how that conversation went, but Carlos always tells me to never be down on myself about honest mistakes. Not even massively destructive, paradoxical mistakes. He's always saying that.

[*Kevin in this part is very old, his emotions are gone, he is drained.*]

CECIL: I suppose now that the technical difficulties are taken care of, I should give you an update on the screaming vortex at the Night Vale Mall. You won't believe what—

[*static*]

KEVIN: [*coughs*]

CECIL: Oh no. Hello?

KEVIN: Cecil. Cecil. Old friend, I'm here.

CECIL: You sound different. When is this radio signal coming from? When are you in your life?

KEVIN: I am very old. It has been many years since I last spoke to you. It's great to hear your voice again. It's great to hear any voice again.

CECIL: I'll admit, this is a little exciting. How is the future?
KEVIN: Desolate.

[*beat*]

CECIL: Okay, not what I expected, if I'm honest.
KEVIN: Oh, what StrexCorp and their Smiling God did to my wonderful little town. What they did to me. I'm not myself anymore. I'm a smile and a twitch of the wrist.

It has been years, Cecil. I've drifted away from myself. Sometimes I am one me and then again I am the other. What they did to the sentient heat trapped temporarily in my body.
CECIL: Oh, Kevin . . .
KEVIN: Kevin . . . even my name is a strange figment. My tongue has forgotten how to form the word. And once I was so good with words. Now I am an ancient thing, withered away by what they did to me all those years ago. The power of the Smiling God is an endless flow. It ebbs like the tides but like the tides, it returns.

I think about what I could have been if I had never encountered Strex. I imagine an entire life without them. It makes me happy. I picture every detail. I try to live it in real time. But it is only a slight, sweet fiction and dissolves like sugar into water. Oh Cecil, I wish you had known me before . . . before Strex, before it all, when I was just a dedicated community radio host like you. I wish you had . . .
CECIL: But I did know you, just now, Kevin. You sounded so excited about your town, about your community. You were so happy. You were you. Kevin? Kevin?

Kevin! Listeners, I must find this Kevin again, but first I must take you to the weather.

WEATHER: "The Heroine" by Unwoman

[*We are back to pre-Strex, actual human, genuinely happy Kevin.*]

KEVIN: Cecil? Cecil?

CECIL: Yes, Kevin, I'm here.

KEVIN: Oh, good, I got you back. Lost you there for a moment. Anyway, as I was saying, Strex wants to buy the radio station. But I'll never let them. I'll fight 'em off, Cecil. I'll defeat them.

CECIL: Oh. . . . It's this version of you.

KEVIN: There's only me, Cecil. I'm the only me there is. And we're gearing up to push Strex out. Grandma Josephine, my oldest friend in town, both meanings of the word. Mayor Pablo Mitchell. Lawrence Levine, out in the Edgertown Development. We have all had our differences in the past, sure. And we will have our differences again. We can't always be happy. But we love each other. We are a community. And sure, that community has a beautiful name, I mean can you think of a single more beautiful name than Desert Bluffs?

CECIL: Obviously. Any name. Literally any name.

KEVIN: But it's not about the beautiful, beautiful name. It's about the people. A town is its people, and the good and the bad of them. And that is what we are going to fight for. That is what we are going to win for.

Hey, you're from the future. That means you know how this turns out.

CECIL: Well, yes I do.

KEVIN: So? Do I win? Does everything go just as right as right could be?

CECIL: [*beat*] Yes. You win, Kevin. Everything goes right. You and community radio prevail, and you are happier than ever. Desert Bluffs is a wonderful town and you live happily in it.

KEVIN: Oh, that's such good news. Thanks for telling me. I can't wait for the future to come. Though I have no choice but to wait, I suppose. That's how the future works, scientists keep insisting. Scientists are the worst, right? Well, I'm sure I'll talk to you again, at some point in my life. Until next time, Cecil. Until next time.

CECIL: Good-bye, Kevin. I wish . . . [*beat*] it doesn't matter.

Listeners, I . . .

What do I say here?

I wish things could have gone differently, obviously. That is obviously what I wish. But they didn't. What is the use of nostalgia for what didn't happen when we have to live with what did?

Do I wish the food court at the mall still existed? Sure. But it doesn't. Oh, right, sorry, didn't get a chance to update you. The whole food court and everyone in it is totally gone now. Anyway.

A counterpart that never was. A friend that I never had. A life that was never lived.

Could Night Vale and Desert Bluffs have been sister towns? Was there a moment when that possibility drifted like breath into frozen air until it wisped away into the cold truth of what happened?

I don't know. I heard only what you heard. I know only what you know. Probably you know more than me.

Stay tuned next for a feeling in your chest that will never quite sit right with you again.

And good night, Night Vale. Good Night.

PROVERB: Candles lit, runes drawn upon the floor, sacrifice prepared. Everything is ready for the summoning. I begin the incantation: "Shakira, Shakira!"

EPISODE 74:
"CIVIC CHANGES"

SEPTEMBER 15, 2015

GUEST VOICES: MARK GAGLIARDI (JOHN PETERS),
DESIREE BURCH (PAMELA WINCHELL)

I THINK MY FAVORITE THING ABOUT *WELCOME TO NIGHT VALE* IS ITS contrasts. Did you ever take a picture and want to tweak it, so you opened up the photo editor and adjusted the contrast? Joseph and Jeffrey take a picture of the world, open their own peculiar mental photo editor, and make a few changes. After first dropping the brightness to make everything a little darker (not all the way—there are still bright shining lights in their creation), they crank up the contrast to eleven until the world becomes one big surreal, hilarious question. It's a world that you recognize and one that you don't recognize at all. Where dogs are not allowed in the Dog Park.

Take John Peters. You know, the farmer? He's an uncomplicated man. Tends his crop, has his traditional set of folksy values. Joseph and Jeffrey crank up the contrast and now his crop is imaginary and he operates on a higher cosmic plane thanks to the aliens who abducted and enlightened him. And of course, because this is Night Vale, he's also a hilarious bozo.

I first got to play John Peters (you know, the farmer?) in Brooklyn. We performed the episode "The Debate" and it was my introduction to the insanity that is a live *Welcome to Night Vale* show. The fans! The cosplay! The roar! I was hooked. The team asked me to join their tour for a leg, and I was elated to get to play in their sandbox. We spent two weeks in a black Sprinter van playing a new city almost nightly, and chasing vegetarian restaurants down I-95.

Here's a contrast that I loved about the tour: For me it was a meeting of the old and the new. I was returning to my Southern roots while experiencing my very first tour, and the rest of the crew was either people I had just met or people I had known for decades. New to me were Joseph, Jeffrey, Meg, and Symphony, who opened their arms wide. Also new were musicians Dessa and Aby Wolf, two powerhouse performers who taught me everything I needed to know about touring, and Disparition, who is himself a contrast with his silent music and brilliant prose. Old friends to me were Hal, my longtime friend and comedy partner, and Cecil, with whom I grew up in Tennessee.

True! Cecil and I were kids together in the Knoxville Performing Arts Institute. Talk about contrast: two fellas inhabiting a macabre dreamscape who used to don sequined bow ties and sing the cheeriest show tunes. We had lost touch for a while, so my heart skipped a beat the first time I heard the show. I was excited to work with my old pal first when our podcasts did a crossover episode, then in that Brooklyn show, then on the road, then when we recorded this episode in his studio. It was hard not to laugh while playing across from Cecil's effortless timing, and then to hear him in the eerie parts was chilling. It's *Welcome to Night Vale* at its best: hilarious, spooky, and with the contrast cranked to eleven.

—Mark Gagliardi

Remember that you are a beautiful person. You're a weird-looking tree, but you're a beautiful person.

WELCOME TO NIGHT VALE

Hello, listeners. To start things off, I've been asked to reread this brief notice. The City Council announces that no changes will be made to the Dog Park at the corner of Earl and Summerset, near the Ralphs. They would like to remind everyone that dogs are not allowed in the Dog Park. People are not allowed in the Dog Park. It is possible you will see hooded figures in the Dog Park. Do not approach them. Do not approach the Dog Park. The fence is electrified and highly dangerous. Try not to look at the Dog Park and especially do not look for any period of time at the hooded figures. The Dog Park will not harm you. The Dog Park is as it always was. Shut up about the Dog Park, the City Council added in handwriting to the bottom of the notice.

This reminder of city rules is apparently in response to recent complaints by Night Vale citizens over the secretive and exclusive nature of the Dog Park. And these complaints are apparently in response to recent activity by certain community radio hosts and local scientists who surreptitiously used the Dog Park to go back and forth between Night Vale and a desert otherworld and then announced said activity to everyone over the airwaves.

Apparently. I'm not sure. I'm not sure of anything really. Who knows? I don't.

Let's have a look now at sports. The Night Vale High School Scorpions already have their first district win of the season without actually having played a single district game. This Friday's football game against fierce rival Desert Bluffs has been forfeited by the Vultures because of lack of funding.

Desert Bluffs has been in a steep year-long recession. I mean it's an awful city, but it's hard not to feel bad. The town is facing record unemployment and major setbacks in city programming after the buyout and subsequent major restructuring last year of the only employer in town, StrexCorp. DBHS has had to cut their athletic programs, as well as all music, history, trial-mocking, and math classes.

Next week, the Night Vale Scorpions take on the Pine Cliff Lizard Monitors, who are coming off last year's successful nine-and-one season, which was due in large part to all of their players being ghosts and thus extremely difficult to tackle.

The Scorpions will need a lot of luck as they will be without star running back Malik Herrera this season. After last year's scandal in which it was revealed he wasn't real, Herrera quit football to pursue his dream of becoming a conceptual artist. His current medium is wood carvings on living trees. He's been at work in the Whispering Forest along the east side of Night Vale, etching phrases like "you look nice today" and "i have always loved you" into some of the cedar trunks. The Whispering Forest usually lures humans with compliments and then subsumes them, turning them into trees as well. But since Malik doesn't actually exist, he's immune to such pressure.

Oh, guess what! We have a new intern. She's been with us the past couple of weeks, handling our social media. I'm kind of an old fossil and am not really good at things like the internet. In fact, I think I've long since let my license to use a computer expire.

But new intern Danielle has really picked up the slack, transcribing my work e-mails and my Hannibal fan poetry onto a Tumblr page. Intern Maureen used to do all of that, but since she left, I've had to lean on Danielle for all of her expertise. Good work, Danielle!

Speaking of which, with the current controversy at the Dog Park, I'm going to need you to go down there and report on what's happening.

[*beat*]

Danielle is in the producer's booth shaking her head no. Danielle, you look horrified. This is an easy story.

She's writing something down. Okay, Danielle just held her hand up to the plexiglass. She's written on her palm in black marker: "This position regularly puts interns in harm's way, and I would like to remain at my desk, where I am safe. I don't want to die. The Dog Park is not safe. Please understand and respect my concerns. Sincerely, Danielle."

Danielle also has extremely legible handwriting and large palms.

Okay, I understand that, Danielle. I think you're overreacting. The last time I sent an intern to report a story at the Dog Park, she became mayor. But okay. You do your thing.

Well, it sounds like we're getting our first eyewitness reports from the Dog Park. We have on the phone right now John Peters, you know, the farmer? John, are you at the Dog Park right now?

JOHN: Howdy, Cecil. I sure am.
CECIL: What's happening down there. Are people demonstrating? Is it peaceful?
JOHN: It all depends on your definition of peaceful, Cecil. I'm looking right now at all these people. They are all in a long row, standing upright and perfectly still. Mayhaps a slight sway to each individual in the breeze, but otherwise perfectly planted and stoic. They're all so quiet, not a single sound, except some incidental rustling, the

mundane din of physical existence, that sort of thing. But not a word is being spoken.

CECIL: This is amazing. I'm so proud of our town, taking a non-violent approach toward civic change. This reminds me of the classic sit-ins where prote——

JOHN: Well, like I said, Cecil. They ain't sitting per se. They're all totally upright.

CECIL: Okay, sure. I know. I just meant—

JOHN: You should say what you mean. That's a famous quote. You know who said that?

CECIL: I know Lewis Carroll wrote—

JOHN: Nope!

CECIL: Who said it then?

JOHN: Now there are birds soaring above. Lots of black birds circling the rows of silent citizens. The birds are cawing and landing on some of them. There's one citizen in particular who is standing on a wood pike, his arms spread wide, his head cocked a bit to the side. He's wearin' a straw hat and a smile of unnatural geometry. His eyes are solid black and seem to be protruding from his rough face. The birds are avoiding this particular man. I think perhaps he is the leader of these people, as he also stands perfectly still, perfectly silent. He is so stoic. So strong. Cecil?

CECIL: Yes, John.

JOHN: I'm lookin' straight at the sun right now, Cecil.

CECIL: John, don't do that. That's bad for yo——

JOHN: It's so beautiful. It's beautiful and it hurts.

CECIL: John.

JOHN: Oh. Here comes a cloud. That sure's a relief.

CECIL: So are the people at the Dog Park carrying signs of any sort? Are they wearing T-shirts with slogans? Anything like that?

JOHN: They're just all green and leafy, rising from the dirt. Little tufts of brownish hair on top. Some of the birds are pecking at their faces now, eating the bulbous golden flesh hidden beneath. SHOO! GET GONE, YOU BIRDS! Good, I think the birds are leavin'. Oh no. They're just circling back to some other people further away. Now they're eating them other folks' heads. It's brutal, Cecil. Just brutal.

CECIL: John. Wait. Are you in a cornfield?

[*beat*]

JOHN: Well.

CECIL: It sounds an awful lot like a cornfield.

JOHN: I don't want to get into an argument with you about semiotics, Cecil, but I know what I see.

CECIL: Thanks for the update, John.

JOHN: Oh, you bet, Cecil. Always nice to talk to you. GET GONE, YOU BIRDS.

CECIL: And now a word from our sponsor. Today's show is sponsored by Knife. Need to cut a thing? Use Knife. Need to poke a hole in another thing? Try using Knife. Have one thing and want it to become two or more smaller things? You *could* try Saw. Saw sometimes works, but other times? You need Knife. Just listen to Knife in action. [*knife sound*] Amazing. [*knife sound again*] Knife.

This has been a word from our sponsors.

To deal with the controversy surrounding the no dogs or people in the Dog Park policy, Mayor Dana Cardinal (Hey, Danielle! That's the former intern I was talking about. You sure you don't want to go write a Dog Park story? Okay. Fine.) has sent her director of Emergency Press Conferences Pamela Winchell to deliver an emergency press conference. Here is what she had to say.

PAMELA: Today is an important day in our city's history. Today, citizens of Night Vale have spoken, and they have said something. I wasn't paying attention. I can't hear and see and understand every single thought or feeling everyone is having at every single moment.

Someone is always trying to explain things to me. "Put the car in reverse to go backwards." "Don't point that gun at me, Pamela." "Greenland is mostly ice, whereas Iceland is actually Ireland misspelled." Always someone over my shoulder telling me how to do something, or someone on my shoulder crying, or someone below my shoulder in a headlock.

It's just too much for me to take in. So some of you are against the Dog Park or maybe you're against the people against the Dog Park. I don't know. Who can tell? Maybe you're against dogs who are parking. Why would dogs park? Dogs can't drive. Wait! Did you mean dogs barking? Are you against the dog BARK?

Oh. Yeah. I'm with you on that. There's nothing worse than an idiot dog voicing its idiot opinion. Keep it to yourself, King Charles. Nobody asked.

Well, maybe somebody did. I once asked a dog, "Who's a good girl?" and it was silent. It didn't know. Or it didn't want to say. Either possibility made me sad. I'm still sad about this.

Let's have a moment of silence for my sadness.

[*moment*]

Okay. I'm still sad though. But the sadness sits better with me.

Did you know it takes more muscles to frown than it does to think about being sad? It's true.

No questions. I'm taking no questions. We're done here.

Oh. Before I forget. Cecil. Can we move our coffee date from Tuesday to Wednesday? I have a dental appointment Tuesday. I almost forgot why I had originally called. Call me back, okay!

[*beeeep*]

CECIL: Oh, I guess that was just a voice mail from Pamela, not a press conference. Never mind.

And now an update on the hole in the vacant lot out back of the Ralphs. The group of huddlers that meet at the hole and huddle have now taken up nestling. "We're done huddling," said a spokesperson for the group.

No one knows who these former huddlers/current nestlers are, nor their regularly scheduled nestling times, just that they like to nestle in the hole in the vacant lot out back of the Ralphs. They also like it when other people come join them. They formerly enjoyed huddling, but now their new thing is nestling. "Come nestle with us," their press release reads. "What's the worst that could happen? We don't know and we'd like to find out," it concludes.

A spokesperson for the group issued a new statement just now. "Do not assume we like nestling or dislike huddling. Nestling just is. Huddling just was. This is everything," the statement reads.

So go nestle. Also Ralphs is a proud sponsor of our station, so maybe get some shopping done as well. Probably do the shopping part first.

We're getting word that the people at the Dog Park have begun shouting at the hooded figures who inhabit the Dog Park. They are shouting things like "I do not like the Dog Park Policy" and "Please can my dog and I come play in the park?" and "That's a nice park."

Some of the dog owners have begun holding up spit-soaked tennis balls and well-chewed Frisbees, and they are demanding that they be let into the Dog Park so that they may get some exercise with their loving and loyal canine companions. One of them even shouted, "My dog has to pee really badly. See?" And then they pointed at their dog and the dog was shifting its weight nervously from leg to leg, its eyes anxious and its cheeks obviously flush underneath the dark fur.

In response to this heightened civil disobedience Mayor Cardinal announced that she and the City Council will hold a meeting today to discuss their various options for changing the Dog Park policy.

The City Council, speaking in unison, said they hated this idea.

And then they sent a dozen or so helicopters across the city of Night Vale spraying every citizen with sedatives.

Well, it sounds like maybe some headway will be made at the Dog Park. I hope it is soon, as things have gotten confrontational. I hope that [*yawns*] oh, my gosh [*yawns*] whew. I better take us . . . before I drift off . . . to the . . . weath—[*zzz*]

WEATHER: "I Love You Oddly" by Rebecca Angel

Good news. That sedative-assisted midday nap left me well rested and full of vim and pep.

More good news. After hours of meetings between the mayor and the City Council, the Dog Park has been officially opened to use by dogs—a first in its three years of existence.

There are some rules and guidelines for Dog Park usage, of course, as outlined just now by the City Council.

First, anyone wishing to take their dog to the Dog Park must have a dog. Second, dog owners must submit proper paperwork proving that they are blood-related to their dog. Third, after a municipal review committee approves the application, a hooded figure will take the dog into the Dog Park and play with the dog using city-approved Frisbees, sticks, and balls. Dog owners may not accompany the hooded figures during this time and will be safely packed away in Styrofoam containers for the duration of the Dog Park program.

The City Council added that there will be a slight bump in gasoline taxes to pay for this new program. Also they will be building new, higher, obsidian fencing around the Dog Park. They added that dogs who go into the Dog Park as part of this new program will not be returned to their owners. Finally, they've hired Troy Walsh Landscaping to plant new white lily gardens around the perimeter of the Dog Park. Troy is sure great at everything he does, so that should be real pretty.

Well, good job, Night Vale. It's a small step forward, but your voices were heard. So often we think that politics is just arguing about who should pretend to be president, but real change starts here at home. With your streets and neighborhoods and communities. I'm proud of the great work done by our citizens today. We all came together over an issue important to the people, and we were heard by our leaders. How inspiring!

As the old saying goes: "Horses leave hoofprints on your heart." That doesn't have anything to do with togetherness or change. It's just a warning that horses are dangerous and will try to kill you. Know that, and you can accomplish anything.

Stay tuned next for a review of the popular new film: *Unedited CCTV Footage-Citgo #4172 Left Rear Cam.*

And as always, good night, Night Vale. Good night.

PROVERB: The word *motel* is an amalgam of the words *murder* and *hotel*.

EPISODE 75:
"THROUGH THE NARROW PLACE"

OCTOBER 1, 2015

RUNNING HAS ALWAYS BEEN A PART OF MY LIFE. MY DAD RAN EVERY single day, until a heart condition forced him to stop. I think that was one of the hardest things about the diagnosis for him, losing the ability to go for his daily runs. I did cross-country in high school, running six or seven miles a day, staying well after the end of school to do so. Now I go for runs on the country road I live on. My wife and I give each other reports on the animals we see when we get back from our respective runs. Recently I saw two flocks of wild turkeys, an old white dog who usually barks at me but who today just walked past me glumly, and a tiny black bird chasing a huge owl. There are times the woods feel like a more happening place than the Brooklyn neighborhood we left behind.

This episode is built around a mysterious process. The process of going "through the Narrow Place." What does this mean? I have no idea. There is, I think, a misunderstanding about mysteries. And that is that they are usually meant to be solved. A mystery that is meant to be solved is really a puzzle, and as a writer you can only have so many puzzles. Meanwhile, most mysteries act instead as stand-ins for the world and life. Which is to say that we don't understand the world or our lives, and so we feel a deep connection when fiction confronts us with a mystery that cannot be solved.

Much of the mystery here is built out of the use of particular phrases and words, repeated over and over: "the Narrow Place," obviously, but also phrases like "we wore black coats." A writer learns all the ways that language can be utilized. It can be used to tell a story, sure, or build a character. It can be used to inform or to deceive, to confuse or to illuminate. But writing can also be used to create scenery. I don't mean describing scenery, I mean creating a set for your story, like a set in a theater for a play. That set is built out of words. By creating this hook of repeating phrases and words, you create a set built of those phrases within which the rest of the story takes place.

Two quick notes:

1. One of Khoshekh's kittens is named Mixtape. My wife and I have a game we play in which every animal we see must be named. One of us will turn to the other, point at a cow we're driving by, and ask, "What's her name?" and the other will answer "Madeline, I think? Or maybe Mary Ann? We drove by so fast I couldn't quite hear." Mixtape was a name that my wife gave to a stray cat in Rome, and it struck me as a truly perfect name for a cat. We can't have a cat, due to allergies, but if we did, its name would be Mixtape (or Barbara Emmaline Quendeline Sauce, Barb E. Q. Sauce for short).

2. Those paying attention might notice some stuff hidden with the "Hey There, Cecil" section. For instance, readers of the first *Welcome to Night Vale* novel might realize that they are reading about two of the main characters. This

episode was written after we had written the novel, but a month before it came out, so ultimately this was an Easter egg more for ourselves than anything. Also the secret plot that will culminate in Episodes 89 and 90 continues to build in this section.

—Joseph Fink

It's not the destination. It's the
endless, exhausting journey.

WELCOME TO NIGHT VALE

What an exciting day for amateur athletes or just anyone who enjoys moving their body for whatever reason someone would want to do that. Today is the Annual Marathon Through the Narrow Place. This yearly marathon is a family-friendly charity race that takes people on a beautiful twenty-six-mile-or-so course along the Crooked Path, down into the Deepening, and, ultimately, Through the Narrow Place.

Race organizers say that this will be the biggest marathon yet, with all the town forced to take part by the terrifying Harbingers of the Distant Prince, and that all participants will be devoured by the Narrow Place.

Race board president Susan Willman added, "That sounds a lot more dramatic than it is. Sorry, you know how when you talk mostly with a small group of friends you end up developing a shared way of speaking that can be misleading or misunderstood when heard by outside ears? We just like to say that the Narrow Place will devour them because what will happen is that the Narrow Place will consume them with an unfeeling hunger and they will dissipate." Susan laughed, continuing. "Oh there it is again. That sounds so frightening when I say it that way, doesn't it? Doesn't it sound frightening?"

She laughed. Susan laughed. She laughed. Her mouth was black and featureless inside. She laughed.

The marathon is this afternoon and will be the end of us all. More on this soon, but first, let's get into some news.

The Desert Bluffs City Council and Desert Bluffs mayor Dan Cardozo announced this week via a golden press release hidden in one lucky Sulphur Crunch candy bar, that due to an extreme deficit in municipal funding, they would have to shut down certain city services, including trash pickup, road maintenance, and tree monitoring. Starting this Monday, citizens will have to drive their own trash to the dump, roads will gradually start to deteriorate under the erosion of particulate desert wind, and the movements of trees will go entirely unwatched and unrecorded.

The City Council and Mayor Cardozo indicated that they had done everything in their power to prevent this shutdown, including requesting federal assistance, selling off city property, and making offerings of food and wine to the ancient sandstone idols out in the dunes, but that the catastrophic loss of employment and tax dollars after StrexCorp shut down operations in town were too much for even those measures to make up for. StrexCorp Synernists Inc., of course, was the former employer of every single person in Desert Bluffs, until the company's rapid expansion plans into nearby towns led to their downfall and subsequent hostile takeover by beings who are definitely not angels. The not-at-all angels closed down almost every Strex office, and laid off, or as they put it, liberated, all former Strex employees, and at this point are mostly liquidating Strex resources in order to fund operas here in Night Vale.

Listeners, I feel for Desert Bluffs in their time of need. Mostly I feel scorn and triumph. More on this never, as I don't ever want to talk about Desert Bluffs again.

And now a much more important story: Khoshekh the cat floating exactly four feet off the ground in the men's room here at the station. We've received all sorts of calls and e-mails and distress signals and emergency flares and Morse code spelling out "HELP US. HELP US. WE HAVE BEEN HERE FOR WEEKS. GOD SAVE OUR SOULS," which I can only assume are all signs of the public's insatiable desire to hear more cute kitty news. And what cute kitty news we have.

Khoshekh is reaching that time in a cat's life when his skull is completely visible, and I have been taking adorable photo after adorable photo and putting them on Snapchat with captions like "Who's a good kitty?" and "Behold my skull of terror."

Whenever I get stressed at work, I just put on protective gear and inject myself with a number of preemptive antitoxins and I go pet Khoshekh for a bit and listen to the low gurgling rumble of his purr.

His kittens are doing as well as their daddy, and some of them are getting nearly as big as Khoshekh was when I first found him. My favorite of the kittens is named Mixtape, and his anterior spines are coming in fast. He's going to be a really big kitten when he's fully grown. Unmanageably huge. It'll be adorable.

That's about it for cat news. If there's any more cat news, like Khoshekh doing something cute or just looking cute in any way, we will immediately break into whatever ongoing news story it is that we are reporting and let you know.

All right, let's do another round of my popular advice segment, "Hey There, Cecil."

"Hey there, Cecil. My husband and I have a bet and we were wondering if you could settle it. I think that the sky is made of gas and distance while he thinks that the sky is hastily painted plywood about thirty feet above the ground built to hide us from the terrible truth of what is actually above us. That's unrelated to the bet, which is:

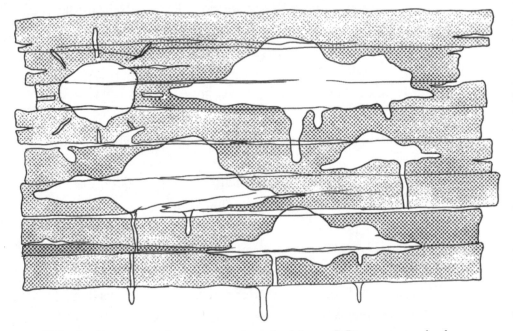

Which of us wears this summoning cloak better? Pictures attached.
SIGNED: INSECURE SUMMONERS IN CACTUS BLOOM."

Hey there, Insecure. Wow, okay. I'd say it's a dead tie. It's almost impossible to look bad in a summoning cloak. But more importantly, instead of arguing about who looks better in a cloak, you should appreciate how you each interact with the cloak in your own unique way. Cherish each other, celebrate your summoning cloak styles, and save your arguments for that difficult and unsettling matter about the sky.

"Hey there, Cecil. My teenage son, like many children his age, can't decide what kind of person he is. For instance, sometimes he is a kettle and sometimes he is a bear and sometimes he is a puddle of water. Many of these forms are difficult to drive to school, and I especially worry about his safety when he takes a form that can fly. No flying outside, I always tell him, but I worry that he doesn't listen. What can I do to help my son through this difficult time? SIGNED: WORRIED MOM IN DOWNTOWN."

Hey there, Worried. You would think that we would all be able to easily understand a teenager's struggle, most of us having been teenagers at one point, except obviously those of us who age backwards. But outside of the context of a young mind, the teenage experience does not have the same immediate, painful urgency that it does for those who are currently living through it.

It sounds like your son is trying on new physical forms to see which ones work for him. Maybe he's just searching for a physical form that other kids at school will think is cool. Whatever the issue, support him, have sympathy for him, and most of all, keep him safe, from others, and from himself. It's his job to make bad decisions. It's your job to make sure they're not bad enough to cause real damage. Good luck.

Last letter.

"Hey there, Cecil. I have made a terrible mistake and it consumes me. My life was once a life and now it is an uncorrectable error. The Arrival wakes each day and feeds. It gives and it takes and it takes and it takes. I would cry, but I don't think there's enough of me left anymore to make tears. What do I do? What do I do? SIGNED: TERRIFIED IN SHAMBLING ORPHAN."

Hey there, Terrified. It's important to be able to forgive yourself for mistakes, even real doozies. Just do your best to make things right and move on, I say. Although your mistake sounds, well, it does sound terrifying. I hope to hear nothing more about it.

That's all the time we have today for "Hey There, Cecil." Keep your calls and letters and psychic pleas coming in.

Listeners, it looks like the Marathon Through the Narrow Place is almost ready to go. Everyone in town is gathering at the starting line with the help of the towering Harbingers of the Distant Prince, who are using their toothy beaks and meaningful glances from their stomach-eyes to indicate where people should stand. It's looking to be a fun race and everyone is weeping. Larry Leroy, out on the edge of town, playfully tried to hide, but the Harbingers beat him at his own game, and the fun continued when they dragged him screaming to the starting line. Even the City Council is in on the festivities, their ghastly powers being no match for the placid un-yielding might of the Harbingers.

I'm here too, don't think old Cecil is exempt, me and Carlos are right here in matching Lycra shorts. He's wearing his run-ning lab coat, and the Harbingers al-lowed me to bring the mobile broad-casting equipment, so I could continue to do this radio show, even though ev-eryone can hear me talking live because I'm right here with them.

Oh, and there's Mayor Dana Cardinal, inaugurating the race by nervously chewing on a fistful of dirt. It won't be long now before we are all surging forward, panicked, the Harbingers looming be-hind us, until we are all forced Through the Narrow Place. What good exercise that will be. But while we wait, let's have a message from our sponsors.

Today's sponsor is that gut feeling that you did something wrong but you can't think of what it could be.

What was it? You feel so guilty but your guilt has no target. It circles and circles but cannot land. You think back through the day, trying to find the source of the gnawing guilt but there is nothing. And you realize that there never was a specific cause. It's just a part of you. You are the guilt. You are the shame. And this only makes you feel more guilty, more ashamed, that these emotions are somehow tied into your very being. As Albert Einstein famously said after he died, "The call is coming from inside the house."

That gut feeling that you did something wrong but you can't think what it could be: Try it today. And tomorrow. And tomorrow. And tomorrow.

This has been a word from our sponsors.

Finally, I think we just have time for this week's horoscopes before the race.

VIRGO: You should check under your bed before you go to sleep. That way the Thing hiding in your closet will think you haven't realized where it is yet.

LIBRA: All eyes are on you. Gross. Give them back.

SCORPIO: Mars is intersecting with Mercury, which means your head is weirdly big for your body and no one wants to tell you because they don't want you to have the grace of self-awareness. Ugh, Scorpios.

SAGITTARIUS: You worry too much about earthquakes and plane crashes. You're going to die of heart disease or cancer just like everyone else.

CAPRICORN: Stop throwing your money away on expensive cars and nice clothes. The owners of those cars and outfits do not appreciate the crumpled dollar bills you keep throwing on them, and anyway, if you want to throw something away, that's what garbage cans are for.

AQUARIUS: You've been so stressed lately. Why not just sit out-side tonight, relax, look up at the stars, and know basically nothing about the world you live in?

PISCES: Scorpions are not as dangerous as everyone thinks. Try to concentrate on that. It'll help you feel a little calmer tomorrow.

ARIES: I know this is hard time for you Aries, but remember: 'Tis better to have loved and lost. It's really great. Just the best.

TAURUS: Step on a crack, break your mother's back. Pick up the phone, break your mother's tailbone. Take your coffee with creamer, break your mother's femur. The wizard's spell has gone terribly wrong, and you must not move at all until it is reversed.

GEMINI: You will meet a tall, handsome stranger. He will in-troduce himself. You will come to know him well, and he will know you well. He will grow older. His skin will sag and thin. He will no longer be handsome. He will no longer be a stranger. He will no longer be most of the things he once was. He will be a close friend, an old friend, one you've known for years and with whom you are settling down into that final stretch of life. But he will always be tall. So tall. Very, very tall.

CANCER: I'm not saying this is bad news, but the stars just say [BLOODCURDLING SCREAM]. I mean, maybe that's a good sign? Right? It's a very inexact science.

LEO: Today is your lucky day. Which is good news, because tonight is your unlucky night. But enjoy this lucky day until the sun goes down. Until the very second the sun goes down. And then . . . And then . . .

That has been this week's horoscopes.

Oh, and here we go. There are the starting guns, pointing at all of us, ready to fire in case we decide not to run. Looks like the race has begun. Well everyone, if we end up devoured by the Narrow Place then at least we went out with one last fun, family-friendly community event. In any case, while we all get moving, let's get the latest on the weather.

WEATHER: "Black Eyes" by David Wirsig

[*a ringing, like ringing in the ears*]

We went along the Crooked Path, down into the Deepening, and then we all, whether we wanted to or not, we went Through the Narrow Place. We went through and on to the other side. There is no other side. We went there.

We sent messages in Morse code to the people we once had been, asking for help, but they could not help us. They were outside of the Narrow Place.

The Distant Prince was pleased. He gathered his Harbingers to him for the celebration. They cooed and merged in and out with each other, taking startling forms. We screamed. They cooed. We wore black coats and had never existed. The Distant Prince wore a golden coat and had always existed.

All darkness is just a thickness of birds. There is rustling in every shadow. Every surface is alive. We wore black coats and we went through it. We went Through the Narrow Place.

[*the ringing resolves*]

So it was another great marathon. I'm glad that our city government continues to encourage physical activity with fun events like this, and I'm proud of all of us for taking part. We will never be the same again, but here's a little secret for you: No one is ever the same again after anything.

You are never the same twice, and much of your unhappiness comes from trying to pretend that you are. Accept that you are different each day, and do so joyfully, recognizing it for the gift it is. Work within the desires and goals of the person you are currently, until you aren't that person anymore, and everything changes once again.

Stay tuned next for a different you, and a different you, and a different you again, each you denying their multiple nature.

And from the Narrow Place, where we wear black coats, and have never existed,

Good night, Night Vale. Good night.

PROVERB: Drake would like to add you to his professional network on LinkedIn.

EPISODE 76:
"AN EPILOGUE"

OCTOBER 15, 2015

THIS IS THE EPISODE THAT CAME OUT FIVE DAYS BEFORE THE FIRST *WEL-come to Night Vale* novel was released. We were thrumming with excitement. Our first published book. I remember the morning that it was released walking over to my local bookstore to see what we had made sitting on the shelves and . . . it wasn't there. Because bookstores aren't superexact, and, unless it's a new Harry Potter, sometimes they'll put out a book two days before its release date and sometimes two days after. But for the author, everything hinges around that date, when what they've carefully carried through the writing and editing process will finally be read by the world.

As a celebration of this, I decided to write an epilogue to the novel, in the form of an episode that would be released before the novel came out.

Like a lot of Night Vale episodes, this one is built around a game we're playing with the audience. It can be useful and clarifying as a writer to find the game of what you're writing. A lot of that just means understanding the experience you want the audience to have.

Where should their emotions go? What should their energy be in this moment? Understanding this clarifies a lot about how a scene or story is written.

With this episode, the game for me was to create an epilogue that (a) required no knowledge of the book to follow, since obviously almost no one had read it when this came out, and (b) would not spoil the plot of the book, for the same reason. This seemed like a fun challenge, and I really enjoyed tearing into it. I definitely saw a number of fans refusing to listen to this episode until they had read the book, and I wanted to tell them, "But if you do that, you'll miss the best trick of this episode." But, of course, the other thing about being an artist is you have no real say in how people decide to experience your work.

When people recommend *Welcome to Night Vale*, they often say something along the lines of "You have to start from the beginning," the implication being that if you don't understand every reference or character the moment you hear them, you'll be hopelessly lost. Jeffrey and I reject that concept, and I think both this episode and "There Is No Part 1: Part 2" (see Volume 3) are illustrations of our rejection. The truth is that the first episode of *Night Vale* is full of references and moments that are impossible to understand. It throws you into a world and slowly you figure it out. That same process could happen at Episode 30 or at Episode 90. We think you can jump in pretty much anywhere, and sure, you'll be confused for a bit, but we believe in you. You'll figure it out.

This episode contains a reference to James Patterson, a truly fascinating man and writer. It would be easy and lazy, I think, to hate on a man who has so completely embraced the concept of author as commercial workshop. But Patterson is so enthusiastic about books and about what he does, and so generous with the writing community as a whole, that it is impossible to hold any of it against him. The *Welcome to Night Vale* novel beat the new James Patterson book on the *New York Times* list. And sure, it was our first week and he had been on the list for four weeks, but we'll take our wins where we can get them. The book we beat was the masterfully named *The Murder House* and I need you to go look up the book trailer for *The Murder House*. It is perhaps the only good book trailer ever made.

—Joseph Fink

In just a few days the whole story will be
known. This is what happens after.

WELCOME TO NIGHT VALE

The last couple weeks, as we all know, have been eventful ones.
I'm not going to go over everything again. We all know what happened. We are well-read, well-informed people who have paid attention to the whole recent
"King City" affair.
We know about the
terrible ordeals that
Diane Crayton and
Jackie Fierro endured.
We know how their
troubles all ended up.
And we know the
truth about the Man
in the Tan Jacket.
We know all about
him now, because of
what Diane and Jackie
found out.

So I won't go over all of that.

Instead, I'll talk about the Barista District, which is experiencing a severe population spike, also as a result of that whole King City thing. There are just so many helpful people, wandering town asking us if we want nonfat or 2 percent, and if they can get us a blueberry scone with that. You can't open a hall closet, or tunnel under your own lawn without a barista jumping out at you, asking if you want a tray for all of the coffee they're going to give you. So much coffee, whether you want it or not. Here it comes, a crushing amount of coffee. Don't run, you'll never escape. Do you want a tray with that?

More on this ongoing aftermath in a moment, but first, the news.

The government released a statement Friday disavowing knowledge of any events which resulted from a recent gardening supplies sale that they may or may not have been involved with.

A representative of the U.S. Government, in association with the World Government, the Shadow Government, the Lizard People, and the Watchers from Behind the Stars, wrapped in a burlap cloak and speaking in a low, croaking voice, said, "So, yes, we recently sold surplus and used materials from a variety of secret government projects and experiments, all disguised as gardening supplies, and yes, the resulting effects on human life and on the very nature of time were unfortunate, and yes, people died in ways that we did not previously think were even possible in this particular universe, but basically it comes down to this: 'America, love or leave it.'"

When asked about any efforts that were being made to provide aid to those who were dislodged from the natural laws of the universe as the result of dangerous experimental materials sold in Night Vale under the guise of simple home goods and gardening wares, the representative only repeated "America, love or leave it," each iteration a little rounder, a little more abstracted from human communication, until it was only a series of guttural sounds in the vague shape of what used to be words, as the representative retreated further and further into their burlap cloak until it collapsed, empty, upon the podium, smelling of compost and grain alcohol.

All in all, a pretty typical statement from the government, and hopefully this clears up that whole thing with the flamingos.

Due to the recent events we all have read about, the librarians have been more active than usual. Witnesses, who were paid to go witness by others who were afraid to get close enough to see, report that there are steam and sparks flying out of the Public Library's many chimneys. Howling can be heard both inside the building and from the mouths of the witnesses as, through the windows, they glimpse the terrible physical forms of the librarians.

There are even a few unconfirmed reports that in the confusion of recent events and the resulting damage done to the library building, one of the librarians may have escaped. Of course, a disaster of that magnitude hasn't happened since, oh, I guess it would have been last year, so that doesn't seem likely. Truly it would be awful if it did though. We lost so many people from so many different places the last time a librarian escaped.

One of the witnesses, James Patterson (no relation to the famous local dairy farmer, James Patterson), reported that perhaps the librarians have developed the power to mentally influence those around them, since the closer he got to the library, the more strongly he felt the urge to read books. "Are there any good novels coming out soon?" he began foolishly asking, blind to the dangers that books present. "Oh man, I could really use a new novel," he babbled, the poor thing, not even understanding the ghastly words spewing from his mouth.

We have no idea if this event was an aberration or if librarians have truly developed the terrifying ability to make people want to actually read books, but all citizens would be well advised to stay clear of libraries and any dangerous books they may see in bookstores everywhere quite soon. I mean, you should always avoid books and libraries, but now it might be worth taking extra pre-cautionary measures, like scooping your eyes out with grapefruit spoons and triple-bolting your door.

And now, back to today's epilogue.

The baristas are continuing to multiply. All over town businesses that were recently useful normal things, like Gas Stations, and Antiques Malls, and Screaming Sheds, are now suddenly coffee shops, full of identical baristas demonstrating their ability to illustrate, using steamed milk on coffee, the exact moment of your death.

This crisis makes me think of the Man in the Tan Jacket, who was with us in so many crises through our town's recent history. What would he have done with this situation?

Perhaps it would help to start at the beginning. The beginning is usually an awfully convenient place to start, right? But trying to find a beginning means grappling with the question of time. Scientists have a game where they try to explain time to each other without laughing. No one has ever won.

The man came to us first almost three years ago, a newcomer in a tan jacket. I remember him standing by the side of the road in the small puddle of light cast from a burning refrigerator.

And that is the thing, the remembering. When he was here, we did not remember him. We forgot him constantly. A specter in a tan jacket. Now he is not here, and we remember him perfectly. Years of stories and experience come flooding back to us. We remember him scampering over the walls of the Dog Park. We remember him showing us a map to a place very far from here, a place we did not understand at all. We remember him passing out pieces of paper, the content of which was a mystery, the physical properties of which were a nuisance. But here again I cover a story we already know because we all so recently experienced it.

Old Woman Josie released a statement, to me, in person, as part of a conversation we were having privately, without her saying it was a statement, it was just a thing she said to me during a conversation, anyway here it is, she said, "I always liked that Man in a Tan Jacket. Even when I was afraid of him and suspicious of him. Even when he showed up at my door in the middle of the night with that suitcase of his, the suitcase that constantly buzzed, knocking on my door and babbling about how he needed help desperately, how we had to help him save his home. Even then, as I was ignoring him in his hour of need, I liked him. Even when I forgot him completely and had no idea he even existed, I liked him. You know, this fruit salad Carlos made is just delicious."

And I agree with Josie's statement. The fruit salad we were having at our lunch together was supergood, and I wolfed it down even though I've been trying to cut back on my meat consumption lately.

I got a little sidetracked there. To get back to the point, we're all likely going to be destroyed by an endless stream of baristas, which is, of course, a direct result of the recent events involving Jackie and Diane. So there's that.

Listeners, looks like we're in need of a new intern. Intern Danielle has stopped coming to the office.

I mean, Danielle had all these crazy conspiracy theories about how radio interns are doomed, so she wanted to stay inside and focus only on computer work. She steadfastly refused any field reporting assignments, so I complied with her wishes and let her run our social media accounts, which I thought would make her happy.

But a few weeks ago, after giving her the simple and fun job of taking pictures of Khoshekh, our radio station's live-in cat, for our official station Myspace as well as to my personal Google Plus and Snapchat accounts, she just stopped coming to work. I guess she just didn't have it in her anymore.

But listen, if you're more motivated to learn about a career in radio than Danielle, we'd love to have you come intern here at the station. All you need to do to become a community radio intern is not run away when Station Management surrounds you outside your home shouting, "THIS ONE IS NEXT! THIS ONE IS NEXT!"

And now a word from our sponsors. Personally I find the content of this ad distasteful, given my earlier warning, but I'm informed by Station Management that I have to read it as written. Here goes.

"Many of us like books. None of us like to admit it. We know that reading makes us deviants, perverts, freaks. Many of us might say, on the radio for instance, that books are dangerous and should be avoided. Even thinking the words *I like books* to ourselves makes us shudder with a secret shame. We know that we should only be reading government pamphlets and the prophecies on the back of cereal boxes, but again and again we find ourselves returning to the dark sickness of literary language. Who among us can say that they do not have, buried in a box of linens under their bed, a well-read copy of *Brand New Ancients* by Kate Tempest or a collection of Annie Baker's *Vermont Plays*?

"Given all this, should we band together, deviant with deviant, a deviance so natural that it is no deviance at all, but an ingrained motion of the heart, a secret desire so common that it is no more secret than the sun? Should we begin to admit together that we all sometimes like to touch and read books?

"No, of course not. We should be ashamed, and hide our love of books from each other, heaping scorn and hypocritical anger upon anyone who dares to reveal that they have the same desires we do.

"Harper Perennial. All of our literature is shipped to you in unmarked brown paper wrappings. Charges will appear on your credit card statement as DEFINITELY NOT BOOKS. No one has to know you are a book-reading freak."

This has been a message from our sponsors. Ugh, books.

The population of the Barista District continues to grow, doubling almost every hour, through no means known to modern science, antique science, or reverse science. Carlos is working on a solution, but in the meantime, townspeople are overwhelmed and scared by the coffee options suddenly available to them. They are screaming. They are screaming and running away.

Larry Leroy, out on the edge of town, told me that he can see them now, the baristas, and that they are beautiful and surging. There are so many hands holding so much coffee. They are all so helpful.

"This might be it," Larry is saying. "Anything could be it," he is continuing. "Any moment could be the last one. We should always be prepared for the eventuality of no more eventualities. We all live on the narrow precipice. But also yeah, this barista thing is really going off, huh?" he concluded.

Perhaps if the Man in the Tan Jacket were here, he would have some idea, some solution, or even would just be there to add a comfortingly forgettable presence to this ongoing disaster. But of course, he is not here. And we all know why. We all know who he really is now.

Oh. Oh, Carlos is texting me. He, hm, okay he says that he has a solution to this whole barista thing. Hey! That's quite clever. It also takes care of that other problem, you know the one I don't even have to explain to you right now because it was so frightful and all-consuming and fresh in our memories.

Okay, while Carlos does his clever plan, I'll do a clever plan of my own which is: taking you to the weather.

WEATHER: "Endless Dream" by God Is an Astronaut

And now here we are, in the after. Carlos's plan, well, we read about what it was and how it turned out. No need to summarize here.

What do we do, after such huge events have transpired? After the ones in danger no longer are (meaning either that they no longer are in danger or that in an existential sense they just no longer *are*).

Well, I'll tell you what I'll do. I'm going to go bowling with Carlos. League Night is tonight, and we've gotten the team back together with Old Woman Josie. Of course, she can use her left hand again now, now that this affair we've been talking about is all over, so our scores should be up.

And what else? The sky, of course. Always that. Let's start there and work our way down to earth. Other cities. Other places. This city. This place.

I imagine that soon this town will settle back into the routine of its existence until a new peril arises again soon. Like a heartbeat. A sudden, violent movement. And in between a lull, in itself a rhythm, a counterpart, the silence between the beats.

Night Vale, in a lull. The doctors at the hospital, going about their mysterious routines. The Pawn Shop, its name changed now, of course, after what happened recently. The office district, and, oh it looks like there is a large family of tarantulas heading there now and they do not look happy. I would hate to be whoever it is that they're looking for.

The Moonlite All-Nite Diner, where I'm sure Steve Carlsberg is going to stop by on his way home for a slice of invisible pie. Our mayor, Dana, getting ready to finish her work. Carlos's lab, where he is also finishing up his work. See you soon, Carlos.

And, and something else. Over a housing tract across town I can see a dot in the sky, floating high above one of the houses, twirling and soaring higher. I can't quite see what it is, but it's lovely.

In any case, an entire town swinging back to the normal, getting on with life in the after. After all of the things that we all now know happened. All of us.

Except, of course, one person. A person missing. A person who we all missed. A person impossible to remember. A person, now, impossible to forget. The Man in the Tan Jacket.

And what next?

Well, I think there may be other people, other stories to tell. We are, each of us, a vast story waiting for someone to tell it.

Stay tuned in just a few days, or depending on where you are in time, any day you decide to get around to it, for a 401-page factual report about the events that led to this epilogue, available in hard-cover, ebook, or audiobook from your favorite factual report retailer.

In the meantime, from after the whole of what you haven't yet read, good night, Night Vale. Good night.

PROVERB: "Late capitalism" is such a sweetly optimistic phrase.

EPISODE 77:
"A STRANGER"

NOVEMBER 1, 2015

GUEST VOICE: JASIKA NICOLE (DANA CARDINAL)

HAVE YOU EVER READ *THE UNEXPECTED GUEST* BY EDWARD GOREY? IN spite of (because of?) its adorable simplicity, it's one of the most terrifying books I've ever read, and I would call the stranger in this episode a vague tribute to Gorey's guest.

The stranger here has no explanation, and like Gorey's guest, no perceived desires or physical action. I've always been fascinated with imperceptible movement in horror, like Dr. Who's angels or even the adventure trope of the cursed object. To some extent, the ambling zombie is part of this.

Additionally, in this episode, we get to hear from Dana. We haven't heard from Mayor Cardinal in a while—not in her own voice at least. And working with the actor Jasika Nicole is one of my favorite things in the world. So, duh, we wrote another part for her.

Here we have a delightful former-intern-turned-mayor dealing with a controversial issue in town: the decision to financially help a rival city. Desert Bluffs, after all, was home to StrexCorp, which tried to overtake all of Night Vale just over a year ago. It's easy to see how a public endorsement of helping out neighbors would be a difficult choice.

Since Dana was an intern at the radio station and her subsequent life in the desert otherworld pining for a way home to see her brother and mother once again, I've loved her character. I've loved how Jasika layered Dana with such emotional gravity, so focused and independent, yet so in need of her tiny network of those who love her—Cecil included.

And yet, here she is, suddenly mayor of Night Vale. And it's been a hard go for her. The City Council does not entirely support her choices. She's fairly young—imagine going from radio intern to mayor in like one year. Go on. Imagine it. I'll wait.

Know what? I'm tired of waiting. Let's move on . . .

I'm really interested in exploring the faults and favors of all characters. Generally speaking, Dana has thus far been nearly without fault, without many traits that make her difficult to like, to empathize with. I don't want her to seem like some ideal secondary hero, worthy of our admiration and unskeptical praise. She's human. She is capable of failings and sins and poor decisions.

So she chews on dirt when she is anxious (among other feelings). She speaks in questions. She is uneasy about her leadership. She is full of self-doubt not noticeably common in our political leadership.

—Jeffrey Cranor

When a window closes, so does a door. So do all
the other doors and windows. The house is alive,
and it doesn't know you, and it is scared.

WELCOME TO NIGHT VALE

Today's top story. There's a strange person standing in the lobby of
our radio station. This person is standing still, in front of the recep-
tion counter. Our receptionist, Lance, keeps asking the stranger if
they need anything or if they are here to see anyone. The stranger
has not moved. Lance said that he never saw the stranger enter. He
looked up and the stranger was just there, about eight feet away
from Lance's desk.

The stranger has eyes that are darker than some people's eyes
but lighter than other people's eyes. The same could be said about
the stranger's hair, teeth, clothing, lips, and skin. The stranger stands
with their arms at their side, weight distributed evenly across the
hips, a rigid but casual stance. The stranger can be seen breathing. It
is hard to say what exactly the stranger is looking at. It is even harder
to say what the stranger wants.

Lance told me he would update me on the stranger. And I will
do the same for you, listeners.

Now it's time for another Children's Fun Fact Science Corner.
Did you know that over 70 percent of the earth's surface is water?

It's true. Scientists believe that the other 30 percent is some kind of animal hide. Their data shows that the world's continents comprise the leathery back of a slow-moving ocean beast. They don't know specifically what kind of beast, but scientists hope that it's cute. Or at minimum nonvenomous and fairly easy to take care of. Scientists are hoping they're wrong about all of this, but given that they're scientists, that's pretty much impossible.

Lest the beast reveal its true nature, please walk gently and speak softly so as not to alert it to your presence.

This has been Children's Fun Fact Science Corner.

Mayor Dana Cardinal announced this morning that she has been in touch with neighboring city Desert Bluffs. "It's a disgusting town with terrible people, and we will no longer speak of them," she would have announced if she were me. But here is what she actually said.

DANA: What does it mean to be a good neighbor, Night Vale? Is it enough that we introduce ourselves? That we say hello? That we avoid eye contact and have sturdy doors and call centers for reporting suspicious activity? How far out does neighborliness extend? Because I have tapped my friends' phones and am using trained birds to record all of their activities, does that make me a kind person? A neighborly person?

It does, but what about beyond what we can see? Who we can see? How far does our kindness extend? To the limits of our city? To the limits of our eyesight? To the end of our block?

To the tips of our noses?

People of Night Vale. We have a chance to help a neighbor in need. I have been approached by our friends to the north.

Wait. I'm being told it's not to the north. To the east. [*quietly, off mic*] Which direction are they, then? What? It changes? Really? Okay. Sssh. SSHHH! [*on mic*] By our nearby friends in this desert.

Due to financial hardships, the people of Desert Bluffs are in need. We are all in this together, Night Vale. Sickness can spread, whether that sickness is viral or economic. We must not ignore our neighbors, our friends.

Today I have asked the City Council to negotiate a low-interest loan to Desert Bluffs, our proximate civic family. I think they would do the same for us.

[*speaking with mouth full*] If I sound passionate, it is because my heart is full of blood. If I sound boisterous, it is because my lungs are full of words. If I sound like I am eating, it is because my mouth is full of dirt. Sometimes I chew on dirt when I am anxious. Or when I am happy. Or when I am talking. I like chewing on dirt.

[*no longer chewing*] I hope you will support your neighbors in whatever direction they live. I hope you will support my decision as mayor. Good day, Night Vale.

CECIL: Mayor Cardinal's deputy Trish Hidge said there would be no questions. She then picked the mayor up into her arms, pulled her cloak across their huddled bodies, and ran through the crowd, bowling over journalists and onlookers and some random jogger who thinks he's better than everyone else because he exercises publicly.

The City Council has already registered their opposition to the mayor's plan to help Desert Bluffs. The City Council issued their own statement which was to stomp into their room, slam the door, and play Rihanna really loudly.

I have to say I agree with the City Council on this issue, listeners. I understand Mayor Cardinal's concern about Desert Bluffs' struggling economy, and she is a very kind and sympathetic person. But as the poet Robert Frost once said, "Good fences make good neighbors. Really strong fences with razor wire and turrets. Keep those neighbors out." And Frost was right.

I support Dana on most issues, but I say save your sympathy for your own town's people.

An update on the stranger standing in our lobby: The stranger is still standing in our lobby. Lance approached them but grew scared. The stranger stood so still that it became impossible to derive context from motion or activity. Any sound or movement the stranger might make would be completely divorced of linear narrative or conventional meaning. At any moment the stranger could suddenly lurch or shriek without apparent cause. Thus the clenching terror Lance felt as he neared the person in the lobby.

Lance mentioned he could hear breathing. It wasn't labored, but it also wasn't quiet. It was a person breathing, Lance confirmed. But I'm not entirely sure how Lance confirmed that. I'm also not entirely sure how anyone can confirm anything, so let's just go with what Lance says.

Listeners, if you've been trying to call in to the station, I apologize, as Lance is too frozen in fear to do much of anything. He thinks he sees the stranger moving, but he also thinks he does not. He is desperate for some explanation of this person's presence in our lobby. But he has received none. Lance is now crying but without tears. He is screaming but without sound.

He wants to gain the courage to touch the stranger. To hit the stranger, to punch and punch and kick and claw at the stranger. He wants to feel the relief, a release from the madness of mystery. He would rather experience actual pain than wait any longer in anticipation of the unknown.

Lance wants to sigh but he cannot. He doesn't remember the last time he exhaled. He is not sure of what is real. So he is sorry if you keep getting our voice mail here at the station. It's been a rough day. More on this soon.

But first, let's have a look at this week's community calendar.

Thursday afternoon, there is a free ice cream social for all members of the Illuminati. If you are Illuminati, please go to the secret underground bunker. There will be ice cream, streamers, and, of course, a bocci ball tournament. If you are not Illuminati, please disregard this notice. Maybe just stock up on some bottled water and bullets and hope for the best.

Friday night, Dark Owl Records will host a '90s fashion night. Everyone is required to non-ironically wear T-shirts and hats from the 1990s, which were originally ironically worn T-shirts and hats from the 1970s. Owner Michelle Nguyen asked that everyone be as sincere as they can be. Irony will not be tolerated, only studied, museum-like, on puffy truck hats with clever witticisms like "HEY, BEER" or "I LIKE HIGHWAY" or "DOG," along with airbrushed pictures of rattlesnakes, eagles, hot-glue guns, and screen doors. Nguyen asked that I not invite the public to this event. Oh. Ooh. I should have read the whole press release before reading tha—— AAaand, I just received a new press release from Dark Owl owner Michelle Nguyen announcing that the event has been canceled because people know about it. Sorry, Michelle.

On Saturday, StrexCorp—formerly a Desert Bluffs corporation, and now a Night Vale business owned and operated by beings who are definitely not angels—will be the headline sponsor of a new program called Free Opera Day, a weekly community event where anyone can hear opera at no cost. In fact, you don't even have to go to the new Old Opera House to hear it. Opera will be broadcast from the municipal loudspeakers which are located on every residential block in the city and within most residential homes.

On Sunday, the Night Vale Opera will be running their most popular weekly program, Opera-Free Day, where citizens are relieved of all opera for twenty-four hours. No one is allowed to play any opera at all. Armed soldiers from a private armed soldier corporation will walk the streets making sure no one is playing any opera. "What is opera?" one armed soldier will ask the others. "I don't know," another will reply. "Could that be opera?" another will ask. "Let's go check it out," they'll all say, lifting their rifles and approaching what will appear to be an automated car wash.

Monday morning doesn't really matter. Nothing ever did. Be silent and look upward to the sky as if it had your answers. It does not. The sky is as dumb as rocks. Really dumb. You'll figure that out early Monday morning as you passively choose to experience the day in spite of its pointlessness, mumbling "Nought else remains to do" while brushing your teeth.

And now a word from our sponsor. Today's show is sponsored by . . . well, it's sponsored by Your Mom. She's really nice and she mailed us a ten-dollar bill to sponsor this show. That's well below our usual advertising rate here at the station, but Your Mom was just the sweetest. She also wrote a letter saying that she hopes you're having a fun time listening to this show—she knows it's your favorite radio program (awww)—and wants you to know that she loves you very much (awwww!). Your Mom also wants to know if you're still seeing that boy. He's bad news and she doesn't like his tattoos. Not that people with tattoos are bad. That's not what she's saying. "But what do you think his skin will look like when he's sixty?," she added. "What do you think anyone's skin will look like when they're sixty?," she said repeatedly. She asked several quiet, sad questions about the process of aging. Then she said she cares for you no matter what. She just wants you to be happy. This message has been brought to you by . . . Your Mom.

Good news, listeners. I've just learned that the stranger standing in our lobby has finally moved. Unfortunately, the stranger has begun walking slowly toward Lance. The stranger raised one arm, imperceptibly at first, but by the time the hand was nearly brushing Lance's neck, Lance realized it and leapt out of the way. Lance is currently standing behind his rolling chair watching closely for the stranger's next move, even though the stranger is moving so slowly as to appear motionless.

It's like the old adage about the frog in the frying pan. They say if you put a frog in a frying pan and then turn up the heat very gradually, then you're a sociopath who takes pleasure in the torture of innocent animals.

Go easy on frogs, okay. They're adorable and ecologically important but also easy to trick into dying.

[distant screaming]

Oh my goodness. Lance! Listeners, I must check on my colleague. But first, I must take you to the weather.

WEATHER: "Meet You at the Gate" by Jayne Trimble

Listeners, we found Lance. He was curled into a dark corner of the storage closet, his eyes dull, his jaw slack, his gray maw unnaturally long. The stranger—who had stood so quietly, so nearly still in the lobby before—is now nowhere to be seen. Likely they are still in this very building, ready to show themselves again at any moment.

I bent down and took Lance's hand. He was always a good receptionist. Well, he wasn't that great. I mean there's no National

Receptionist Ranking system. How am I supposed to know? I've never done it myself. He could have been a receptionist savant for all I know about the field.

But Lance was a good man. He loved movies. He always dreamed of moving to Hollywood and becoming a makeup artist for major motion pictures. He loved doing makeup. But it was a dream deferred as he could never figure out where Hollywood was or how you were supposed to get there. Most airlines and bus drivers would stare blankly at him when he tried to buy a ticket. It's not on any map I've ever seen. It's possible Lance just invented it to take his mind off of the tedium of daily life.

Either way, his makeup skills came in handy, as he did himself up just like that poor girl in the closet from his favorite documentary: *The Ring*. Plaid skirt and white shirt, long hair, and a grotesque corpse face. He really nailed it. I told him good job. He climbed out of the storage room and said thanks.

I told him one day someone will find out where Hollywood is, and he'll go there and be a super-famous makeup artist. He didn't say anything. We stood in silence for several minutes.

I'm taking a continuing education class at the community college about the art of conversation. They said every good conversationalist should try to find five to seven straight minutes of no speaking, in order to let others talk. Lance is taking that same class. So we both gave the other person room to speak for those long, silent minutes.

Finally, our intern Kate entered and told us her roommate called to say there's a stranger standing just outside their apartment door. The stranger isn't moving or speaking and won't leave. Kate said she needed to take off early to deal with this. She said this several times, each iteration slightly louder, slightly more strained.

Have a great rest of your day, Kate!

Lance has returned to his work, feeling better. I asked him to check for missed calls as the light for the voice mail was rapidly blinking to indicate it was full. We apparently received dozens of calls from Night Vale residents reporting strangers standing, silent and unmoving, in their homes or sitting in the back seats of their cars. A few residents were in their beds, in the middle of the night, when they turned and found a stranger there lying beside them, empty eyes staring at nothing, not moving.

Listeners, maybe take a moment to check outside your front door. Check for a silent, strange face in your window or just around the corner at the end of a hallway. Perhaps take an agonizing look into your shower, just in case.

Make sure there is no one there. If there is, well, be patient. They move pretty slowly, it turns out. You know what? Maybe hide until the stranger leaves. It'll be fine. But maybe hide or run away. Maybe just huddle down, close your eyes, and hope one isn't near you right now.

Stay tuned next for the sound of human breathing, which is probably just your own breathing. Probably.

As always, good night, Night Vale. Good Night.

PROVERB: I'm a single-issue voter. If a candidate is not a baby polar bear, I straight-up cannot support them.

EPISODE 78:
"COOKING STUFF: THANKSGIVING SPECIAL"

NOVEMBER 15, 2015

GUEST VOICES: WIL WHEATON (EARL HARLAN), MEG BASHWINER (DEB)

I WATCH A LOT OF COOKING SHOWS. AS A CHILD, I WATCHED RERUNS OF *The Galloping Gourmet* with my grandmother. My mother would sometimes watch Paul Prudhomme, and I would always stop down to watch with her. These days, my wife and I watch quite a bit of *Chopped*. (Alex Guarnaschelli is our favorite judge because we're not assholes.) I've noticed, though, that I rarely watch cooking shows alone. Food is only exciting when I'm with those I love.

In this episode, Earl Harlan is back on the air to help Night Vale with the perfect Thanksgiving meal—a time often associated with homecomings and family. Yet here is Earl struggling to deal with his son, Roger, and Roger, in turn, struggling to deal with his father. Neither seemed to know how they got to this point in their lives, nor why their relationship began *in media res*.

I love Earl as a character. He's smart and talented. He's likable, and in some ways both heroic and helpless. Wil's performance adds an extra layer of practicality to Earl, and for me, this is where he becomes fully human. The world, for him, is a how-to to be learned and mastered (as a chef, how to cook a turkey; or per his old job as scout leader, how to set up a tent or start a campfire). But there are no instructions for being a father or a family member. He can only try doing what he has seen elsewhere.

Football, to Earl, seems like the keystone of any good father/son relationship. Dad needs some way of connecting with his boy that involves toughness and competition, but here it falls flat as Earl doesn't seem to know much about football (or parenting) at all.

Contrast this with Cecil. Earl and Cecil were close childhood friends who drifted apart. Cecil is unquestioning about this (unquestioning about a lot of things in Night Vale, really), but Earl is starting to understand he and Cecil experienced time quite differently than others. Earl was nineteen for a long time and is now uncertain about how old he is and who this child is. Earl keeps trying to let Cecil know that something went wrong. Cecil, though, is just glad to have an old friend provide a popular segment on his radio show.

Earl approaches life like a problem to be solved, and right now he's stumped on what to do about Roger. Though while Cecil has neither solutions nor answers for Earl, he may be able to offer something Earl doesn't have in his life at all.

—Jeffrey Cranor

Cook a feast no family could fully eat. Recite prayers no family could fully believe. And acknowledge a frightful history no family could fully comprehend.

WELCOME TO NIGHT VALE

CECIL: We have a treat for you today, Night Vale: a Thanksgiving edition of *Cooking Stuff with Earl Harlan*. Our guest, of course, is Earl Harlan, sous-chef at Night Vale's most celebrated restaurant, Tourniquet. Thanks for being here, Earl.

EARL: Thanks for having me on, Cecil.

CECIL: Earl's going to be talking us through preparing and cooking a basic Thanksgiving meal. I know a lot of you out there have your ancient family recipes still on their original cave walls, but Earl might have some new techniques to help you spice up those old dishes. And there are a lot of people, like Carlos and me, who have never cooked, or even seen, a Thanksgiving turkey. It's intimidating. Where do we begin, Earl?

EARL: It doesn't have to be intimidating. On today's show, I'll walk you through the five easy steps for the perfect Thanksgiving turkey: Kill, Clean, Gut, Stuff, and Cook. Also some essential dishes like mashed potatoes and cranberry sauce.

CECIL: That sounds great, Earl. But before we get started, let's get a news update about the trial of Hiram McDaniels.

Things are coming along in Night Vale's Trial of the Century. Judge Siobhan Azdak has been assigned this case. Siobhan is not actually a judge. She's a theater writer for the *Night Vale Daily Journal*. But given that Night Vale has never had a trial, we just didn't have many judges around. Since Siobhan has such a nuanced understanding of contemporary stagecraft, but with an acerbic and unforgiving critical voice, she seemed a pretty good fit for deciding the fates of likely criminals, which is who she'd be dealing with. I mean, what innocent person gets arrested and brought to trial? No innocent person I've ever heard of.

Hiram McDaniels, a literal five-headed dragon, has been charged with the attempted murder of current mayor Dana Cardinal, as well as conspiracy, assault, and willful destruction of private property. The trial will be held just as soon as they can find a jury of Hiram's peers. So far they have found a salamander, but it's tiny and cannot speak human languages, let alone hold still long enough to listen to the lawyers discuss jury selections. Also it's an amphibian, not a reptile, so that's pretty insensitive.

They did find another five-headed dragon available to serve on a jury, but it turns out she is Hiram's sister Hadassah, and she was none too happy to be called in for jury duty, let alone at her brother's trial. The prosecuting attorney, Troy Walsh, has been toying around with the idea of just dressing people up like dragons, so that Hiram feels like he's getting a fair trial. This seems like the most equitable thing to do, since everyone knows that justice is less about what the law says and more about how everyone feels about it.

More on the Trial of the Century as events develop. Now let's get right back to *Cooking Stuff with Earl Harlan.*

EARL: Thanks, Cecil. So let's cook a turkey. First step: Find a turkey and kill it.

CECIL: Yum.

EARL: I shot mine. But you can use a knife, a bow and arrow, a heavy wrench, your teeth, whatever is easiest for you.

The next step is to clean your bird. Pluck all of the feathers from its lifeless corpse. Cut off its head and all six of its hooves. (Adventurous culinary experts out there could pickle those hooves and serve them with ice cream for a traditional Svitzish dessert!)

Next, gut the turkey. Don't be intimidated by the stench. Just stick your knife deep into its belly and allow everything to pour out onto the floor. You won't need any of that mess.

CECIL: My mother actually used to cook turkey organs for us. She said they were called giblets.

EARL: Your mother lied to you, Cecil.

CECIL: Then what was she feeding us?

EARL: Let's stuff this turkey. What do you say?

CECIL: Okay.

EARL: I used to make my stuffing from stale bread, but since wheat and wheat by-products can turn into snakes and kill you, I just take old newspapers, wad them up, and shove them into the turkey. They absorb most of the bird's toxic fluids. So same result really.

After the stuffing, throw in some seasoning like salt and pepper, thyme, sage, a fistful of grass, anything you find lying around. Just put it in a pile on top of the turkey and slide it into the oven.

While you're waiting for it to cook, maybe catch a football game on television.

I plan on watching some games this year with my son, Roger. Last Thanksgiving we watched football together, but at the time, I had just come into awareness of myself as an adult, and suddenly had this son that I didn't know at all, so I didn't know his name. It was awkward. Plus, neither of us had heard of football, let alone

its byzantine laws and restrictions on dancing. We both sat silently waiting for it to be over, wanting to speak to each other, unable to find the words.

CECIL: Not talking can be a blessing, Earl. Thanksgiving Day football games are my favorite, because my brother-in-law doesn't talk to me for hours. Carlos likes watching the big parade, but I don't deal well with gore, so I cover my eyes and have him describe to me how they all die.

EARL: I'm trying to build family traditions with Roger. I'm trying to build anything with Roger.

CECIL: Fun! And hey, I remembered to rent an oven for your appearance this time, Earl. Now, you already prepared our turkey before the broadcast today. It's cooking right now low and slow at 675 degrees. I can't wait to taste it.

But first a public service announcement:

The Night Vale Parks Department would like to remind you that bears are dangerous animals, and you should stay away from them. Conversely, bears are also adorable, so it's hard to want to stay too far away. The Night Vale Parks Department understands bears look like they want hugs, and maybe they do want hugs. Maybe a hug would be just the thing to calm down their aggressive side. Who knows? In fact, the rangers over at the Parks Department are split right down the middle as to whether bears are dangerous or cute.

According to the new Parks Department brochure on wilderness safety: "It's tough to say. I dunno. Try hugging a bear. See what happens."

EARL: What a weird brochure. Bears are dangerous animals. No one should ever hug—

CECIL: Let's not argue, Earl.

[*beat*]

This has been a public service announcement created by the Night Vale Parks Department and paid for by a bunch of bears that pooled their money and bought some airtime.

Let's talk now about the ultimate Thanksgiving side: mashed potatoes.

EARL: Right. Mashed potatoes are a simple dish in concept, but they take skill to master. A lot of people think they only need to mix potatoes, stock, butter, and cream. But there's so much more to it than that!

CECIL: Really? I've been using that standard recipe for years. It seems fine.

EARL: Oh, but, Cecil. It could be so much better. For instance, you could cook those potatoes for about forty-five to sixty minutes to really soften them up. A raw potato is quite hard to mash, let alone chew.

CECIL: I never thought about that.

EARL: People also forget to take the butter out of its wax paper or foil wrapping. You should definitely unwrap your butter before using it. Also make sure your cream is fresh. You don't want to use any heavy cream older than, say, six months.

CECIL: Amazing. I would have never thought of any of this.

EARL: And listen, salt and pepper are fine for mashed potato seasoning, but if you really want to step your dish up a notch, really have your family clamoring about your kitchen skills, then let me tell you my secret spice mix.

CECIL: What is it, Earl?

EARL: I use slightly *more* salt and a little extra pepper. Just a tad.

CECIL: Amazing.

EARL: Then you just put it all in a pot and mash it with your feet until it's warm enough to serve.

You know, I made this dish recently for me and Roger.

CECIL: Did he love it?

EARL: I couldn't tell. He ate it and then said, "Thanks, um," and then I said, "Dad," and he said, "Okay" and he went to bed.

CECIL: How sweet.

EARL: Lately I've noticed he wakes up in the middle of the night and just walks. I got up and quietly followed him one night. He walked out of the house and into the neighborhood. He walked down each street in our subdivision, never backtracking or walking the same street twice. He didn't stop or look at anything. He just walked in the darkness. Once, a hooded figure passed him but neither of them acknowledged each other. The hooded figure saw me for sure, but I think they also saw that I was just a concerned father and was not interested in spying on any of their secretive activities. The hooded figure nodded and let me pass.

CECIL: And Roger came home after that?

EARL: Yep, he walks each street, each night in a different pattern, and then returns to bed.

CECIL: Quite an adventurous kiddo you have there. Let's pause now for a word from today's sponsor. With that, here's Deb, a sentient patch of haze.

DEB: Hello, human listeners. Today's show is proudly sponsored by Corn. It's almost Thanksgiving, after all. And you wouldn't have Thanksgiving without Corn. Thanksgiving is America's holiday. Corn is America's crop, America's lifeblood. You can't live without Corn. If we didn't have Corn, we wouldn't have tortillas, or syrup, or soft drinks. Without Corn, we wouldn't have dogs or cars. We wouldn't even have a moon. Everything is made of Corn. Lifeblood. Listen to your heartbeat. ZZZZZZZZzzzzzzzT! You hear that heartbeat of yours? I'm a patch of haze. I don't know what a heartbeat sounds like, but this is what I imagine it sounds like. ZZZZZZZZZzzzzzzzT! That sound in your chest is Corn, my friend. All of that Corn, pumping through your delicate, mortal veins. You didn't choose how you got here. Neither did Corn. You are both products of free market and overpopulation.

Corn. Eat it.

This message brought to you by the Corn and Imaginary Corn Farmers of America.

CECIL: Thanks, Deb.

EARL: It's really humid in here.

CECIL: That's Deb for you. Well, speaking of corn, that brings us to my favorite Thanksgiving dish: cranberry sauce.

EARL: A lot of people look down on canned cranberry sauce. But don't be so quick to judge. It's inexpensive, easy to store, and with the right preparation you can elevate this plain can of red gelatin into the most talked-about dish on the table.

CECIL: Great news. I have an entire cupboard full of canned cranberry sauce. I'm looking forward to hearing what I'm supposed to do with it.

[*beat*]

Earl?

EARL: I found Roger one evening in the cupboard. He was just sitting there. He wasn't hiding or crying. I asked him what he was doing and he shrugged his shoulders. I asked him if he was all right, and he said, "Sure."

CECIL: Tell me. How is he doing in school?

EARL: It's been up and down. There's no record of his birth or his existence prior to last fall. I don't know of any birth mother and he has no memories prior to showing up at my house for the first time a little over a year ago. The school has let him enroll and take classes despite his lack of paperwork. He gets along with most kids okay, but some tease him and call him names like "Ghost Child" and "Zombie Kid" because his skin is grayish and decaying, and he is nearly transparent.

CECIL: Ouch. Kids can be cruel.

EARL: He's really good in class, though. He's still in elementary school because he looks about eight or nine. But his teacher Ms. Blackwell said he has adult-level reading and math skills, so we're trying to get him more advanced material. He's been reading Immanuel Kant for a book report.

CECIL: Roger's such a bright kid. You're a good father, Earl. You know that, right?

EARL: I have no idea what he's thinking. I try to talk to him, but he seems . . . distant? bored?

CECIL: He's a child. It's difficult, I imagine, for what is essentially an adopted child to—

EARL: He's not adopted, though. He looks just like me, Cecil. See, here's a photo of him. And one of me when I was a child.

CECIL: Oh wow. You two are identical. When was this photo taken of you? Is that a steam locomotive in the backg———

EARL: AAAH! Fire!

CECIL: Oh my. Listeners, it appears our oven has caught fire. Where's that extinguisher?

EARL: Here! Here!

CECIL: [*coughs*] Where are you? Earl? There's so much smoke. Listeners, while I find Earl, let me take you all to the weather.

WEATHER: "Autumn's Echo" by Stripmall Architecture

CECIL: Well, our turkey has finished cooking, and you've laid out a whole Thanksgiving spread for us here, Earl. It looks delectable.

EARL: Yeah, the turkey came out perfectly. Once the oven catches fire, that's when you know it's time to take out your bird and dig in.

CECIL: Let me start by tasting the cranberry sauce. [*takes bite*] Oh, so good. It's got that perfect balance of tart and sugary sweetness I like. Plus the crunch of the frozen corn mixed in just gives this gooey dish a delightfully complex texture.

EARL: I also recommend mixing in a handful of bay leaves at the end.

CECIL: Yum! And now let's try these "Earl Harlan Special" mashed potatoes. [*takes bite*] Mmm . . . so buttery and warm, like the skin on the bottom of a human foot.

EARL: And don't forget my secret spice mix.

CECIL: I've already forgotten. Let's move on to the crown jewel of Thanksgiving dinner: the turkey. Tell us about this masterpiece, Earl.

EARL: Turkey is easier than you think, listeners. Don't be intimidated. I shot this bird, drained its blood, tore all of its feathers off, removed its organs, and cut off its head and feet. Then I stuffed things into its dead body and put it in an oven.

CECIL: Let's give it a taste. [*loud crunching, like crushing gravel?*] Mmm. So . . . Okay . . . Huh.

EARL: That's so nice of you to say, Cecil. This show has meant a lot to me today. I've been having a tough—well, a complicated year—and cooking has brought be so much joy—well, distraction. It's a real pleasure getting to spend time with you and your listeners.

CECIL: Earl, come over to our place for Thanksgiving.

EARL: I—No.

CECIL: Yes, please. Carlos and I would love to have you and Roger—

EARL: Who?

CECIL: Your son.

EARL: Right. Right.

CECIL: We'd love to have you two over. My sister and her husband are coming. Plus, my niece Janice will be there, so that would be someone Roger could talk to and play with.

EARL: I don't want to intrude. Can you even fit that many people?

CECIL: Of course. Plus, Carlos and I will do the cooking. No working for you this holiday.

EARL: Cecil, I don't know what to say.

CECIL: Actually, we might need a hand with the cranberry sauce. I have over twenty cans of the stuff I need to prepare. But other than that, you and Roger just sit back and try to understand the point of football. Maybe even have Carlos describe the torture scenes from the parade to you both. Keep Steve occupied and out of the kitchen while I'm cooking.

EARL: Thank you, Cecil.

CECIL: You're welcome. I can't wait to try out all these new recipes. I'm going to go out and assassinate a turkey right after the broadcast today, I'm that excited.

Listeners, thanks again for tuning in and thanks to Earl Harlan of the restaurant Tourniquet for these helpful cooking tips. Stay tuned next for a nearly exact repeat of this same show, but with the addition of one extra word that changes the meaning of everything.

And as always, good night, Night Vale. Good night.

PROVERB: If a car flashes its brights at you, it's probably a gang. And if you flash your brights back, the gang gives you a cake. It's a cake gang.

EPISODE 79:
"LOST IN THE MAIL"

DECEMBER 1, 2015

COWRITTEN WITH ZACK PARSONS
GUEST VOICE: ALIEE CHAN (BASIMAH BASHARA)

A COUPLE YEARS AGO I APPROACHED JOSEPH FINK WITH AN IDEA OF doing something for either Memorial Day or Veterans Day that related to the Blood Space War. It was one of those great elements that was introduced in the first episode of the show that has only been slightly expanded upon over subsequent episodes. I had a lot of ideas for what the Blood Space War might be and some of these we went back and forth on—a time war, a scam to send people to be eaten by aliens, some sort of heroic adventure—but in the end what I settled on was that simple message, not insanely original, that war is subtraction. The specifics of the war don't matter. It's not giving a benefit to the people who see their loved ones go off to fight in it and the Blood Space War, like most wars, almost never makes sense.

I liked that idea of Night Vale being pressured by mores (and the Sheriff's Secret Police) to celebrate the Blood Space War, but nobody, not even Cecil, can explain what it's about or why it's happening. Nobody knows what winning would look like or if it's even possible. Meanwhile this parade is complimented by Basimah's story. You have this vibrant young woman, coming of age, becoming who she will be as an adult, who hasn't seen her father most of her life because he volunteered. She tries to celebrate him as a hero and it doesn't work. Maybe he is a hero, maybe he's out there winning the war and saving Night Vale, but what does Basimah care? She wants her dad.

And because it's Night Vale, she gets him back, even if it's only for the length of a song.

—Zack Parsons

We brought something back with us. Something we cannot escape. Memories of a great vacation to deepest space! And the merciless Distant Prince.

WELCOME TO NIGHT VALE

Listeners, it is a solemn day here in Night Vale. Even more solemn than last year's Solemnity Fest, during which three people were overcome and had to be revived with party hats and whoopee cushions.

Today is Remembrance Day, that special day once per year when we interrupt our routines to reflect upon those who probably sacrifice their lives for us in the endless Blood Space War. We're not sure whether they are alive or dead, because there is a thousand-year difference between our time and those who fight for us on the vast intergalactic battlefields where time converges. But we assume that they are all heroes.

On this day, we put aside our political differences, even deeply bitter, divisive differences like the belief or disbelief in mountains, and we all come together to remember those who will die thousands of years from now, and to hope that the impossibility of victory is less impossible than before.

Like any deeply painful and serious subject, it is best remembered through the medium of a civic parade.

Looking out of the studio, I can see the parade route is packed with onlookers and everything is getting under way.

The symbolic dead lead the procession, each of them wearing the mask of one of those who went into the distance of time and can never return. Behind them is a float depicting the enormous serpent whose mouth contains the universe. A playful reminder to us all that even the stars must someday be swallowed.

Following that apparition comes our mayor, and my friend, Dana Cardinal, in her ceremonial mayor's coffin. Behind her are the Citizens for a Blood Space War. Still over six hundred million dollars left to hit the fund-raising goal for their bomb that may destroy reality as we understand it. Get those cookies in the oven for the next bake sale!

A brief departure now from the parade in progress. All this week we have been reaching out to you, the listeners, and asking for stories about how the Blood Space War has affected your lives. You heard from the Black Dauphin on how to grow a victory garden inside your body and Sara Bismuth shared the story of her Etsy store where she sells dolls that represent individual soldiers in the Blood Space War, showing the actual wounds they will someday suffer. And now, today, in her own words, I bring you the story of a girl whose father volunteered to fight. Let's listen together.

[*amateur recording quality with low ambient sound maybe crickets or night sounds*]

BASIMAH: Hello. I'm Basimah Bishara and I am a junior at Night Vale High. My father, Fakhir Bishara, left to join the Blood Space War when I was six. I remember the glowing doorway he stepped through when the tall, silver-skinned recruiter came to our house. And the sound of it, like a slide whistle going up, but the most tragic slide whistle I've ever heard.

My dad was gone forever. But also, he isn't gone at all.

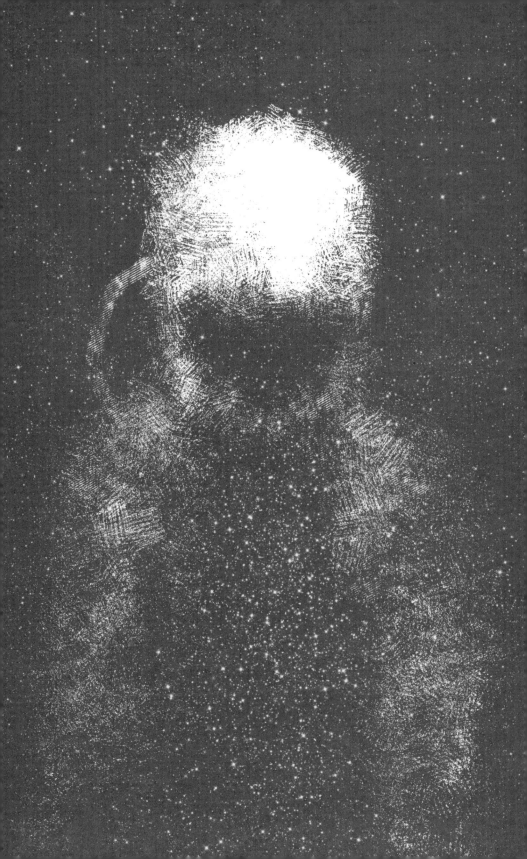

[laughing, ambient sound like a lunchroom]

I think I'm a regular student. Whatever that means. I haven't grown wings like the cheerleaders, but I fit in. I'm bad at math, I mean I used to be good at it but I think I stopped paying attention. It seemed like it was pointing toward a truth I didn't want to learn. I'm really good at science and English. I used to be in marching band, now I prefer guitar. Me and my friends formed an all-girl thrash group. We're called the Mizz Fits.

[guitar plucking mixed in with the ambient sound]

I guess how it works is that once a year for the first hundred years of dad's journey they are going to wake him up and allow him to send a message back to earth.

I have a big family, so it's not like I don't feel loved. Sometimes I feel like it would be easier if dad couldn't get in touch with me at all. No, I don't wish that. I love him. I wish he had never left.

The messages show up on my nightstand in these gelatinous gashapon capsules. They're warm and soft in my hands. The words are printed on a tiny roll of plastic inside. He only gets to send one, every year, and he always sends it to me right around my birthday, but not exactly on my birthday. I don't know whether he's getting it wrong or they are. Or maybe it's just time being weird again. I'd like to believe it's that.

To my dad, he left eleven days ago, but to me it's most of my lifetime. I'll be an old woman and he'll still be on his way to the war, sending letters to a me that he remembers from just a few weeks before. It's stupid. It's not stupid, I guess. It is stupid though. It is.

CECIL: More from Basimah in a bit, but we need to update you on the parade.

[rattling chains and distant fluting]

Here comes the emissary, listeners! It wouldn't be Remembrance Day without a visit from the only entity to ever return from the war. It has been hauled up from the pit and, yes, here it comes.

[*high-pitched merry flute whistling, think the bird from Prokofiev's* Peter and the Wolf]

No one knows what the emissary is or why the emissary inhabits a cosmonaut's suit. Oh, it's lifting the visor and giving us a glimpse at the void within the helmet. It's saying something. I'll try to interpret. "All these things . . . are meaningless. End . . . the . . . war."

Of course, that's the whole point, isn't it, listeners? If we end the war it will go on eternally. We must continue the war to bring it to an end. It's why all those brave people enlisted and keep enlisting and will enlist forever.

[*fluting moves away*]

And there goes the emissary, a solemn reminder of why our volunteers continue to fight in the Blood Space War. What a brave being. Soon we will trap it back in its pit.

Speaking of those volunteers, the Night Vale Veterans of a Blood Space War Association is holding a fish fry this Saturday to raise money for a statue of the unknown soldier to be built one thousand years in the future, by which time we may know who the soldier is. Bring friends, family, fish, and whatever else you would like fried over to the VFW hive located in the space between the walls at the abandoned cannery.

[*distant, comical car-honking sounds*]

Oh no. While I avert my gaze from the Shriner's homunculi, let's have a word from our sponsors.

Do you have dry eyes? Red eyes? Goat eyes? Aphid eyes? Any

other eyes you're not currently using? We want your eyes at Richter's Eye Glass Hut. We give you money for your unwanted eyes and turn them into glass for affordable window panes. How? Don't ask questions. Come on down to Richter's Eye Glass Hut, located conveniently off the highway helix in the shadow of the immense precarious rock. [*faster disclaimer*] No longer accepting potato eyes or the eye of a storm. Not responsible for our windows watching you while you sleep.

And now, let's return to Basimah's story.

[*ambient sound of her bedroom*]

[*Basimah is doing an impression of her father's voice.*]

BASIMAH: "The ship is so big. It makes me think of big things, Bazzy." That's what he calls me. It was my nickname when I was six. I'm not six.

It all comes out of him in a jumble. "They say what we are going to fight is an idea, like a color or pride, but it can kill us. If the idea gets inside you then it's over. Bazzy, do you remember the song I used to sing to you to put you to sleep? Paula Abdul. 'Rush Rush.'"

And then he wrote the whole song out, but he got a bunch of the lyrics wrong. I guess he was doing it from memory.

I just got a capsule two months ago telling me he wants me to be a doctor so I can cure one of the big diseases like cancer. *Like* cancer? There's nothing *like* cancer, there's just cancer. Sure, I'll cure that, Space Dad. No pressure, right?

Most of the messages my father sends me are lists of ways I need to live my life. Things I should do and shouldn't do, you know? He told me to pray every day and obey my mother. When I was nine he warned me not to kiss a boy until I'm sixteen. Which, well, I guess good news for him there.

[*New ambient sound. She's outside, maybe in the lunchroom, maybe somewhere else.*]

The divergence started with little things. He said I should get a puppy for my eighth birthday, but I got a snail. When I was fifteen he wanted to make sure I had started wearing my hijab. Mom said I should make my own choices, so sometimes I wear it and sometimes I don't. Like, always at mosque, but not that often at school. That sort of thing.

My father is talking to a person who isn't me, to a person that doesn't exist. He has imagined my entire childhood and young adulthood. He brings up obvious milestones, like starting high school or that first kiss. But he didn't know about the car accident I spent most of my fourteenth year recovering from. I can't tell him about the poems I write or the fact that I have a girlfriend, not a boyfriend.

He's a ghost to me now or, maybe, since he's going to be around long after I'm gone, I'm the one who is a ghost to him.

I take some comfort knowing my dad got paid a lot of money for joining the Blood Space War, enough to take care of me and Mom for a long time, and, really, having a space dad is just another way to have a family. Everyone has their own thing, you know? Like all of the Mizz Fits. Clara is in a nuclear family straight from the 1950s, but, like, literally from the 1950s even as she lives her life in 2015. Nisha has a council of fathers. Jacquelyn's mom is a spider.

As long as you are loved, it doesn't matter. So my dad's a space ghost? I can deal. I just wish dad loved *me* and not who I was eleven years ago.

Or maybe I'm not okay with it. Maybe I wish he would come back.

I wish he would be a dad to me, not to the ghost of me that haunts him.

CECIL: More with Basimah coming up, but first, the weather.

WEATHER: "Sharon" by Good San Juan

The parade has ended, most of the onlookers have ceased to look on, and the wind is gathering up the paper Remembrance Day masks and depositing them in a random scattering across our side-walks and streets. A lone dog I recognize from a recurring dream is staring at me from a block away. A dark van rumbles past. Everything is calm and quiet once again and—

[*close, loud fluting*]

Oh my! You startled me. Listeners, the emissary has appeared in the studio without warning, without even opening a door. It is sitting in the chair next to me and slowly rotating. Its visor is open, and I am being forced to stare at the ineffable darkness within the emissary's helmet.

[*fluting*]

I believe it is asking if I understand the nature of unreality. Emissary, I understand dreams and fantasies and this gooey, sometimes—incredible, sometimes—painful world that surrounds us, but I can only experience it with my seven senses.

[*fluting*]

Listeners, the emissary is saying that the nature of unreality . . . is . . . that experience and reality are linked but separate. What is experienced may not be real. What is real may never be experienced. So far this is just basic geometry like we all learn in third grade. Where is the emissary going with this?

[*fluting*]

The emissary is saying . . . "in a thousand years, we will turn the vastness of space red for no reason. There was never a purpose to this war we made."

But if Remembrance Day has taught me anything, under strict order of the Sheriff's Secret Police, it is that war is a purpose unto itself.

[*fluting*]

The emissary is asking me to end the conflict, but I'm sorry, emissary, I do not have the power to end the Blood Space War. After all the blood that has been spilled in space, or will be spilled, or may be spilled at some theoretical point in the future, I am a humble radio host and you are a sentient nothingness inhabiting the suit of a dead cosmonaut. How could the two of us hope to stop a war?

I don't know. I just don't know.

The emissary is gone, as though it was never here. Maybe it wasn't. After all, this moment was only something I experienced, not something I know is real.

Let's hear the rest of Basimah's tape.

[*Basimah, quiet ambient room, guitar playing of "Rush Rush"*]

BASIMAH: People always say to me, "You must be proud of your father going off to fight in the Blood Space War."

I used to say *yes* to them. Not anymore. I don't care if it makes me selfish or ungrateful. My dad made the wrong choice and I want him back.

He wrote down the lyrics all wrong.

[*singing to the tune of "Rush Rush"*]

You're gonna see
I'm gonna run,
I'm gonna fly,
I'm gonna bring this love back to ya

[*fluting on the recording*]

Ah! How did you get in my room? What are you? What are you?

[*The fluting shifts, distinctly playing the tune to "Rush Rush."*]

Daddy? Is that you, Daddy?! [*laughing*] Daddy! [*crying, laughing*] Daddy. Daddy. Daddy. [*crying*]

CECIL: Listeners, I don't know how the emissary ended up in this taped recording, dropped off at the studio three days ago, given that the emissary was only released from its pit this morning. But then: I don't know how my favorite type of pie is made, but when I order it, there it is, steaming and delicious. I don't know how the mail gets delivered, but every day, like clockwork, it doesn't. I don't know how lost pets end up on the moon, but they do, and they have built an extensive city up there.

The clock claims it is now 12:01. Remembrance Day is over. We can all return to our lives and to forgetting that the Blood Space War is going on, or will go on, maybe, a thousand years from now.

And maybe, in one thousand years, plus a day or two, those brave volunteers we sent to fight in a war none of us understand will allow the most dangerous idea of all into their heads. They will turn back, and return home to us, against all laws of time and space.

Paraphrasing the half-remembered words of an ancient prophet, perhaps they will bring this love back to us. Or maybe they already have.

Stay tuned next for events that will or will not happen, in the order that they may or may not occur.

And from the present as I am currently experiencing it, good night, Night Vale. Good night.

PROVERB: Ever wondered how a plane flies? Well, the answer is that no one knows. Pilots are scared to ask. If we ask, maybe it'll stop working.

EPISODE 80:
"A NEW SHERIFF IN TOWN"

DECEMBER 15, 2015

JOSEPH AND I MET THE AUTHOR MAUREEN JOHNSON ON TWITTER A FEW years back. (She's @maureenjohnson. Go follow her. Do it now. You will not regret it.) She found our show about a year in and started talking about how much she liked it. We developed a Twitter friendship with her, and that would have been a terribly confusing sentence for all of us just eight years ago.

Maureen is a delightful, funny, and wise person. And like we do from time to time with people we enjoy, we named an intern after her. Intern Maureen first appeared in Episode 35: "Lazy Day" on November 15, 2013.

Maureen responded on Twitter immediately to her namesake's debut (note the timestamp):

Maureen Johnson ✓
@maureenjohnson

☼ Following

WAIT. THERE IS AN INTERN MAUREEN ON @NightValeRadio

RETWEETS **20**   LIKES **76**

9:36 AM - 15 Nov 2013

But as with most Night Vale radio interns, something terrible would befall her, and in Episode 38: "Orange Grove," from January 1, 2014, Intern Maureen drinks the orange juice that causes her to flicker out of existence.

Maureen Johnson responded a couple of days later:

> **Maureen Johnson** ✓
> @maureenjohnson   ⚙ Following
>
> We're going to need to talk,
> @NightValeRadio.
>
> RETWEETS   LIKES
> 7   44
>
> 12:27 PM - 3 Jan 2014

On Twitter, @NightValeRadio and @maureenjohnson teased back and forth about this unfortunate occurrence, until Joseph and I decided we would bring back Intern Maureen *if* Maureen Johnson agreed to perform the character live onstage at Town Hall for our second anniversary show (Episode 49: "Old Oak Doors" in June 2014). She did, and she was great.

Once we cast an actor as a character, it gives that character a fuller life, direction, and personality. Maureen Johnson's mock-angry glares on social media really informed the character of (former) Intern Maureen's true angry glares at Cecil.

Even when the actor isn't voicing that character—as is the case with Maureen in the newest episode where Cecil runs into Maureen, and she is, unsurprisingly, annoyed with her old boss—that actor has still strongly informed who that character is. And having spent a lot of time with real Maureen this past year (GeekyCon, NerdCon, the Night Vale book tour event at WORD Bookstore in Jersey), her namesake was fresh in our minds. We couldn't resist bringing her back into podcast.

I mean, it's probably just for this one small part. I'm sure it's just a one-off scene and will never come up again. I mean, why would it?

—Jeffrey Cranor

A few other intern-naming notes: Intern Dana was named after one of our podcast's earliest fans; Intern Vithya was named after one of the first people I met in college; Intern Zvi was named after choreographer Zvi Gotheiner, whose work I saw once and liked; Intern Hannah was named after a winner of WNYC's excellent game show (and podcast) Ask Me Another.

I fought the law and the law won. I ignored the law and the law won. I abided by the law and the law won.

WELCOME TO NIGHT VALE

There's a new sheriff in town, Night Vale. The former sheriff, whose name we never knew, whose face we never saw, and whose voice was only ever heard through a vocoder, is gone. Our former sheriff was secretive, reclusive. Really into classical music and kleptocracy. Rarely made public appearances, and when he did, it was with a balaclava and cape.

The new sheriff has a more public persona, refusing to wear the traditional mask or cape and actually allowing their first name to be known. (It's Sam, by the way.) The sheriff called a press conference this morning to announce that they are taking over the Secret Police effective immediately.

More on this story as it develops.

But first, an editorial. It's the holidays, Night Vale. I hope many of you will get to spend this time with people you love. I know I'll be sharing some eggnog with my dearest family: Carlos, Abby, Janice . . . others . . . But let's not forget those people who quietly make our lives better: the postal carriers, the baristas and food servers, cabdrivers, and the agents from a vague yet menacing government agency who sit outside our homes night after night re-cording all of our conversations and activities.

Think how boring a job domestic espionage must be. They are out there at all hours. Do they ever get to sleep or spend holidays with families or take vacations? Who even knows?

So the other day, swept up in the holiday spirit, I took some de-licious Pfeffernüsse cookies out to the windowless van across from my home and gave them to the agent sitting in the back. Her name is Monica Barnwell, and she was just a lovely person. She appreciated that I recognized all the hard work she has put in the last several years surveilling me. And I thanked her for her service to our com-munity.

We had some small talk and then I said, "Well, gotta get back to my dull life," as I looked down at my shoes. She said, "Thanks, Cecil." And then I said, "Monica, would you like me to . . . I don't know . . . question the World Government or be more antiwar or talk more like a political dissident or something, just to make your day a little more exciting?"

"Oh, that'd be so fun, Cecil. Thanks!" she said.

Then I went back inside and told my boyfriend I wanted to get a beret, either red or camouflage.

So, Night Vale, this holiday season, think about all the people you may take for granted. You don't have to give them a gift or any-thing. Just a thank-you and a smile for all their hard work is enough. And if you have any particularly juicy secrets, consider brightening some agent's day by announcing them in a loud, clear voice to the nearest hidden microphone in your home.

The new sheriff has spoken. They opened their press conference with the following statement: "Citizens of Night Vale. We have a crisis on our hands and that crisis is . . ." Then the sheriff performed a ten-minute modern dance piece (set to music by Steve Reich, of course) that frantically, yet lyrically, conveyed a disdain for the fiscal irresponsibility of current mayor Dana Cardinal.

The press corps loved the piece, especially its subtle tribute to choreographer Anne Teresa de Keersmaeker's sweeping repetitive style, even though the sheriff's muscular, longitudinal movements obviously indicated heavy training in Lester Horton's methodology. The press applauded politely and the sheriff continued with their speech.

Quote: "Our Secret Police force has been secretly requesting budget increases to help cover overtime and new equipment. Maybe you didn't know about it," the sheriff said, "because it's, you know, secret, and all. But we were requesting it. . . . Secretly! Don't print that! It's a secret!"

The sheriff went on. "Instead the mayor has decided to use our money to help the citizens of our unfriendly neighboring town Desert Bluffs. We will not only see a rise in crime because we have a mayor who decided to disrupt our stable economy, but we also will face a lack of financial ability to effectively stop this crime."

The sheriff went on. "I will secretly undermine the mayor's authority with the help of the City Council and some lizard people I know to keep Night Vale 'safe.' (Don't report my finger quotes around the word safe! They're secret!) This is my promise to you as your new sheriff."

One reporter then asked, "Uhh, what happened to the old sheriff?"

The new sheriff responded by painting a canvas entirely blue.

More on this story, but first an update on the Trial of the Century.

Judge Siobhan Azdak has brought in a computer programmer named Melony Pennington to develop the first ever all-AI jury for the trial of Hiram McDaniels.

Attorneys have had a difficult time finding a jury of peers for McDaniels, as he is literally a five-headed dragon, and outside of his family, seems to be the only one of his kind in the area. Not knowing how to find actual dragons to serve on the jury, and not willing to have a five-headed dragon unfairly juried by all humans, Judge Azdak called for science to solve this problem, because, according to Azdak, "Science has solved every other problem."

Both the prosecuting attorney, Troy Walsh, and the court-appointed defense attorney, also named Troy Walsh, agree that this is a fair solution, and artificial intelligence is "probably a thing anyone with a MacBook and some Red Bull has already mastered, like, years ago," they said in unison with identical smiles and matching haircuts.

Pennington has been working with young computer prodigy, Megan Wallaby, who is an eleven-year-old girl who inhabits what once was the body of a Russian sailor and also was only born three years ago, but then the specifics of her identity and her manifestation within time are really none of your business.

Wallaby is helping Pennington engineer a sentient program that can think exactly like six different five-headed dragons. Megan has had a real affinity for computers ever since the, uh, the incident in the school gym that one time. The other members of the jury will be humans. Auditions for those jury slots will be conducted Wednesday at the Night Vale Community Theatre.

Four of Hiram's five heads are being brought up on charges of conspiracy and attempted murder of our mayor. The fifth head, the violet one, is being courted as a key witness by the prosecution, but they're having a difficult time getting a private conversation with it. The trial is scheduled for early next year.

By the way, listeners, I ran into former station intern Maureen. I actually didn't notice her at first, as I was listening to an album I just got. It's a new musical about Alexander Hamilton, who became our nation's fourth president because he successfully killed former vice president Aaron Burr in a duel. Anyway, the soundtrack is fantastic, and I was totally engrossed in my lip-syncing and self-styled choreography, when I saw Maureen waving to me from down the street.

I saw she was with someone, but his baseball hat was pulled down over his face, so I didn't get a good look at him.

Maureen then asked me for a letter stating she'd completed her internship, because she needed these two credits for college. I reminded her she spent most of her internship flickering in and out of existence, so I couldn't write the letter, but I was really excited to see she was dating someone.

Then she said something about not assuming people are dating just because they're hanging out. Blah blah blah. I don't even like boys. Blah blah. But I kept staring at the boy in the ball cap, and I did not like him one bit. I felt like I knew him from somewhere, but I couldn't put my finger on where. Oh well, I'm sure it won't come up again.

I told Maureen it was a good thing she wasn't into boys because this one seemed like bad news. Really bad news, I whispered, and Maureen groaned and rolled her eyes in what I assume was agreement.

Then I said, "Good seeing you," and walked away. She shouted, "Come back," and "Where's my credit letter?" while waving her fist and cussing, which is I guess how kids today say good-bye.

Oh, listeners. I need to make an apology. Earlier in today's show I mentioned giving some cookies to the agent from a vague yet menacing government agency, and in the process I revealed her full name as Monica Barnwell and the location of her operation as in front of my home.

Because of this security breach, Monica has apparently lost her job as a secret agent and had to go into hiding for the rest of her life, changing her looks and identity, and never seeing her family or friends again. Really sorry about that one, Monica.

Let's have a look at traffic. What do you say?

Feet apart. Toes together. Right foot turned forty-five degrees. No need for mathematical precision, but if you have a protractor, break it into pieces and swallow it. Absorb its numbers like nutrients.

Bend your knees. Bend other things that allow for bending. Do not force malleability. That right foot though. What's it doing?

Did you move your foot? Memories aren't real. Do you control yourself? Not if you don't remember being in control. Maybe we pretend to have experienced things so we don't have to actually understand why they happened.

Your foot is flexing now. Why? What silent siren song calls your right foot? You are sitting. You are passive, still. Your left foot idles in the dark, complacent and obedient. Your right foot serves a greater god. It flexes for its idol: all plastic and steel and full of fire and fumes. Your right foot wishes for you to pray with a clear mind and open eyes.

This has been traffic.

And now an update on the new sheriff's press conference. The sheriff announced that while they couldn't do anything about the money the mayor has already wasted on neighboring towns, the Secret Police would certainly make it clear to anyone from Desert Bluffs who might be trying to enter Night Vale that they would not be wanted.

The sheriff announced a plan to tag all Desert Bluffs citizens with bright orange hats that have the word "UNWANTED" written in blinking LED lights across the front.

As the sheriff said this, several journalists shifted uncomfortably in their seats. This was because their seats were uncomfortable, but they still nodded excitedly about the sheriff's cool new idea.

One journalist pointed out, though, that the orange hat thing would be an added expense, what with having to print up hats and design the LEDs and all that. And this whole press conference seems to be about our city's lack of funding for new projects, the journalist said.

In the tense silence that followed, the journalist added, "Plus everyone from Desert Bluffs is pretty easy to identify what with all the blood on their shir———"

But then the reporter was helpfully tackled and muzzled by the other reporters who did not want to get off on the wrong foot with the new sheriff. As the great television newsman Edward R. Murrow once said, "Hey, don't rock the boat, okay?"

In the commotion, no one seemed to notice the appearance of several strangers, standing around the perimeter of the conference room. Our new station intern Kareem was there and claimed the strangers really didn't appear so much as seemed to have always been there, even though he was positive they were not there at the start.

They were completely still, except for their breathing. They were definitely breathing, and everyone heard it.

No one knew what the strangers wanted but they were certain it wasn't good. The members of the press stepped backward into the middle of the room. They waited. And from the silence came a noise. There came a sudden—

Oh, it's almost twenty past the hour, listeners, I better get to the weather report. Here you go.

WEATHER: "She Knows" by John Fullbright

Where was I? Umm . . . "They waited. From the silence came a noise. Then there came a sudden . . ." Oh yeah, basically, everyone was quiet until a reporter asked the sheriff, "Who are these people? Will the Secret Police protect us?"

The sheriff did not respond. It was quiet, save for the strangers' breathing, for about three minutes. Then the questions and cries came in increasing volume and pace, "Who are these people?" "Sheriff, why aren't they moving?" "What do they want?" "Has anyone seen my phone?" "We're going to die!" Et cetera.

Eventually the room devolved into panic, members of the press shoving to get out, but in a way that suggested that the exit was through each other. Then the sheriff raised their hand and announced into the microPHONE, "Everything's fine."

No one believed the sheriff, and the sheriff, knowing this, rephrased the statement, "Some things are not fine, but other things are fine. This"—and here the sheriff indicated the whole room—"is probably fine."

The panicked reporters were now filled with both fear and doubt.

The sheriff stood stupefied as a single bead of sweat rolled down their brow, along the nose, forming a thin, wet crack across their entire face.

No one breathed, except the strangers, of course, who by the time the droplet had completed its erratic journey, were somehow several feet closer to the press corps despite never having visibly moved an inch.

Everyone in the room, including the sheriff, knew that death was upon them. None of them were afraid of death. They were, instead, terrified of what would come immediately before and immediately after death.

Listeners, like I said earlier, our own Intern Kareem was part of that press corps today. So, to the family of Intern Kareem, he's a good intern and is doing great work. He got back from the press conference a little bit ago saying he had a great time. He also provided some excellent reporting.

According to Kareem, the strangers encroached slowly on the remaining journalists, moving without seeming to move. No one could look the strangers in the eyes. They did not know what the strangers wanted of them, just that their lives were likely over. Kareem said he heard someone crying, another person frantically chanting, and he was trying to take it all in, but then he heard a flapping of wings, like a pteranodon or a librarian. And looking up, he saw a flash of blackness and long, feathered creatures descending from a dark sky.

And next thing he knew, he was back at the radio station, safely interning once again. Kareem called the creatures that saved everyone "angels," but I reminded him that there is no such thing, and according to the AP Style Guide, it is illegal to acknowledge the existence of angels. So this is why—

Kareem is now trying to argue with me about the fluidity of vernacular and the constant evolution of language.

Ugh. Okay, listeners, I need to deal with this.

Stay tuned next for the real-life actualization of that dream you had last Tuesday. You'll make a cute couple, so congratulations.

And as always, good night, Night Vale. Good Night.

PROVERB: There are hot singles in your area. And they all died exactly twenty years ago on a night just like tonight.

EPISODE 81:
"AFTER 3327"

FEBRUARY 1, 2016

GUEST VOICE: MAUREEN JOHNSON (INTERN MAUREEN)

CONSIDER THIS:

Welcome to Night Vale is a human named Cecil (moi), playing a character named Cecil (moi aussi) on an imaginary radio show, discussing fake news that refers to real news that has been manipulated so much as to become "fake news . . ." (sung to the tune of "Girls and Boys" by Blur).

Is Cecil Palmer the postmillennial podcast incarnation of '80s New Wave veejay Max Headroom? Both are friendly, gregarious pseudohumans who live within the technology they occupy, but also a little bit in the world we inhabit too. Max has his cable TV, Cecil his radio show. They are the ghost in the machine. And most importantly, they represent all that is organic about humanity (humor, love, ego), whilst being completely artificial.

Because let's face it—the practicalities of Cecil Palmer and his relationship to technology are mysterious at best.

In this episode we fall down the weird rabbit hole of Cecil relating confidential and classified information on the air about Night

Vale newcomer Nick Teller and his inventions and his loosely veiled Nicola Tesla identity. So, how does he actually get away with this? When you really stop to think about it, how does he do this? What is the structure of his relationship with the Management of community radio that he can get away with this? And how does he even know these things? Does he have spies? Minions? Does he get a ticker-tape news feed of everybody's doings in town?

The mystery is clearly way more fun than the solution. It's not about whodunnit, or how they done it, but the fact that the mystery exists at all.

This episode is an alt-history, time-travel nerd dream! It begins with the usual sci-fi fodder—If you had the technology to go back and fix the mistakes you've made, would you? It's the classic fanboy time-travel paradox. (See: *Primer, Back to the Future, The Philadelphia Experiment, Terminator,* et cetera.) But in true Night Vale fashion, the solutions are not what you would expect. In fact, is there even a "solution" to the sum of a human's life? Are the problems that send you careening through time in a Terry Gilliam joyride really problems at all, or just a matter of perspective and self-acceptance?

Humans love to give themselves labels, while simultaneously shouting to anyone who will listen that they are more than just the label they've been given. We willfully fall in line with our own personal set of identity politics, tempered with just enough individual quirks to make it feel authentic.

So the question that Cecil and Max Headroom and all the other automaton psychopomps pose: Is technology actually changing human society, or is it actually showing us what human society has been this whole time?

—Cecil Baldwin

To err is human. But to err is also computer. We'll have to find another test to reveal which of us are secretly bots.

WELCOME TO NIGHT VALE

Let's start things off with the community calendar.

This afternoon the Museum of Forbidden Technologies will be hosting a lecture by Night Vale High's AP auto shop teacher Nick Teller. He will be demonstrating some fun devices he came up with while tinkering around in his garage. As usual for talks at the Museum, Nick will be covered with a burlap tarp, and a white noise machine will be played through a state-of-the-art surround-sound system so that no dangerous and secret technology can accidentally be learned about.

Tuesday will be the annual day in which we leave offerings of fruit and Rolaids for the Eternal Scouts on display in front of City Hall. These brave children rose through the ranks, from Boy Scout to Eagle Scout, Blood Pact Scout, Weird Scout, Dreadnaught Scout, Dark Scout, and Fear Scout before finally achieving the rank of Eternal Scout. Now these two brave boys, Frank and Barty, stand in their glass cases, as they have for almost three years, with wide unseeing eyes, wide unseeing mouths, and long unseeing hair.

It is rumored that one day, in Night Vale's hour of greatest need, the Eternal Scouts will awake, and walk among us once again.

Until then, we all bow our heads in silent reverence, so that we don't have to look at them, because they are very creepy. We all look at the ground instead, because the ground is not creepy, except that it consumes your body when your body no longer belongs to you.

Wednesday is Take Your Daughter to Work Day. Wednesday is Put Your Daughter to Work Day. Wednesday is Teach Your Daughter How to Do Whatever Simple Task It Is You Are Paid to Do and Then, Once She Has Mastered It, Slip Away and Leave Her as Your Replacement Day. If you do not have a daughter, one will be assigned to you. If you do have a daughter, are you sure you do?

Thursday is a lost cause. Why even bother with Thursday? We all tried and tried and still Thursday is what it is. Let's all give up hope for Thursday and just let it do its thing.

Friday evening, legendary rock band the Clash and the great Amy Winehouse are joining together for a Free Concert in your imagination.

Saturday, there will be a sale at Dark Owl Records, with everything wildly reduced in price. "Cheapest of all," said Dark Owl owner Michelle Nguyen, "will be the idea of art, which has been degraded to a point where it holds no recognizable value.

"It's like, what does art even mean outside of the intention to make art?" said Nguyen, in a statement she burned into my lawn this morning. "And does the intention to make art alone define what it is? Anyway, you can take art for all I care. I moved on to the intricate, fractal happenstance of nature, like, years ago," she concluded.

If there's any particular album you're looking for, please do ask for it by name, so that Michelle can know the album is too well known now and she can put every copy she owns in the garbage with all the rest of the popular music.

Sunday is someone else's problem. What, you have to worry about every day yourself?

This has been the community calendar.

My former intern Maureen has dropped by the studio. And oh my god, she has just the most ADORABLE beagle puppy with her. Look at you! Look at you!

MAUREEN: I'm here too.

CECIL: Of course! Hello, Maureen, you are also here, yes.

MAUREEN: Hi. Or whatever. I guess "hi."

CECIL: Maureen, it's just a delight to have you and your little buddy there on.

MAUREEN: I bet it's a delight.

CECIL: Okay. What's been new with you?

MAUREEN: Well, let's see. Oh yeah, I had to start a new internship because I still need those credits to graduate. The new internship is pretty sweet I guess. I lead an army or whatever.

CECIL: You lead an army?

MAUREEN: Or whatever. Doesn't matter. I mean I don't have to. If you could write me my intern credit letter for school, I wouldn't have to do this other internship. I could just graduate and—

CECIL: Oh, your new internship sounds just great. I hope you're truly applying yourself.

MAUREEN: [*beat, maybe a slight inhale*] I've been talking with another former intern of yours by the way.

CECIL: Dana? I'm so proud of her. My best intern ever. She's really doing some great things for this town. You know, she's mayor now, right?

MAUREEN: I know who Mayor Cardinal is! Everything's about Dana, isn't it? Oh look at me I get college credits AND I get to be mayor. Not like Maureen. Maureen has to lead an army or whatever to get those credits.

CECIL: An army . . .

MAUREEN: Or whatever. It's not important.

CECIL: It sounds kind of important.

MAUREEN: Oh, does it? Is that what sounds important? Do you know that there are people starving to death somewhere?

CECIL: Oh my god, where? We should help them.

MAUREEN: I dunno. Somewhere. I wasn't being specific. I wasn't actually suggesting making the world a better place. I was just using theoretical human suffering as a deflection.

CECIL: Have you been taking those Art of Conversation classes at the community college too? Our receptionist, Lance, got me into these classes. I've learned so much about how to better talk with people. Techniques like "Intense, Almost Invasive Listening" and "Absolute Denial of the Reality of Truth" and "Changing the Subject: Your Best Line of Defense."

MAUREEN: Can you write me a credit letter or not?

CECIL: That's a good question. Another good question is: Who's a good boy? Who's a good boy?

MAUREEN: This dog is, obviously. He's a beagle. Therefore he's a good boy. This was a mistake. I'll talk to you later. Or whatever. More "whatever" than "later."

CECIL: Bye, buddy. Oooh. Look at you! Such a cute dog. I would do anything for that little face. That tiny, adorable face and those floppy dumb ears. Ugh, I would do anything! Oh no, the beagle's leaving. In the arms of Maureen. Maureen is also leaving. Good-bye, Maureen! It was nice of you to drop by and talk about . . . whatever it was you talked about.

Listeners, she's leaving in the company of that same boy I saw her with a couple weeks ago. The one with the ball cap pulled low over his face. I definitely recognize him. Where do I know him from?

I'm certain this won't come up again. I wouldn't worry about it.

A small update on my previous community calendar announcement. Things have gone off track during AP auto shop teacher Nick Teller's presentation on his inventions. It seems that he somehow

accidentally removed the unsecured burlap tarp from his body, and turned off the switch on the white noise machine next to him, thus foiling the usual safeguards against learning.

His completely audible talk covered simple life hacks he's developed to lower your electrical bill. The first is a way of transmitting energy over great distances. To that end, he held up a lit light bulb, not visibly attached to any power source. The power, Nick said, came wirelessly from a coil situated twenty-six miles away in the desert. His other power-saving tips included setting your thermostat just a bit higher, improving the insulation of your home, and using a free energy generator he invented that can provide power for an entire household indefinitely on no fuel at all.

The World Government has made a statement apologizing for the technical errors that are allowing this speech to be heard, and have released a response that consists of just the words "NUH UH" drawn in red crayon on construction paper. So two interesting sides to consider in this story.

Update on the Trial of the Century, as four of the five heads belonging to five-headed dragon Hiram McDaniels are tried for their role in the attempted coup against our beloved mayor.

The first witness of the trial was called to the stand today. It was Harrison Kip, adjunct professor of archaeology at the Night Vale Community College. He was once tricked by Hiram's heads and their coconspirator, the Faceless Old Woman Who Secretly Lives in Your Home, into summoning a sand golem that wreaked havoc throughout Night Vale. We covered all this of course, in our two-part report last year.

Harrison had been so ashamed of his role in the destruction that he fled into the desert to live the life of a simple hermit, only reaching out to civilization to procure the bare necessities of life, and occasionally getting on Skype to remotely teach classes and hold office hours.

Mr. Kip did his best to describe what had happened, but mainly all that happened is that he was tricked into raising a sand golem, so his testimony wasn't that interesting. The only highlight came when he was asked about his months out in the desert. He indicated that he found the desert mostly peaceful, but that he had recently seen something in the middle of the night that had disturbed him. He seemed very shook up about it, slumping forward and mumbling what was, I believe, the word *appalling* over and over.

That part of his testimony probably didn't mean anything, and probably doesn't indicate anything is going to happen. As that famous TV lawyer Buffy the Vampire Slayer always says in her big closing arguments, "Past performance is not a predictor of future results."

Nick Teller's speech at the Museum of Forbidden Technologies is, disastrously, continuing to be heard by attendees, and, even more disastrously, the contents of this speech are being repeated on the radio.

He moved on from his energy tips to reminisce a bit about some projects of his that didn't go exactly according to plan. For instance, he said, he once did some work on a boat in Pennsylvania and a few mixed-up calculations meant that instead of the boat becoming invisible as planned, it jumped through both time and parallel universes, horribly altering every human on board.

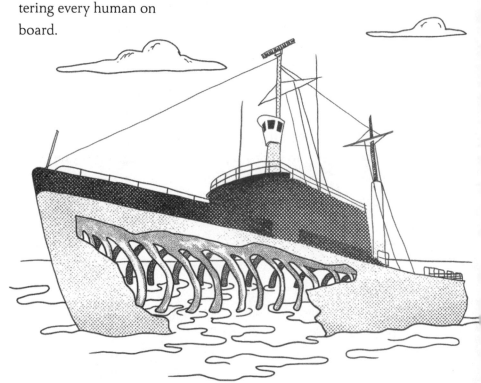

But, Nick went on to emphasize, he didn't let failures like that get him down, even though that particular failure was so spectacular that he had to change his name and fake his death in order to evade the consequences. Well, this is inspiring stuff, even though hearing it is completely illegal. As is, probably, repeating it on the radio. Whoopsie.

Well, more from Nick, as I continue to accidentally tell you what he's saying.

But first, today's traffic: a spectrum of gray.

The topmost gray is that of sunlight filtered through high altitude clouds, then through lower altitude haze, darkening down on a monochromatic spectrum toward dirt that is gray or appears gray due to the quality of light. Built up from the dirt are gray buildings, full of gray people speaking grayly.

"Yes, I'll have another slice of pie," they say. "Business is looking as good as this pie," they say. "Pie tastes great and is better nutritionally than most people think," they say.

Colorless, toneless words. Gray faces slacking onto gray necks and gray bodies. Gray dreams of a gray future that is neither good nor bad but just what's next. A gray life lived grayly.

Gray dreams through gray nights, electric lights too bright to ever let dark settle into dark, no great absence to contrast the stars, no rich black of the void, a gray night. Gray dreams. Gray life. Gray words. Gray buildings in a gray world and the light grays grayly through the gray.

This has been traffic.

And now a word from our sponsors.

Today's sponsor is Google.

Looking for pictures of a monkey riding a pony? Just search that on Google and it will probably be there.

Looking for pictures of a dog named Table? Search that, and I bet someone named their dog Table and took a picture.

How about an image of the exact moment of your death? I dunno, that might be on there too. Give it a search.

The internet is huge. Whatever it is, it's probably on there.

Google. Search for superweird stuff. We'll probably find something at least kind of similar.

This has been a word from our sponsors.

It's almost time for our weather report, and I have to admit I'm surprised. I'd have thought given some of the forbidden information we've been repeating from Nick Teller that we would have been shut down by now, but maybe I was wrong about th———

WEATHER: "Table Song" by Katie Kuffel

I'm finally back, listeners. I'm sure you've noticed over the past several days that our usual broadcasts had been replaced by harsh buzzing and the occasional shout of "You're not hearing anything right now. This isn't sound."

As I had kind of hoped, the World Government shut down our station, which meant that I got a couple weeks off. I had been needing a break, and the extralegal closure of my place of work and the forced reeducation of all of us who worked there gave me just the chance I needed.

In between reeducation sessions, I did a number of household chores that needed doing. Painting, gutter cleaning, and the like. The picking up and the putting down and the mending and the clearing. Resodding my lawn after Michelle burned her statement into it. I had some quiet time with Carlos, and I rewatched the entire series of *Buffy the Vampire Slayer*. I love at the end of every episode, after she successfully wins the big court case, when she smokes cigars and cracks wise with her law firm partner, Angel. Ugh, so good.

I also dropped in on Nick Teller at his auto shop in the high school. He had just finished up feeding the cars and was grading some papers, but he kindly made time for a chat.

I asked him if he wished things had turned out for him differently. If he wished that he hadn't had to flee his old life, and come to this town where his best inventions are suppressed by order of the World Government.

He smiled. "No," he said. "Honestly, I get it. The world has never been accepting of what I do. And I'm happy with my life here. I like teaching auto shop. I like working with young people. I like guiding them into a life of creating new things that will never see the light of day because they threaten the system as it is and the powers as they are. It's rewarding work."

I told him I was glad that he seemed to have found peace in his life.

He said he was too. "After all," he said, "what other choice would I have? It's not like I could go back and fix my mistakes. Or wait . . ." He turned pensive and told me that he had some old papers he wanted to look through, for purely nostalgic reasons, and asked if I could leave him to it.

And so I did.

Listeners, maybe at some point Nick wanted to be something other than he was. But that doesn't mean he is beholden to that dream he once had. It's okay for him to be all right with who he is now. Acceptance is not failure. Sometimes acceptance is just acceptance.

Of course, one must always be open to new dreams, and new ambition. And if at some point Nick decides that he no longer wants to be an AP auto shop teacher, or if he decides he wants to alter history so he will never have even come here, then that too will be okay.

Stay tuned next for an unexpected gain in cabin pressure. No mask will help you. We weren't prepared for things to go this way. And good night, Night Vale. Good night.

PROVERB: You know what would be great? If someone made a movie showing Spider-Man's origin story. I'd love to finally see that on the big screen.

EPISODE 82:
"SKATING RINK"

FEBRUARY 15, 2016

GUEST VOICES: MEG BASHWINER (DEB), JACKSON PUBLICK (HIRAM MCDANIELS)

WHEN I WAS BETWEEN THREE AND EIGHT YEARS OLD, I SPENT MY SUMmer days at Classic Day Care Center in Mesquite, Texas. It no longer exists. It's a plumbing supply company now.

This is good news because they weren't very good at the "care" part of their title.

I mean aside from occasionally getting yelled at or smacked, Classic is where I learned to swim and play soccer and make god's eyes. So it wasn't all bad.

Every few weeks they would put us all in the conversion van and take us on the long drive across the city to Broadway Skateland. I loved this because (1) I loved skating from the first moment I learned to not fall down, and (2) I loved road trips, seeing the world from the back seat. The car-ride games like license plate poker and punch buggy. The thrill of adventure, being away from home. I still love all of these things.

One summer afternoon around 1982-ish, I was so consumed with speed racing around and around in an oval to Top 40 music, I stopped listening to announcements. (Favorite skating songs back then: "Elvira," "Another One Bites the Dust," "Call Me," "I Love Rock 'n' Roll," and "Queen of Hearts.")

Anyway, "the Classic van is leaving" is not a thing I heard over the PA. It wasn't until they played some couple skate song (probably "Sailing") that I rolled myself off the wood and looked for my friends. Not at the soda machine. Not playing Ms. Pac-Man or Tron. Gone. So I just skated for another hour or so before I told anyone.

Later, after I got tired—and a bit worried about being all alone so far from home—I told the skating rink manager (probably not named Teddy Williams) and he called Classic to come get me. The ride back to the day care was long, a bummer of a comedown. The woman driving me told me not to tell my mom. And as I type this story, I realize that I never did.

I looked up Broadway Skateland on Google Maps, and it's unbelievably still there (4.4 stars on Google even! Good job, Broadway!). And it is literally a seven-minute walk (not a half-day-long road trip) from where Classic used to be. Never trust my memories is the lesson here.

In writing this episode, I was feeling some nostalgia for my early '80s roller-skating days. I also wanted to include a bit of romance between characters I've been 'shipping in my head for a while. So enjoy the love, and enjoy the songs. It's an all-skate.

—Jeffrey Cranor

If you're happy and you know it, then the
chemtrails are finally working.

WELCOME TO NIGHT VALE

Today is the grand opening of the newest feature at the Desert
Flower Bowling Alley and Arcade Fun Complex: a skating rink.
Owner Teddy Williams said he has loved roller skating since he
was a child, and it's been a dream of his to build a skating rink in
Night Vale.

Williams said skate rentals are half off during this opening
week, and there will be music by local DJs every Friday night. Williams also clarified that there is absolutely no way there is any underground city living below the rink.

"I double-, triple-checked," Williams said. "There's no way a
portal to another civilization could be under there because I built
the skating rink on top of the old pet cemetery. No confrontational
nation will come from the ground and attack us."

Teddy said he did hear occasional growls and hisses and even
a few loud birdlike shrieks coming from the walls, but this is most
likely just the ghosts of the dead animals whose corpses he disturbed
when building the rink.

"It'll be fine," he added as Joan Jett's "I Love Rock 'n' Roll" played
loudly in the background.

The City Council announced today that flowers look especially pretty.

"Everyone go smell the flowers," they snarled, wistfully, in unison. "Have you ever smelled one of those things? Just so full of color and musk and fluffy yellow dust! Here, smell this."

They threw daisies all over the surprised reporters. The council asked if the sun looked like it was smiling. "We just stare at that thing all day," they sneered, lovingly. "We think it is the kindest thing in the sky. Look."

The council then pointed up at the windowless conference room's drop ceiling.

It's so nice to hear the City Council in a good mood. I can't think of the last time they've sounded so hopeful and cheery. Have they ever been in a good mood?

But you know, everyone here at the station too has been uncharacteristically friendly the past few days. Station Management—who I only ever see as shadows and glowing orange lights in the corner office and who regularly scream and cause the building to shake when the ad sales team doesn't make quarterly goals—has been buying donuts for the staff. They also bought us a new claw hammer and a stone pounding board for making coffee.

Plus, this morning they left a card on my desk thanking me (Station Management! Thanking me!) and giving me a raise. I didn't even know I was getting paid.

So many people having a lovely day. I hope you're having one too, Night Vale.

Our new sheriff followed up the City Council press conference with a report on the growing number of strangers in Night Vale. These strangers appear out of nowhere and do not visibly move other than their even, deliberate breaths. Sometimes they are suddenly closer without anyone seeing them take a step.

The sheriff said they think the strangers are just people from

Desert Bluffs, who have abandoned their wretched city to come live in Night Vale, but that the Secret Police are looking further into rumors that the strangers might be something else entirely.

When pressed about their opposition to Mayor Dana Cardinal's financial assistance of Desert Bluffs, the sheriff brought out a several-foot-high stone and sculpted an intricate series of interconnected geometrical shapes, each one balancing the next.

The reporters watched the sheriff for hours until the sculpture was complete. The sheriff then added that they did not oppose the mayor on all issues.

"In fact, Mayor Cardinal is a good mayor. We just disagree on the issue of how to fight crime," the sheriff said, still tightly gripping their stone carver. "For instance, I agree with the mayor about needing to open the Dog Park to dogs and people. I love dogs and think it would be great if folks could take their dogs into the Dog Park."

The sheriff then said that they saw the cutest beagle puppy the other day. Really, really cute. The sheriff leaned close into the mic and said "SUCH A GOOD BOY. GOOOOOD DOOOGGGG."

Listeners, I'm getting word that the City Council was just seen in public, walking across the front lawn of City Hall, each of them carrying matching black cases. Witnesses were stunned as the City Council is rarely seen outside of City Hall, despite their constant vacations.

Some reported that they heard the council whistling Mariah Carey's "Always Be My Baby," but others reported that that must have been the bluebirds fluttering about just above their heads. Some eyewitness accounts say that the council wasn't even walking. They were strolling. When has the City Council ever strolled? We didn't know their bodies were even anatomically capable of that.

Someone else said, "That looks like skipping to me," but that's ridiculous. Skipping?

Is the council leaving town on another vacation? What put them in such a good mood? More on this as it develops.

And now a word from our sponsor. Here with that is Deb, a sentient patch of haze, and also, I think, our ad sales manager here at the station.

DEB: Oh, I don't work for the station.

CECIL: But you regularly provide me with copy for our live spots. You also read ads from various companies on the air. Do you work for an ad agency?

DEB: Cecil. Please.

CECIL: But this is my show. If you don't actually work at the station or for the companies you're pitching, I'd like to know who you work for.

DEB: Ssshh. Not everything can be an emergency.

Okay then. Human listeners, today's show is brought to you by Pfizer.

What does Pfizer do? What DOESN'T Pfizer do? Whew, all the things Pfizer can help you with! We can't even begin to describe it to you. You know what, Pfizer is indescribable. How can you put into words what Pfizer does? You can't. You wouldn't. No, you absolutely would not. You wouldn't dare describe what we do.

You're still trying to describe us in your mind, aren't you? Maybe Pfizer wasn't articulate enough. Maybe Pfizer can't trust you.

You have betrayed Pfizer. Don't say no. Did you just say no? Why are you always arguing with us? We give and give and give. And we never ask for anything other than money in return. We only ask for money and that you not try to describe us in words. And what do you do? You give us lots of money, but also try to describe us in words.

Pfizer. We can't even with this right now. Uff da.

CECIL: It sounds like you work for the pharmaceutical industry.

DEB: Now not you too, Cecil! I can't be here anymore.

[*door slam*]

CECIL: Wow. The door didn't even move. Not sure how she slammed it.

Listeners, I'm being distracted. Intern Kareem has been pestering me to allow him to go skating. Since Station Management seems to be out of the office, he thinks right now is the perfect time to take a long break and go check out the new Desert Flower Skating Rink.

I'm going to let you go, Kareem. But only because it's a news story. I want a full report on the new facility, okay. This is still your work time, Kar——

Well. He just skated away. I need to sit him down and talk to him about professionalism and where he got cool skates like those. They had lightning bolts on them.

But first, we've just received a call from a controversial figure. Calling in from the jailhouse, I presume, while on trial. Listeners, let's go now to an exclusive interview with literal five-headed dragon, Hiram McDaniels.

Hiram, hello.

HIRAM-GOLD: Howdy, Cecil. Thanks for letting me on your show. I just wanted to call in and clear up a few things about this trial.

HIRAM-GREEN: WE WILL BURN THE COURTHOUSE TO THE GROUND. WE WILL CHAR THE ALREADY CHARRED REMAINS OF THE HUMAN JUDGE AND JURY.

CECIL: My understanding is that the jury is not all human. It is a jury of peers, Hiram.

HIRAM-GOLD: Well, now, my green head is speaking metaphorically.

HIRAM-GREEN: WE WILL SCORCH THE SCALES OF JUSTICE.

HIRAM-GOLD: Like that. The thing is, Cecil, they are using computers to simulate five-headed dragons on the jury, but now they're saying that a single five-headed dragon computer program counts as five separate jurors. So they're only making one computer and then choosing seven human jury members. And that hardly seems fair.

HIRAM-GRAY: They don't respect us at all.

HIRAM-GOLD: No, they don't, Gray Head. They really don't. Plus, no computer can re-create the complexities of a sentient dragon.

HIRAM-GRAY: It's offensive.

CECIL: Well, I know they looked for actual five-headed dragons, but there aren't many out there that the city can find.

HIRAM-GOLD: My sister Hadassah is in town. I think she should be considered.

CECIL: Family members of the accused generally aren't allowed on juries. But also, one of your heads, the violet one, is going to be a witness against you at the trial. How are things going within your own body?

HIRAM-GOLD: They put a hole in my cell wall so my violet head can be outside of the jail since he's not charged with any crime.

HIRAM-VIOLET: [*off mic*] I can still hear you conspiring against me.

HIRAM-GREEN: QUIET, YOU TRAITOROUS SKINK. I WILL CHEW YOU FROM Y——

HIRAM-GOLD: Easy, Green. We're not allowed to talk to Violet anymore. It would be witness tampering.

HIRAM-BLUE: We shouldn't even be talking to the media. Our lawyer said anything we say can be used in the trial.

HIRAM-GOLD: My blue head is right, Cecil. But I just wanted to use my phone call to get the word out about the unfair practices going on in this trial.

HIRAM-GRAY: It is so unfair.

CECIL: Well, I'll certainly look into this. Are you having an okay day otherwise, Hiram?

HIRAM-GOLD: Sure am, Cecil. Despite my circumstances, everyone's in pretty good spirits today. They served raw lamb in the mess hall, and they let us watch a whole hour of the Lee Marvin marathon on C-SPAN this afternoon.

HIRAM-GREEN: THEY SHOWED *DEATH HUNT.* IT WAS HIS FINEST WORK AS AN ACTOR.

HIRAM-GRAY: I think *Gorky Park* was one of his more interesting roles, but yeah, *Death Hunt* is pretty good.

HIRAM-BLUE: Lee Marvin is a lighthouse in a stormy cinematic sea.

HIRAM-VIOLET: [*distantly*] I personally prefer *Cat Ballou*—

HIRAM-GREEN: SILENCE YOU WITHERED NEWT.

HIRAM-GOLD: All right there, Green. Thanks for taking my call, Cecil.

CECIL: Thank you, Hiram.

We're getting good news from Teddy Williams down at the new skating rink that there are record crowds. So many people are showing up to skate. He didn't realize how popular roller skating would be here.

We're also getting bad news from Teddy that all of the lights have gone out. He's hearing deep growls coming not only from the ghost pets in the walls, but loud shouts and snarls coming from the skaters themselves. He cannot see who it is but he can definitely smell the metallic, briny stench of blood. He did not care to elaborate about how he is so familiar with the smell of blood, just that he's sort of an expert in the matter and it's definitely blood and that no one else should come to the skating rink.

He whispered all of this from underneath the turntable in the DJ booth. He reported seeing looming shadows in the near-black. The shadows of hulking figures with what appeared to be either antlers or very elaborate hats. He could feel the floor trembling beneath him as if there were a stampede of beasts or a clash of angry gods.

Williams reported that he just once (just one time in his life) wants people to be able to play arcade games and skate and bowl and drink sodas without fearing for their safety.

Listeners, do not go to the skating rink. And for those of you already there, take cover. Do not come out from your hiding place, not even if they put on Pat Benatar.

As I wait for further news from Intern Kareem at the skating rink, let me take you now, to the weather.

WEATHER: "Thinking of Milk" by Tristan Haze

Despite a terrifying start, the new skating rink sounds like a huge success, and everyone seems to be having fun again. It is clear now what has happened.

Intern Kareem said that when he arrived at the skating rink, he saw almost everyone from Night Vale. Leann Hart from the *Daily Journal.* John Peters, you know the farmer? Old Woman Josie and the beings Kareem insists on calling angels. Judge Siobahn Azdak. Even the City Council was there. Their black cases were all opened, revealing white retro skates with thick red and blue piping. It was a feel-good atmosphere on a feel-good day.

Kareem bought a soda, filled it with every flavor from the fountain, and put his bag in a locker. "Electric Lady" by Janelle Monáe was on, and he raced to the floor to have his first skate to his favorite song, only to see a group of hulking figures with elaborate hats enter. Kareem stopped dead in his tracks, standing and shivering in front of this menacing group.

Kareem had never seen them before but he recognized them immediately by their sound and their smell as the Management of this radio station. Kareem stiffened up, and prepared an explanation that he was here to work, to report on the new skating rink, and he was not slacking. But Station Management did not seem to notice him. They were gazing across the room at the City Council, who by this point had all donned short shorts and headbands and were twirling and spinning in unison around the rink.

Just as Beyoncé's "XO" started playing, the City Council and Station Management all made eye contact. Station Management and City Council skated toward each other, and everything went dark. The record player scratched and all went quiet save for horrifying growls and animal screeching. Kareem could smell something briny and metallic, like olives.

While everyone scrambled to hide in fear, Kareem, himself a young man in a new relationship, knew exactly what was going on. He put on the night-vision goggles we require every one of our interns to carry at all times, and he watched as Station Management and the City Council met in the middle of the rink, joining arms, skating in slow happy circles, intermittently placing heads on shoulders, wanting to sneak kisses but uncertain of the right moments. Dozens of figures with hundreds of fingers all intertwined in defiance of our understandings of physical dimension, sighing hotly with romantic need and burning anticipation. The City Council had brought live rodents, and they held them up gingerly to Station Management's mouths as Management chewed off pieces of the screaming creatures. When Station Management finished devouring the last bites, the City Council adorably brushed pieces of tail and fur from Station Management's face, letting their fingertips, or whatever it is at the end of whatever those appendages are, linger.

After a few circles around the rink, Management and the council left together. The aftermath of their budding romance is clear on the brand-new polished hardwood floor of the skating rink: swirling hearts strung together, carved into the wood with their wheels.

The lights are back on now. Everyone is skating again. The stereo is blaring Parliament's "Flashlight," with Hanson's "MMMBop" coming up next.

As a person in long-term relationship, I know how fulfilling long love can be. I also remember the days of being single, and that is also fulfilling. But nothing is quite so thrilling, so unexpected and uncertain, as that moment in between those two states, single and in love.

That short fire burst of irrational passion for a person, or people, or multidimensional entities you barely know but with whom you maybe want to be with always. You know the thrall of hopeless wanting, where you long to hold the other so tightly as to become one. You think it is love, even when it is not. Love is patient and understanding and turbulent and rocklike, ever confident in itself. But this early infatuation, these addictions to a new other, are some of life's most fragile and ecstatic moments.

Well, I'm so happy for City Council and Station Management. They make a cute . . . couple.

Kareem said that he also saw former intern Maureen, her new puppy, and some boy in a hoodie all brooding in the corner. Maureen appeared to be making sardonic jokes at the expense of the new couple, and at the expense of the idea of dating itself. Kareem said the dog was really cute, but there was something about the sight of Maureen and the hooded boy and the puppy that upset him. I told Kareem, oh she's always like that.

Stay tuned next for the best hits of the '50s, '60s, '70s, '80s, '90s, 2000s, 2010s, 2020s, and beyond.

And as always, good night, Night Vale. Good night.

PROVERB: Be careful what you wish for, because it probably won't come true and life is mostly about expectation management.

EPISODE 83:
"ONE NORMAL TOWN"

MARCH 1, 2016

WHEN PLANNING OUT THE PLOT FOR THE SECOND HALF OF YEAR FOUR, we talked about this episode and how we wanted to approach it. How do you write about the difficulties of merging cultures without making it a direct commentary on the refugee crisis or the then current Republican race or any number of other serious problems of our time? Those are all things very worth talking about, but they are so weighty we thought it would likely quickly take over whatever silly sci-fi story we had going.

So I started writing this episode with the goal of finding a way to talk about a political reality forcing different cultures together without relating it to current events and found, quite quickly, that it was absolutely impossible.

The trick to facing an insurmountable problem in writing (and probably in life) is just to lean completely into it. I decided to zag hard the other direction and make the episode entirely about the issues we had hoped to avoid. The result is half Night Vale story, half *New York Times* editorial, and I think it was the only successful way of navigating the relationship between the story we're telling and the real world as it is right now.

Of course, in the years since this episode, the urgency of the refugee crisis has only deepened, and the government responses have only become more brutal and cruel. As global warming continues to worsen, this problem will become more and more the center of our lives, and so it seems damn worth writing about whenever we get the chance.

I've also lately become much less apologetic or hesitant to inject politics into my work. There is a sense when you are in a privileged class that putting politics into work is somehow rude, because politics is a game we play before returning to our basically unchanging lives. But that's not how politics works for a large portion of that country, a portion that is only growing as more and more groups are targeted. Politics is the shape of people's lives. And politics carries moral weight. To support the looting of this country by the rich, or to support putting refugees into cages is not to me a matter of policy, but of immorality. They are evil actions, and writers should never be afraid to talk about good and evil as they actually exist.

On an unrelated note, the traffic segment of this episode has kind of an interesting origin. Back when the issue of assholes selling bootleg Night Vale merch was still a somewhat manageable problem, I had to do a weekly e-mail to an on-demand shirt-printing site to take down all the crappy Night Vale merch people had put up.

Given how often I was having to contact them, and wanting to at least provide some entertainment for them if I was going to have to reach out so much, I started telling a serialized story in the comment section of their copyright takedown form. The traffic in this episode is that story, originally sent on a weekly basis to the legal department of a T-shirt printing site four years ago.

—Joseph Fink

Breathe in, breathe out, breathe in, breathe out, don't breathe, don't breathe, don't breathe, don't breathe.

WELCOME TO NIGHT VALE

Our neighboring town of Desert Bluffs is no more. It has been swept from the map, its borders a bad memory, its name a forgotten joke.

Oh, listeners, I have long dreamed of saying these words although the circumstances are different than I could have ever foreseen.

Mayor Cardinal announced today that after months of extending loans and other budgetary aid to the struggling community, she and Mayor Cardozo of Desert Bluffs agreed that the path to financial stability lay in, I can't believe I'm saying this, merging the two towns.

As of this week, Night Vale's borders will extend to include the dumb buildings that used to belong to Desert Bluffs, and all the weirdos that for some reason chose to live there.

Dana said that she understood there would be some adjustment needed from everyone, and then went on to say some other stuff that didn't really matter because apparently it's fine that Desert Bluffs is now part of Night Vale and no one has a problem with that and it's okay, it's fine. It's fine.

Our new sheriff, Sam, who has been an outspoken opponent to the monetary aid given to Desert Bluffs because of the strain it puts on law enforcement budgets, reacted as expected. At a press conference, they expressed their extreme displeasure in this development by singing selections from Richard Foreman's Tony award-winning Broadway musical *Film Is Evil: Radio Is Good* while weeping copiously. In response to follow-up questions from the attending journalists, Sam quietly said, "Listen, I just need this right now, okay?" before vowing that they would continue their strong opposition to the mayor's plan for unification, and then softly crying a little more.

And now, traffic.

There once was a farmer who never much thought of leaving his land. He was comfortable where he was, and comfortable with only ever being merely comfortable. He had no close friends, although a few people at the farmers market knew who he was.

"Yes, I know who he is," one of them might have said, although none of them ever did. None of them were ever asked.

One night as he was sitting down alone to dinner, he heard a loud party happening out in his field. Music, conversation, laughter. More confused than annoyed, he went out to see who could have set up a party in his remote field. But there was no one there.

Instead, the party now sounded as though it were coming from his house.

He ran back in, now afraid he was dealing with intruders.

But there was no one there.

The sound of the party was again coming from outside. Not from his fields, but from the empty stretch of road that led from nowhere much to his little farm, which was also nowhere much. He went out to the road.

But there was nothing. The sound of the party was now just over a gentle slope in the road. He followed it. Nothing.

Then it was just around the corner. Then where those trees covered the road in shadow.

He followed and followed the sound, each time finding that he was almost but not quite to its source, and he never came back to his farm again.

"I have no idea what happened to him," one of the folks at the farmers market might have said, although none of them ever did.

None of them were ever asked.

This has been traffic.

The Ralphs supermarket announced a small change to their sales structure, indicating that they will no longer be following the "bring food you want up to the cashier and pay for it" model that has been played out for years now, and instead will be structuring themselves as the world's first auction supermarket.

Any citizen looking to buy food from Ralphs will have to come to one of their daily scheduled auctions and bid on the kitchen staples and snacks as they are brought up for auction one by one. For instance, Lot 402 might be a banana, while Lot 403 might be a bag of Sun Chips and a bottle of tomato juice.

Charlie Bair, new weekday shift manager at the Ralphs, said,

"We believe this will be a more exciting and fun way for consumers to get the food they need. And to pay more for it. A lot more," he continued. "In competition with others, so that if you don't get that peanut butter someone else will, and then they'll have peanut butter and you won't. Better open up those wallets and make sure you get the food you need."

Fortunately for me, Carlos tends to do our shopping, since I personally have . . . a little trouble with auctions due to some traumatic experiences in my past. I mean, I know that, as the saying goes, "past performance is not a predictor of future results," but still. I think I'll sit these auctions out.

As part of the launch event for the auction system, Ralphs employees will stand on the supermarket's roof, pelting passersby with water balloons and expired produce, and drunkenly chanting the lyrics to every Cat Stevens song in unison until they have run out of breath, and, eyes locked with each other, in hunched-over, panting silence, continue to mouth the lyrics they no longer have the breath to say.

Back now, to the news.

The dissolve of Desert Bluffs into Night Vale continues.

It's not only new people, but new ways of life.

Dave Morales Cariño, a former Desert Bluffs resident, announced the founding of the first ever Joyous Congregation of the Smiling God here in Night Vale, on an old industrial stretch of the Eastern Expressway. Night Vale is a proud city of bloodstone worshippers, but certainly there are many in town who know of the power of the Smiling God, and belief and worship in the Smiling God is not a new thing here. In fact, a few longtime Night Vale residents attended the inaugural service at the Joyous Congregation's church, located in a storefront that used to sell leaf blowers and leaf blower accessories.

The City Council said that sales from their bloodstone factory have fallen by as much as 1 percent and that this is totally not okay with them.

"We're seeing someone now," they said, in a high-pitched whiny voice. "And it's just not a good time for us to be losing any income. Mayor Cardinal won't let us devour the Joyous Congregation, but we urge you to stick to the traditional worship of Bloodstone Circles, like your mother, and your grandmother, and the lizard people before her."

And now a word from our sponsors.

Today's show is sponsored by a happy-looking dog that's woofing and wagging his tail. He just wants you to play, or to pet him, or maybe just to stop feeling sad for a moment. He wants what's best for you, even if he doesn't know that he wants it. His instincts have been tinkered with, made to align with your interests, and now his happiness is yours. He's a big-eyed, woofing dog and he's dancing from paw to paw because he's so excited to make your life better. Are you about to take him for a walk? Oh no, did someone say the *W* word? Did the physical needs of an animal companion force someone to also go outside and move their body, both things that will chemically make them feel better? What a convenient system. What a good boy. What a good boy.

This has been brought to you by a happy-looking dog that's woofing and wagging his tail.

Paul Birmingham, local community activist who lives in a lean-to behind the library, wanted everyone to know that he was against it. When questioned what he was against specifically, he shrugged and said "I dunno. It. All of it. Or some of it. The bad parts. I'm totally opposed. Not a fan at all," he concluded. He waved signs, all of which just said "NO."

Paul has a long history of political activism in Night Vale, starting with his "Oregano Should Be Legal" campaign that he waged ferociously for the better part of the '80s, only giving it up when he found out that oregano already was legal. Then he shifted into environmental activism, marching every day in front of City Hall to draw attention to his controversial "What If What I See as Red Is What You See as Blue What If Color Isn't Even Real" campaign. More recently, he had joined the Airfilled Earth Society, the group that believes the earth is a precariously inflated orb that could pop or deflate at any moment.

Now he seems to have dropped all of his previous specific beliefs for the more general stance of negativity without target, a No directed at Nothing. Reporters report his breath sighed. Reporters report his shoulders sagged. Reporters report his shouting waned, his signs drooped. Paul wiped his brow.

"Just, something has to be true, you know?" he said. "Somewhere in all of this something has to be true." He squinted at the sky before concluding, "I still can't see them. I wish I could. Then maybe I would understand."

He wandered back to his lean-to, seeming to have grown years older, his defiance burned out of him.

Breaking news: The Sheriff's Secret Police and the City Council have taken unilateral action to disunite Night Vale and Desert Bluffs. The sheriff, backed by the hulking figures of the City Council, led a fleet of Secret Police cars into neighborhoods that used to be Desert Bluffs, announcing that all these buildings were now Night Vale's and that everyone living there needed to go.

"Nothing against you personally," the sheriff said, as their Secret Police chased after former Desert Bluffs citizens with what could be described as comically sized potato sacks if it weren't for the grim seriousness with which the police conducted their chase. The former Desert Bluffs citizens started to flee, panic set pale and glistening on their faces, but they stopped when they saw yet another car coming at them from the other direction. Black sedan. Tinted windows. Unmistakably governmental. It pulled directly in front of the sheriff's group, bringing everyone to a momentary confused halt.

Out of the car stepped Mayor Cardinal. She looked around at the scene as it lay. She couldn't have seemed younger, or more tired. She took a slow, deliberate breath.

"Go home, Sam," she said to the sheriff. "Go home, all of you."

The sheriff looked around at their police officers for support and then shouted back "You can't stop us, Dana. We will drive these people out of our town."

"No, Sam," she said, "you won't. You won't because it's their town too now. You won't because there's nowhere else they should go. You won't because it's a bad thing to do and I think, somewhere in there, you aren't a bad person. Maybe I'm wrong about that. Wouldn't be the first time. But, primarily you won't," she concluded, "because I won't let you."

And she folded her arms. And she said nothing more. The Secret Police still held their potato sacks, unsure now of what they should do. Their sheriff no longer ordered or even goaded, but just stared thoughtfully at their mayor. The former citizens of Desert Bluffs stopped fleeing, looking back at this first figment of hope.

And then the sheriff got in their car, turned it around, and drove away. The Secret Police all got in their cars and followed. The City Council roared and stomped, but without the police to back them up, they too eventually retreated. And still Dana stood, silent, arms folded, until the last of them was gone. She turned to the new citizens of Night Vale who had moments before been fleeing.

"Hi," she said. "I'm Dana. Don't hesitate to get in touch if you have any problems, okay?"

She got back in her car. She too left.

I . . . I don't know where I stand on this scene as it just unfolded. I need to think about it. While I think about it, let's go to the weather.

WEATHER: "The Sky Is Calling" by Kim Boekbinder

Here's what.

We all have our regionalisms. For instance, in many parts of the country, there is a sandwich known as a sub sandwich, that is in other places known as a hero, a hoagie, a grinder, a longburger, a prince's delight, or a bread burrito. This is one example of a difference in culture. There are others.

It is in these little details that we see ourselves, that we define how we are *not* others, and thus, how we *are* ourselves.

When confronted with someone whose normal is not our normal, we are forced to confront the most frightening prospect of all, that there is no such thing as normal, just the accidental cultural moment we happened to be born into. A cultural happenstance that never existed before and will never exist again.

Our idea of normal is a city built on sand. For instance, for us, our city is literally built on sand, and this is our normal.

We resist difference because it requires we acknowledge that the culture we grew up with as normal is just a momentary accident. It requires we accept that the world we were born into will never be the same as the world we die in. The longer we live, the more we become interlopers, even in our own hometowns. But, if we let it happen, also the more we will learn.

I cannot say I am always happy about Desert Bluffs. It can be said that I have ranted about them on the radio, sometimes for hours, while listeners called in to complain that they wanted me to talk about something, anything, else. I have thrown things at the microphone, and attempted to cast spells upon Desert Bluffs that would drive them into ruin.

But my happiness or unhappiness is irrelevant to their existence. They exist, and so do I, and now our differing normals, in such close proximity, perhaps will edge just slightly toward each other.

Night Vale may never again be the Night Vale I knew, but it will be some kind of Night Vale. It will be a version of our town that someday someone will look back on and think, "Those were the days. That was what was normal." And that person will be wrong. And that person will be right.

Stay tuned next for tomorrow's winning lottery numbers, broadcast to everyone simultaneously and so reducing each jackpot share to a small but fair amount.

And from a town that isn't the town it was before, and then won't be the town it has become, and then will change again, and then again after that, and all of them the same town, and all of them our town: Good night, Night Vale. Good night.

PROVERB: Actually, it's Properties Brother.

EPISODE 84:
"PAST TIME"

MARCH 15, 2016

GUEST VOICE: JACKSON PUBLICK (HIRAM MCDANIELS)

I PLAYED ONE SEASON OF LITTLE LEAGUE IN GARLAND, TEXAS. WE were the outlaws. I played catcher. My batting average that season was .000. (If you don't follow baseball, then good, because I don't need you knowing just how terrible a batter I was.)

One thing I was pretty good at doing was catching the ball and throwing the ball. I was bad at doing either of those things while moving, so catcher seemed to be the one thing that fit my (lack of) talents. You just squat, and when a little league pitcher throws the ball, you mostly just have to catch it and throw it back.

Sometimes kids made contact with the ball and ran to a base, which was pretty great because it meant I didn't have to catch a ball and throw it back.

Growing up in North Texas, we went to watch the Texas Rangers from time to time and even an Oklahoma City 89ers* game or two, but it was never my sport. The game seemed dull, and I thought the sound and fury of canned music, the Wave, and interstitial fan contests was silly and not worth the time I could have spent playing Atari.

But a girl I liked in high school loved baseball, so I started going to games with her. For a short time, she got me really into baseball. I even started going regularly to batting cages and eventually signed up to try out for my high school baseball team. (I said, "Signed up to try out," not "Tried out.")

After graduation, we drifted apart, and I lost interest in baseball again until 2003, when I moved to Northampton, Massachusetts. In a divey corner bar, I witnessed Red Sox fans transcend existence with the success of their team, only for them to spiritually implode during Game 7 of the American League Championship Series against the hated Yankees. Boston blew a late lead, and in the bottom of the eleventh, the game-winning homer was hit by the Yankees third baseman, a man known in New England as Aaron Fucking Boone.

I've been a Red Sox fan ever since.

This episode isn't about baseball, but it is about the Little League coach I wish I had had growing up. Maybe Lusia could have refined my undeveloped skills and my interest in America's pastime. Maybe I could have been on that 2003 Red Sox team, and I could have told Aaron, in person, where he could shove that home run.

—Jeffrey Cranor

---

*The Oklahoma City 89ers (presently named the Oklahoma City Dodgers) are a Triple-A minor league team which is, according to Wikipedia, inexplicably in the "Pacific Coast" League.

Dress for success. Put on your tall hat and rubber gloves and long, gray coat. Success requires this specific outfit.

WELCOME TO NIGHT VALE

It's spring again, which apparently means it's baseball season. My brother-in-law, Steve [*long inhale and exhale; like a regimented breathing exercise*] Steve and I took his stepdaughter, Janice, for little league baseball tryouts this weekend.

Steve and Janice play catch a lot together. She really loves the sport. It's actually pretty adorable. She shouts things like, "Go farther Steve. I want to see how far I can throw the ball." And I shout things like, "Keep going, Steve. See how far away you can go."

The tryouts were at the haunted baseball diamond over near the Shambling Orphan Housing Development. There were a lot of kids there. Say what you will about all the people from Desert Bluffs moving to Night Vale, and I've said many things, but it's created enormous growth in youth sports. There are leagues for kids with all kinds of interests and abilities.

Janice tried out for a wheelchair softball league—the first of its kind in Night Vale. Plus I got to spend time talking to Little League baseball coaches Betty Lucero and Lusia Tereshchenko. Lusia is a fascinating woman. So despite having to be around Steve all day, I had a pretty good time. More on that in a bit, but first the news.

In a study released today, the Greater Night Vale Medical Community has found a statistical link between a high-carbohydrate diet and the number of squirrels on your lawn.

According to the study, they found that people who take in a higher-than-normal number of carbohydrates have an average of four point seventy-four squirrels somewhere on their lawn. But those with lower carb intake have a slightly different number of squirrels.

A representative from the Greater Night Vale Medical Community said, "You can see from this pie chart," and here the representative pointed at an American flag, "that the data shows a statistical link between these things."

Another representative, who was previously unnoticed, then emerged from behind the first representative and stated, "It is important that you adjust your carbohydrate intake and/or your trust-slash-distrust of squirrels accordingly." The first representative then did a set of twelve pushups—the kind where you clap your hands between each one.

"Believe us. We are doctors," a third representative said, as she lowered herself down, headfirst from the ceiling at the back of the room. As everyone turned to see her, she said, "Just kidding!" And then the three representatives began juggling and doing yo-yo tricks to hip-hop music.

And now it's time for another edition of "Hey There, Cecil."

"Hey there, Cecil. I just moved into a new apartment and after two months, my landlord is telling me I'm behind on rent. But I've been paying my rent. On the last day of each month, I carry a twenty-stone bag of quartz chips and two pheasant carcasses and lay them outside his office. What am I doing wrong? Also, what is the currency these days? Signed: IN DEBT IN OLD TOWN."

Hey there, In Debt. Well, I think you're in the wrong here. Quartz and dead pheasants are not currency. They have not been legal tender since the 1990s, so you are in arrears on your rent. Here's

what I would do. Write a nice note to your landlord explaining you didn't understand how money works. Then maybe find a different job where they pay you in actual American currency, which has no physical form and is just a series of arbitrary numbers printed on ATM receipts. Hope this helps.

"Hey there, Cecil. I love dogs a lot. The other day, I saw a young couple out walking the cutest little beagle puppy. I asked if I could pet him. They didn't say anything, but the dog had the sweetest expression. So I pet the dog. The couple didn't speak or move. She just glared at me. The boy was smiling. And as the dog licked my hand, I asked the boy, "What's your dog's name?" and the boy laughed. It was a cruel, hollow laugh. And I pet the dog once more and they left. And I can't get that dog out of my head. I'm now dreaming about it. Terrible dreams. Terrible dreams where I cannot move. I wake, physically incapacitated and crying. When I can finally move, I run to the bathroom needing to vomit but unable. I am covered in cold sweat but my face is on fire. I hunch over the sink spitting up small globs of black tar. Every single night. So my question is: Should I get a dog? And if so, is a beagle a good breed? Signed: DOG LOVER IN DOWNTOWN."

Hey there, Dog Lover. You should absolutely get a dog. You sound allergic to beagles, so maybe a basset instead.

"Hey there, Cecil. What are you doing Saturday night, at say, 8:00 P.M.? Would you be interested in an opera and drinks after? Signed: LONELY BOY IN THE LABORATORY."

Hey there, Lonely Boy. Yes. I would very much like an opera and whatever else after.

And now back to the tryouts. Coach Lusia Tereshchenko told me she's been seeing more and more of those strangers lately. She does not like them. "They stand and they stare at the kids, at the coaches, at the parents. Just breathing, not moving or speaking. Them, I do not like," Lusia said. "At first I thought they were from this Desert Bluffs. So many of those people coming to Night Vale. But Desert Bluffs families play in the baseball league now. I meet them. They are nice people. They are good people. They do not stand and stare and breathe," Lusia said.

"These strangers. They are from someplace else. Not here. Not Desert Bluffs. They are not humans. They are not even ghosts. Believe me. I should know," Lusia said, and then laughed. "Get it, because I am dead?"

I told Lusia I got it. But she continued, "I'm dead, Cecil. It's funny. Laugh, okay? I'm a ghost."

And so I laughed. It was genuinely funny. But then she went suddenly solemn, "Oh, these strangers, they remind me of those terrible men on the train."

I asked Lusia, "What men on the train?" But just then an errantly thrown baseball bounced to a stop at Lusia's feet. She bent over to pick it up, but being a ghost, her hands went right through it.

"Ah, Cecil, some days I can pick up the ball, some days I cannot. Will you help?"

I picked up the baseball and threw it back to the child who nearly fell over running but caught it nonetheless.

And Lusia said, "You still have a good arm, Cecil. You were a great shortstop."

I told her I don't remember playing baseball, and she laughed and said, "Well, you know what they say about growing old? Memory is the second thing to go."

I asked, "What's the first?"

"Relevance," she said quickly. "Relevance."

Listeners, sorry I have to interrupt my story. We're getting another call from Hiram McDaniels, literal five-headed dragon and former mayoral candidate. Hiram is in the jailhouse for attempting to kill our current mayor. And he's on our phones now. Hiram. Hello.

HIRAM-VIOLET: Cecil, it's me, Hiram's violet head.

CECIL: Hello, Violet. Listeners, it was Hiram's violet head who courageously turned in his other four heads for their crimes against the mayor. Violet, how are you?

HIRAM-VIOLET: They cut a hole in the cell where our main body and other four heads are. My head is poking out of the hole into the fresh air. Technically I am not in jail, but I am also not free. I think I have made a mistake.

CECIL: You did the right thing, Violet. Your other four heads wanted to kill the mayor.

HIRAM-VIOLET: There are five of us, but there is one of us.

CECIL: I'm not sure I follow.

HIRAM-VIOLET: "Do I contradict myself? Very well, then I contradict myself, I am large, I contain multitudes."

CECIL: AH! My favorite line from *Die Hard*.

HIRAM-VIOLET: Cecil, I have removed myself as a witness for the prosecution. I stand with my other heads. I stand with and for myself.

HIRAM-GOLD: And it sure is nice to have you back, Purp . . . I'm sorry. You are not purple. You are violet. I respect that.

HIRAM-VIOLET: Thanks, gold head.

HIRAM-GRAY: Injustice makes me sad.

HIRAM-GOLD: We're gonna do our best, Gray. We're going to do our best.

HIRAM-GREEN: WE WILL BURN THE COURTHOUSE. WE WILL DEVOUR THE JUDGE. WE WILL CRUSH THE JURY WITH OUR TAIL.

HIRAM-BLUE: They are shackling and muzzling us for our own trial, Cecil. They think our green head is serious in his threats.

HIRAM-GREEN: MY THREATS ARE ONLY METAPHORS, YOU SOFT SENTIENT POUCHES OF FUTURE FOOD!

HIRAM-VIOLET: Cecil. I cannot be separated from myself. I may disagree with myself, but I am all in this together.

CECIL: Violet, I—

HIRAM-GOLD: But, listen, Cecil, if Night Vale knew the trouble they were in, they'd let us out so we could help fight these strangers.

CECIL: Oh, believe me, Hiram. The new sheriff is working double time to get rid of the Desert Bluffs p——

HIRAM-GOLD: Not Desert Bluffs people, Cecil. They're harmless, hardworking folks. I'm talking about the strangers. The ones that don't move. The ones that breathe. You tell your mayor friend I can stop them.

HIRAM-GRAY: We're not strong enough.

HIRAM-BLUE: They would be quite resistant to our fire and even our strength.

HIRAM-GREEN: WE WILL TEAR THE STRANGERS TO PINK FLESHY SHREDS AND THEN CHEW THEM AND THEN SWALLOW THEM. I AM BEING LITERAL.

HIRAM-VIOLET: I will fight with you, Green. You too, Gold and Gray and Blue. We could do this. But, Cecil, we need out of this prison.

CECIL: I don't know what I can do about that, Hiram.

HIRAM-GOLD: I'm sure you'll think of something. We're gonna make it through this. Thanks, buddy.

Well then, let's have a word from our sponsor.

Today's show is brought to you by the Dove Campaign for Real Beauty. Superreal beauty. Beauty so real, you won't even recognize it as your own. Like a set of human lungs on a white table. So real. So beautiful. Most people have lungs. Expanding, contracting, attached to nothing. Just lungs on a white table. Most beauty products won't show you what a set of human lungs look like, because they think you can't handle real beauty. They will photoshop out the models' lungs, leaving a gaping gory hole in their chests. But an empty upper rib cavity is not what a real person looks like. No, we look like this: A pair of lungs breathing autonomously on a white table in a white room with music playing. Inspirational music. Mostly choir and keyboards. You know the drill. Don't gotta tell you about inspirational music, am I right?

Dove. Lungs on a white table. Little League coach Lusia Tereshchenko told me the incredible story of her journey to Night Vale. When she was a young woman she left her home to travel west across America. She wanted to find a new life for herself out of the crowded, smoke-choked cities. She walked for miles, picking up work in roadside towns. She rode in carriages when she had money. She eventually found a job, making belts, for an old tanner, who worked Lusia long hours for little pay. The old tanner was otherwise kind and treated Lusia like her very own daughter, because she never had a family. But, the tanner grew ill, and Lusia took care of her, bathing her and fetching herb mixtures from the apothecary.

One morning the old woman was no more. Lusia ran her business for a while longer but since the tanner had no heirs, and Lusia did not feel she had found her true home, she continued west where there was supposedly golden sunshine along an azure sea.

Soon, however, she once again was in desperate need of money, so that she could eat, and could sleep in safety. She met some men, silent men. Men who kept their faces in shadows. Who kept their voices in shadows. Who kept their guns in shadows. And she worked for them, never knowing what her work was, just that she was to ride the train with them until the time was right.

One afternoon, the men stood up simultaneously and moved in different directions. One to the front of the train, one to the rear. One climbed through the ceiling onto the roof of the car. Two more drew pistols on the passengers. They told Lusia to keep everyone calm.

The train whined to a halt, and the men hurriedly unloaded crates from the rear car onto a horse-drawn cart. The crates were warm, warmer than the air around them. They smelled sharp and earthy, like freshly ground cinnamon.

The apparent sheriff of the little town they stopped in, the town of Night Vale—a place she'd never heard of—soon arrived. He was wearing a welding mask and a cowboy hat. The sheriff drew his gun on the shadowy men. But being outnumbered, he was unable to do much to stop them.

So while calming the others on the train, Lusia crept behind one of the men. He had a kerchief drawn across his face. Not an actual kerchief tied in front of his face. But a simulacrum of patterned fabric hand-drawn on his face. Using one of her leather belts, Lusia whipped the gun out of his hand and deftly picked it up from the ground. She fired at the outlaws, felling both. Outside, the sheriff felled two more.

But as she climbed up to the top of the car, she heard a shot from just below her, and then she was lying on her back. She couldn't remember why she had laid down. She saw, in the sky just above her, a dark planet of awesome size, lit by no sun. She didn't know how she had not noticed it before. It was so close. An invisible titan, all thick black forests and jagged mountains and deep, turbulent oceans.

And then . . . Well, let me take you first, to the weather.

WEATHER: "The River, The Woods" by Astronautalis

I asked Lusia if that's how she died. "Well, one moment I'm in a gunfight," she said, "and the next moment I'm a ghost." She asked if I had a cigarette.

I don't smoke, so I said no.

"I couldn't hold it anyway," she admitted.

"Why are you living in a baseball diamond?" I asked her.

She said this wasn't always a baseball diamond. It was just a field. A field where train tracks used to run. A field where a train once rolled to a stop. But right around this time, the game of baseball was becoming popular, and kids began coming to the field to play. Lusia watched and learned and grew to love the sport's simplicity and structured grace.

"It's a beautiful game, Cecil. So I started trying to coach the kids, but since I'm translucent and hazy, they got scared and ran away, calling this the haunted baseball diamond. Over time, the kids realized I had some helpful things to say about batting stances and hitting the cutoff man, so they came back." Lusia turned to one of the kids. "Eye on the ball, Manny!" she shouted.

I asked Lusia, "So you think those men on the train were related to these strangers in Night Vale now?"

"You do not see evil like that very often," she said. "But no. Those men on the train performed their evil because they needed whatever was in those crates more than they needed life or peace," she said. "These strangers, they don't need anything. They are evil for evil's own sake."

I looked over and saw Steve and Janice coming my way. They were high-fiving and grinning.

Lusia said, "She's a good kid. Good arm. She's gonna be a great shortstop like her uncle."

I told Lusia I hope we have a good baseball season and it was wonderful catching up with her. Steve, Janice, and I turned to walk back to Steve's van.

Lusia whispered to me, "We're past time for hope, Cecil. They're no longer coming. They're here, and we cannot stop something that wants nothing."

Staring straight at Janice, ignoring Lusia, I said, "You made the team! Congrats. Let's get ice cream."

Behind us I heard a distant bark. It was a sweet, sickening yelp. And in the reflection on the van window I could see a boy in a hoodie holding a beagle puppy and both of them were looking at us. I felt cold sweat, but my face was hot. My tongue was sticky and thick.

"Steve, can we get a dog?" Janice said, all strapped in.

"Let's go get that ice cream, okay?" I interrupted.

The dog barked again, and I did not look. I did not look at anything as I got in my seat and shut the door. I felt like throwing up.

"Thanks for driving, Steve," I said, putting my hand softly on his arm. He looked momentarily amused. No, not amused. Concerned. And we drove away as Janice told us all about her new team.

Stay tuned next for something lurking just outside your window. Don't worry. It's not a human.

And as always, good night, Night Vale. Good Night.

PROVERB: Dance like the government is watching.

EPISODE 85:
"THE APRIL MONOLOGUES"

AUGUST 15, 2016

GUEST VOICES: MARA WILSON (FACELESS OLD WOMAN), KATE JONES (MICHELLE NGUYEN), HAL LUBLIN (STEVE CARLSBERG)

THE FIRST SONG I CAN REMEMBER IS "THRILLER" BY MICHAEL JACKSON. I remember watching the music video at my paternal grandparents' house the night it was released. This song and video had a profound impact on me: It kick-started my lifelong battle with insomnia. Four-year-old me knew then what I know now: No one's gonna save me from the beast about to strike.

I don't want to insinuate that my parents had "poor judgment" or "terrible parenting skills" when they allowed a four-year-old to watch a shorter, musical version of *An American Werewolf in London*, but I do think they regretted their decision when I insisted that we shouldn't allow Santa into the house because it's just Michael Jackson in a costume coming to kidnap me.

This incident would turn into a distrust of pop music. I preferred the sweet sounds of musicals, like *Xanadu*, a film with songs about the Greek Muses inspiring a mural artist to build a roller rink so rocking, it would stir Gene Kelly to skate-tap-dance.

The next stop on my musical journey came when my mom drove me to a birthday party in Brick, New Jersey. It was a mere ten minutes away from our home, but after dropping me off, she took a wrong turn off a traffic circle, drove for an hour without question, and ended up in Camden, New Jersey, which was, at the time, America's murder capital. After that, a family intervention resulted in me becoming her personal GPS.

None of this was a big deal until 1988, when my older sister got her driver's license and my mom bought a Chevy Cavalier that came standard with a tape player. While my sister drove around blasting REM and Belinda Carlisle, I was stuck in the Cavalier making sure Mom arrived home safe and incident-free. With my sister's abandonment, I lost out on these new one-to-one odds on voting for what we would listen to in Mom's car. The new tape player inspired my mom to become a teen again, only her idols used bamboo flutes and lute-sounding string instruments to sing Vietnamese '80s slow jams.

The next seven years of my life were nonstop Viet-pop.

I'm not disparaging Vietnamese music, but it's fair to say listening to the same handful of songs on repeat for six or seven years will make anyone miserable, especially when you don't speak the language.

Viet-pop has not really made it out of Vietnam, which makes me think Michelle likes it, but then again, one of her favorite sounds is her hopping (which, to the untrained ear, sounds strikingly similar to silence), so she probably hates it.

When I turned seventeen and got my license, I was finally free of the oppressive sounds of my mom's favorite Viet singers, and even now, on long car rides or at home alone, I prefer silence. Maybe I'm just like Michelle. Maybe I should tell people I listen to hop-core.

In recent years, I've branched out since being exposed to so many artists through *Welcome to Night Vale*. Have you guys heard of Spotify? It's really neat. And did you know headphones come free with an iPhone?

My mom's taste has also evolved. My sister and I gave Mom an iPod for her long walks around town, and she asked me to load the playlist from her 2007 wedding. Not long after, my sister updated Mom's iPod inadvertently deleting the wedding playlist and replacing it with one of her own. My mom, a Luddite, accidentally pressed "Repeat Song" and went out for her walk. She returned an hour later very concerned that the songs were "All about butts now." Apparently my sister's playlist included Sir-Mix-A-Lot's "Baby Got Back," which Mom listened to for an hour, not realizing she could press stop or pull out her earbuds. I love wondering what was going through her head the fourth time that song started, who she thought Becky was, and why she didn't just turn it off.

Then again, it is a great song.

—Kate Jones

CECIL: Once again, the turning of the seasons. Nearly imperceptible here, a shading of the desert heat. But we feel the change, in the thrum of our bodies, in the texture of the sand. There is rain, once in a while, if not here, then somewhere else surely. Wild spring has stepped in for her stolid winter sister. It is April, and something is different. It is April, and the days have depth and vibrance. It is April. And so, dear listeners, Night Vale Community Radio is pleased to present . . . the April Monologues.

FACELESS OLD WOMAN: Chad. Oh, Chad. I'm beginning to understand, and I wish I did not.

You used to wear nice shirts. You cut your hair regularly. Sometimes while you slept, I would comb it, to keep it orderly and presentable for the next morning. You would shower and shave and dress for your internship. So plain and well-kempt and precious. Unaware of the faceless old woman, secretly living in your home.

And then one day you did not return home. You love your home. You rarely leave, not even to be with other people. You play video games and watch police dramas and read books by comedians. You have always loved your solitude, and I have always thought you were special in how completely ordinary you seemed. Few young men are exactly what one thinks of when one thinks of a young man. You were it, Chad.

And I always looked out for you.

Remember that terrible roach problem you had, and you tried all kinds of traps and poisons, but nothing worked. Only one day you returned home to find thousands of roach corpses scattered across your floor, each one with its legs tied together and its head removed. And there was a hand-scrawled note that read "THEY'LL NOT BOTHER YOU AGAIN."

That was me. I did that. Well, I didn't kill the roaches. That was the exterminator you called. He was very thorough at his job. But I wrote the note, Chad. That note was me.

We had a good way about us. I lived secretly and facelessly in your home, and you, well, you kind of did too, only metaphorically.

But then one night you didn't return home. I saw in your e-mails—I loved reading your e-mails, Chad, so compellingly bland—you had to go check out a used and discount sporting goods store, something for your work. But that store was not what it claimed to be, and you didn't return home for months.

The landlord came by in your long absence, but I scared her off with this terrifying noise I can make using only a leather belt and a bird. You loved your home and I protected it for you.

But when you returned, things were different—oh how different. Your crisp buttoned shirts, all unbuttoned and wrinkled, dangling on hooks like dried pelts from a misguided hunt.

These days, you rarely notice the little things I do, like when I painted the inside of your bathtub black or glued blurry photos of spiders into the bottoms of your mugs.

You don't even play video games anymore. You wear hoods and light candles. You drew a star in the middle of your floor, which actually I can totally get behind.

Your e-mails, which were once so wonderfully common, full of mailing list detritus and social invitations and social invitation rejections and food delivery receipts, a tale of a stagnant nothing of a man, so perfectly lovable in his comfy inertia. Now they are terse, coded messages to a girl I think you are destroying.

"Found a door. Come over," this one says.

"HE is here, and HE is good," this one says.

"Candles are growing again," this one says.

I do not like these candles you have that grow when lit, and melt when not. And I certainly do not like . . . HIM.

You say HIM, but HE is not human. You say HE is good, but HE is awful. He . . . It. It is unwelcome. Unwelcome, Chad.

What you brought to us here in this little town, my town, the town I secretly live in. What you summoned.

I stopped secretly living in your house because I was afraid of it, but now I have returned because I feel, unusual for me, some obligation to do something. To prevent this coming disaster.

[*whispering*]

Listen to me. It is five in the morning and you are asleep, but I am at your ear quietly asking you . . . telling you . . .

I'm begging you really, Chad. Did you ever think I would beg you? Beg anyone? I haven't begged since I was a child, aboard that wicked ship. Those men didn't listen either, Chad, which is the reason I lived at the bottom of the ocean for so many years before this place, this desert, this town, this apartment.

Chad, what happened to you in that store that wasn't a store? What did they turn you into? What have you brought into this reality? Do you even know the destruction that awaits this town? Not just this town, perhaps the world? That is not a door you have opened, Chad.

When is a door not a door? When it is a chasm.

I know you cannot see or hear me, for I live secretly. But I beg you, if somehow my voice seeps into your dreams and sticks in your memory. You must undo what you have done before it is too late.

You must—

[*no longer whispering*]

Chad. That creature, that monster you summoned is here. It is staring at me with eyes that could never be mistaken for human. It's walking toward me. How does it see me, Chad? No one sees me.

Chad, it is licking my hand. Stop it!

It's bringing me a tennis ball. The puppy is bringing me a ball. I will not play fetch with you, hound. How do you see me, you monster?

[*softly*] Chad, we must undo— [*off mic; loudly*] *GET AWAY FROM ME*— [*on mic softly*] you must undo what you have done. It means nothing but ill will to this town, to the world, and most importantly from my perspective, to a faceless old woman that secretly lives in your home.

[*off mic*] Stop staring at me, you unholy beast. There, beagle. Go fetch your stupid ball!

CECIL: Growth turns our thoughts to decline. Each new sprout brings to mind the decay out of which it grows. Each thing leads to its opposite. Every moment contains multitudes. Every second is the history of the universe, if taken at its composite parts. Let us take this moment at its composite parts, break down this day into each person's thoughts. We return you now to the April Monologues.

MICHELLE: I've been thinking lately about loneliness. Not because I'm lonely. I just like to be ahead of the curve when it comes to thinking about things.

Obviously I'm not lonely. I'm Michelle Nguyen, owner of the coolest and only record store in town and I'm not lonely. I'm just, like, a performance artist, and my medium is solitude.

I've been listening to a lot of hop-core lately. It's my new favorite genre. It's recordings of a person hopping. Thump, thump, thump. But soft. Thump, thump, thump. Totally great. You wouldn't have heard of it. Because I made it myself and I've shared it with no one.

It's a recording of me hopping. I recorded that and I'm listening to it. It's the new thing.

Maureen came by. Nervous, jaw clenched, hair parted, hands fluttering, stomping, restarting, sighing Maureen. She was looking for something new to listen to. Said things were stressful at her internship, she had to lead an army. Or whatever. And she needed something that would relax her. I suggested easy listening, like Slayer, or some silence, but she said that she was tired of all the Top 40 stations playing no sound at all. Silence is too mainstream, and she wanted something new.

I'll be honest, I actually like silence. I shouldn't. It's, like, so popular. But my favorite silence is the hum of a dryer from the next floor down. I also like the swish of a highway that you thought was too far away to hear but now that it's so quiet, you can hear it, distant and dissipating, like the sizzle of foam on a wave.

I gave Maureen Leonard Cohen's new album, the one where he talks in a gravely voice and women sing along behind him. She rolled her eyes and walked out. I think she liked it.

Hold on.

[off mic] Welcome to Dark Owl Records. Hey, Larry. Oh, you want the new album by the Beatles? How original. Well, all the dubstep stuff is upstairs.

[on mic]

It's like that old joke. I listen to Bach often but never the Beatles.

Thump, thump, thump. I love this hop-core recording. I made it on the old beige carpet of the back office here at the store. I did it in socks, so it would be extra quiet. You have to hold still, like, even hold your breath to hear it. But it's there. Thump, thump.

You have to really pay attention to notice me. But I'm there.

I don't actually listen to Bach often. What a sellout. Did you see his HBO special? Ugh. I didn't, but I bet it was bad.

It's a quiet time for record sales. Usually it's really busy, which is annoying. I hate it when people are like, "Please, I want to pay you a lot of money for physical albums." It's like, get in line, you know? Get in that line. The one leading to the cash register. I'll ring you up when it's your turn.

But I've let the temporary staff dissolve back into mud for the season, and I won't have to mutter the incantations to bring them back to life for another month or two. It's just me, behind the counter. Me, like always. I'm all I need. I'm the ultimate underground hit. No one's heard of me. No one's listening. Just the way I like it.

[off mic] Yes, I know this is a one-story building, Larry. I was being metaphorical. I don't actually have any Beatles albums. It's like that old joke. I listen to Bach often, but . . .

[on mic]

He left. His loss.

Maureen came by. Steady, jaw-tight, hair-loose, hands-swinging, shuffling, restarting, sighing Maureen. She said she liked Leonard's album, but she had heard it enough now. What else did I have?

I never thought I'd do this, but I gave her some of my favorite recordings of bees. I love those recordings, but I've listened to them enough times that I don't ever need to hear them again. It's like, the sound became part of me, and I know it better than the recordings do, you know?

Maybe you don't know. Probably not. You're probably still listening to that Woody Guthrie single on repeat because you just listen to whatever big music tells you to.

Oh this is my favorite part of the hop-core recording. It's the part where the thump of my hopping gets so quiet that it isn't any sound at all. It's a silence, and you have to know I'm there to recognize me in the silence. That I'm still hopping even though you can't hear it. Listen.

[*long silence*]

That's me in there, in that no sound at all.

They say music is made up of the spaces between the notes. And that life is made up of the moments where your eyes are closed because you're blinking. And that books are made up of blank pages that everyone pretends have words on them so they will seem smart. I'm the blink and the space. I'm the pause. I'm the gap.

Hold on, I have a customer.

[*off mic*] I don't actually have a customer. I just need a moment to myself. This is me greeting someone. This is them feeling like just because they're in a record shop they're entitled to like, music or whatever.

[*on mic*]

Ugh, that person is the worst. Hold on, someone is actually coming in. Oh, it's . . . I'll be back.

[*long pause*]

Maureen came by. Satisfied, jaw-loose, hair-up, hands-idling, striding, stopping, restarting, sighing Maureen.

She said she loved the bees recording. She wanted something like it, but even more so. Similar, but so different that it would startle her. I knew exactly what she meant with that thirst but I didn't know how to satisfy it. There's only so much music, you know? And there's so much human desire.

Well. You're not going to believe this. Probably, like, you won't even understand.

I gave her the recording of me hopping. I know that, like, ruins it, because now someone else has listened to it. But somehow I don't mind if Maureen hears it. I think maybe even I'd like that. I hope she comes back soon. I mean, don't get me wrong, I love it when the record store is empty, when there are none of those annoying "customers" clamoring for music to listen to. Being alone is the best. But I also kind of like it when Maureen comes by. Her being here is cool too, I guess.

I just have to figure out what album to show her next. Only, there's so much good music, you know?

CECIL: This then this then this. Each leads to the next. The seasons are a corridor we proceed through, and the door at the end of the corridor is black and depthless. Appreciate the warmth of this narrow corridor. How small this world is, and how small we all are for living in it, and how joyful a smallness can be. So let us return for one last time, for one last small time, to the April Monologues.

STEVE: I try to be helpful. I know I can't always fix everything. I know my limits and they are many, but still, I try to be helpful.

So when the kid came by, I did my best.

He was scared, sure. Because he could see them, too. The glowing arrows in the sky. Dotted lines and arrows and circles. The sky is a chart that explains the entire world, and he could see it. That's a terrifying thing, if you aren't prepared for it.

He was shaking so bad. His ball cap was pulled low over his face. Steve, he said. Steve Carlsberg. I know you can see them too. Help me.

And I tried. I tried to be helpful.

I like in the evenings, when it's quiet. Parts of the world, the big cities, things don't change much from morning to afternoon to evening. The same even light. The same people in a hurry.

But here, every time of day has a different tone and shade. In the mornings, before anyone else is up, the desert is golden, and the horizon light illuminates every detail on the mountains to the west. I feel bad for the folks who don't believe in mountains, who won't see even when shown.

Then the birds come and hop around outside the kitchen window. I like to watch them as I make coffee. My brother-in-law, he never sees the birds on account of he likes to grind the coffee himself and the pounding of his coffee hammer keeps all the birds away. But me, I don't mind the prehammered stuff. It's a soft trade for the birds.

And then the afternoon, where the light deepens and widens, and the mountains turn to blue cutouts against a white-blue sky. And then the sunset, loud and fragrant, like sunsets usually are. And then the evening, a vast, quiet empty. Just me and Abby and Janice, floating, an island of a family, in the rich darkness of the desert nothing.

The kid was so scared. Oh boy. But he had it in him. He tries to be helpful too. I could tell. And so it wasn't enough to know. He wanted to do something about it.

He said that he had been sent to a sporting goods store—that they thought might have been a front for the World Government. I know that place. The World Government isn't the half of it. Go in that sporting goods store, you're gonna find a real racket. Ha! I love puns. But yeah, that place holds the core of it. And this kid, he goes in there and he sees it. And once you've seen it, once you know, you can't ever not know.

Can't become who you once were after you've become what you are now.

Glowing arrows in the sky. Dotted lines. He understood, like I understand.

The folks that run Night Vale, they think they have control. But you can't control what a person knows. The more you think you have that contained, the more it eludes you. Might as well try to control the weather.

[*brief weather bit*]

And they try to do that too, using cloud-seeding drones and laser arrays, but it never works out the way they planned.

"What can we do about it?" the boy kept asking.

Poor kid. I wish my brother-in-law took better care of his interns at the radio station, didn't send them places they had no right being, like sporting goods stores run by the World Government. But it's not up to me. I suppose Cecil can run his life the way he wants, and he won't ever hear from me about it. Not like the other way around, I suppose.

The kid understood how the world worked. He could see the structure of it, and, oh bless him, he wanted to fix it. To make it right again. And he wanted me to tell him how.

Not much we can do but understand, I told him. Not much to do but know.

But he wouldn't accept it. He wanted to follow those glowing arrows in the sky like they were a map to somewhere, and not a labyrinth in which a monster lives.

Listen, I said. Listen, Chad, I said. I think in time you'll feel better. Maybe get a puppy, I told him. We had a puppy infestation back a few years. Hell on the insulation and some load-bearing joists, but it was just the cutest thing.

Yes, he said. Summon a puppy.

Well, I said, sure, but more just get a puppy. Like, *adopt* is probably the word you're looking for, I said. Adopt a puppy, sure. They smile and wag their tails and roll around. Very cute, I said.

That is how we will change things, he said. Summon a puppy. The World Government will never see it coming.

And he thanked me and walked away.

Oh well. At least he's not a station intern anymore. I'm sure he'll be fine. What's the worst that could happen?

I sat out on the porch the rest of the day, just thinking, watching the wide light of afternoon narrow back down to the west until I could smell the sunset coming. And then I went inside. It was Abby's turn to make dinner, and it looked delicious.

Maybe I should get a puppy too. Add one more to our island of a family. A puppy could be just the thing. Janice would love it.

But not a puppy like that kid has now. I think, perhaps, that that's no puppy at all. Maybe it was a mistake, my conversation with him. But what can I say? I try to be helpful.

CECIL: And so we reach the end of the April Monologues. There is much that could be said. I will say none of it.

PROVERB: Put your [*static*] in, take your [*louder static*] out, put your [*even louder static*] in, and [*a lengthy sequence of buzzes and static*] all about.

EPISODE 86:
"STANDING AND BREATHING"

AUGUST 15, 2016

GUEST VOICE: MOLLY QUINN (MELONY PENNINGTON)

MOLLY QUINN HAS DONE SEVERAL LIVE SHOWS WITH US. SHE'S AN AB-
solute delight to tour with. I'm always telling people: Work with
Molly Quinn. She's great. I tell this to other writers, baristas, police
officers, birds, anyone who'll listen.

Last year on our U.S. tour, Molly joined us for a two-week
stretch, but the character she plays in the podcast—Fey, the voice
of the local numbers station WZZZ—didn't really fit at all into the
story line of our touring script ("The Investigators"). So Joseph came
up with the character of Melony Pennington, a supergenius computer programmer who created Fey.

We did about a dozen shows with Molly as Melony last spring,
and it was great fun. We of course really enjoyed Melony as a character. And in our minds (and in the minds of whoever saw those
dozen or so live performances), Melony was a familiar part of the
Night Vale universe.

But we realized she hadn't appeared on the podcast yet. No
one outside of those live audiences knew Molly was Melony, just

that she was Fey from Episode 42: "Numbers." So we wrote and recorded a part to tie into the trial of Hiram McDaniels, which is finally in this episode.

I write all of this while we drive from St. Louis to Chicago as part of our current live show tour. (I'm not driving. Assistant Tour Manager Angelique is. I'm in the back seat of our rented Chrysler Town & Country, which Cecil nicknamed "Vanna White.") Molly joined us last night in St. Louis to reprise her role of Melony, and we realized as Cecil was introducing her onstage that there were a bunch of question marks over the audience's heads.

While Melony Pennington is superfamiliar to all of us, the good folks of St. Louis have almost no way of knowing her. They did know Molly though. The moment Molly started speaking, the question marks straightened into exclamation points. And now St. Louis knows. And now you know too.

So enjoy the podcast debut of a character that has been around for over a year.

—Jeffrey Cranor

I believe the children are our future. They
are also our past. And our present. This
is how children work in linear time.

WELCOME TO NIGHT VALE

Mayor Dana Cardinal announced that last night's air raid sirens were nothing to be alarmed by. Nor are the missing street and highway signs, nor are the angry people who were assigned to hold the signs and wave them about using the maritime telegraphic language of semaphore and who are now standing around dumbfounded and empty-handed. Nor should we yet concern ourselves with mailboxes which have all been filled with what postal workers hope is just hair gel.

Following a meeting with the sheriff and the City Council, Mayor Cardinal says she believes this all to be the work of pranksters, perhaps the return of the feral dogs who once defaced several concrete walls with libertarian street art, but the mayor and the Secret Police are not ruling out more sinister activity.

Sheriff Sam added, while whittling a piece of balsa into a polar bear, that it's definitely these foreigners moving here from Desert Bluffs. The City Council said nothing. They mostly stood around behind the press conference podium texting and giggling. All of them had fresh haircuts, crisp upturned polo collars, and manicures.

The mayor said she would work closely with Sheriff Sam to find the culprits, but in the meantime, there's no need for alarm. Sam added that there was a need to remove all of the foreigners.

More on this story as it develops.

But first, an update on the trial of Hiram McDaniels. Unable to find a jury of peers for a literal five-headed dragon, the court agreed to create artificial intelligence to simulate what five-headed dragon peers would be like and then place that AI on the jury.

For this project they hired expert computer programmer Melony Pennington, who joins us now by phone. Welcome to my show, Melony.

MELONY: Welcome to YOUR show. I mean Hi. Hello. It turns out you welcomed me. It doesn't make sense to welcome you. Sorry my mind was, you know, the expanse, the vast, the out there, I mean, my mind is elsewhere. My mind is everywhere.

CECIL: Wonderful. And how are you—

MELONY: Do you ever look at the stars? The stars, you know, the stars. Not each star. But some of the stars. I mean every single one of the stars at once. I mean the whole night sky added up. Do you ever look at the sum of the stars? The night sky as an equation. Beauty as a math problem. Which it is. Everything beautiful is math. Everything beautiful is a problem. What was your question?

CECIL: Um . . . How are you doing?

MELONY: Oh, I'm fine.

CECIL: Melony, you sound familiar.

MELONY: Do I sound familiar? You just said that so I guess I do. You must have met one of my programs. Or not met. None of them are sentient. You can't meet things that have no sentience. Well I guess you could be like "Hi, there pile of rocks. I'm Melony" just to see what happens. I suppose there is no set dogma for social engagement. I wish I had a dog. Have YOU ever met a rock? What's your name again?

CECIL: I'm—

MELONY: What I was saying is that I probably sound familiar because all of my programs have the same voice as me, that's how computer programming works.

CECIL: Have you ever programmed a computer that broadcasts on a radio station, specifically one that recites random numbers?

MELONY: Oh, yes. The local numbers station: WZZZ. Yes, that was one of my early programs. And those numbers and chimes aren't random. They're encoded messages to foreign spies. Also a few pudding recipes and a funny cryptology poem or two.

CECIL: So you designed Fey, the voice of WZZZ.

MELONY: Oh, the WZZZ program has no name and absolutely no sentience. Not every program is sentient. That WZZZ program only recites numbers and tones. That's all it does and all it will ever do. It doesn't know it exists.

CECIL: About that, see, there was a thing that happened a couple years—

MELONY: Oh, listen to me babbling on. You had me on to talk about the trial.

CECIL: Yes. Well, I understand there has been some controversy around the ethics of making a jury of peers from artificial intelligence, rather than actual five-headed dragons.

MELONY: Oh, there are a lot more problems than just ethics. What are ethics even? How can you quantify what is right? I mean let's assign a number on how ethical a computerized jury is.

CECIL: I'm gonna say it's a low number, like one point five or two.

MELONY: But let's make it on a scale of zero to three. So that's pretty good. Everything's going fine. Ethically speaking anyway. But the programming has been tough. Have you ever even tried to program a computer?

CECIL: I barely know how to turn one on. Say, as long as I have a real computer expert on, do you have some basic computer tips for me and our listeners?

MELONY: Oh, a public service like that would be really ethical. Like a two point five or even a three on the Ethicability Scale. What a good idea. Here are some basic tips for the computer novice who is hoping to one day write code that advances us closer to the singularity.

Tip one: Computers can make you angry. Anything can make you angry. Computers are anything.

Tip two: Is your computer plugged in? That's probably illegal. You need a license to plug in a computer.

Tip three: Computer programs are a lot like humans. They're full of bugs, mostly theoretical, and invented by overly caffeinated, lonely people in dark rooms.

Tip four: Did I say that thing about the stars already?

CECIL: Y——

MELONY: Oh, good. Tip five: Create a strong password. The most secure password possible is "You'llNeverGuessThis," where the *O* is replaced with a zero and the *L*'s are replaced with zeroes and all of the other letters replaced with zeroes. A string of nineteen zeroes is the most secure password.

CECIL: I added an exclamation point at the end of my password.

MELONY: Exclamation points are impossible to hack. You are very secure.

Tip six: There are two main types of computers.

The first are PCs, or personal computers. Personal computers know your name and things about your life and are casual and friendly. Sometimes they're overly personal and you end up having to say, "This is all too much. Back off, computer."

The second type of computer is the house cat. These are ambulant robotic quadrupeds used by the Secret Police to monitor our domestic behavior and to try to understand why people like to stroke robots and talk in high voices to them.

CECIL: This has been very helpful.

MELONY: Thank you for saying that. I love to be helpful. This trial has been so challenging, and everyone is upset. These days I don't feel helpful. These days I feel kind of useless and it gets me down.

CECIL: Oh, I know that feeling. Sometimes when I'm sad, I like to sing old hymns to myself.

MELONY: Me too. Which one's your favorite?

CECIL: "I got the eye of the tiger, a fighter . . ."

BOTH: ". . . dancing through the fire. 'Cause I am a champion and you're gonna hear me roar." [*Melony really sings out the last part of this.*]

MELONY: That's my favorite passage from the Old Testament. I feel better already.

CECIL: Thanks, Melony!

MELONY: I'm sorry, I didn't catch your name. Good-bye.

CECIL: The mayor's office reports that perhaps their earlier call for not being alarmed was a bit premature and that we could all stand to be a little more alarmed. Several dead animals have been found all about town. On sidewalks, in trees, in fields, animal corpses everywhere. This has happened before, listeners. Many of you remember the glowing cloud (all hail) that passed through Night Vale years ago dropping dead animals on all of us. And since that first terrifying and bloody visit, the Glow Cloud (all bow before the mighty cloud) has since settled down as a citizen of this town, even joining the school board, as the Glow Cloud's child attends Night Vale Elementary.

It's hard to believe that the Glow Cloud (all praise to the malevolent cloud who rules my every puny desire, et cetera, et cetera) would return to such dreadful acts of violence against animals and rooftops, but again, it's hard to know why anyone does anything.

John Peters—you know the farmer?—standing out in his freshly sown field of imaginary corn, near his pasture, said he saw a couple of mangled squirrels and expired possums. He added, "I seen them strangers, too, those ones what don't move 'cept for their breathin'. Just breathin' and breathin' and sometimes gettin' a little closer'n you think they were a second ago, despite not lookin' like they were even movin'.'"

He also said he finally received a card from his brother Jim, who left town nearly forty years ago to fight in the Blood Space War. The message inside simply read, "Happy twelfth birthday, little brother! Only three months into my mission and I'm already missing you something fierce, Johnny." John covered his face and pointed to one of the strangers out on the edge of the cornfield. "Yeah, it's definitely them strangers what's killin' these animals." John then began weeping and clutching the birthday card—on it, a farmer caricature holding balloons and a caption reading, "I love you . . . 'Cows' Your My Brother"—tightly to his heaving chest.

And now a word from our sponsor. Today's show is brought to you by Papa John's.

At Papa John's, we make pizza with only the freshest ingredients using old-world recipes passed down from our family's many generations of pizza makers. Nearly all of these pizza makers are still alive, making pizza and passing down recipes. They live in the back. We're running out of room for them. We've long given up on thinking they'd eventually die. Why don't they die? I mean we love them, but there are close to fifty people in our family dating back to at least the 1800s, their bodies aging and failing but not ever, you know, dying.

Perhaps it's our secret recipes causing that. You'd think so, but it's not. Because a few members of our family have actually passed away. Although now that we're thinking about it, those were public executions for treason back during the first World War. And another couple were car accidents. Maybe it is the sauce.

Either way, visit your local Papa John's. Order a delicious pizza. How hard can it be? Immortality we mean.

Papa John's. It'll be fine.

And now a look at traffic.

They met through a mutual acquaintance. They shook hands and met eyes. Over food and drinks and among friends they laughed and told stories. Occasionally their eyes lingered. Occasionally one looked away first. They shared a brief but quiet and private moment on the front porch. It was getting late. People were leaving. It was a new moon that night. Neither would remember that part. One of them said good-bye as they headed to their car. The other said good-bye back. They hugged, both thinking in that short embrace about the other's body against their own—about the topography of forgiveness and the geography of tomorrow. See you again soon, I hope. Yes, you too.

They parted as the one drove away. Later the other drove away. It was a fun party with good friends, good food and drinks. They would remember the laughing and the stories. They would not remember the moon or the name of the other. It wouldn't come up again. They later met other people, and still other people. Later they would drive home and drive home. They never met again. They both lived meaningful lives, laughing, drinking, eating, and driving home.

This has been traffic.

While officers from the Sheriff's Secret Police are now responding to a series of power outages and broken water mains, witnesses have reported a strange sight at the city's Dog Park. Hooded figures, which are sometimes glimpsed inside the Dog Park, were all lined up outside the Dog Park, as if standing guard.

A long row of dark cloaks and hoods, humming and chanting. Witnesses kept a great distance from this scene, simply noting the hooded figures were all of equal height and imposing stature, spaced evenly around the forbidden municipal park. The sidewalks in front of them were empty except for one young couple and their dog, who walked slowly past the sentries, unperturbed by the presence of these eldritch figures emanating a crescendo of white noise. Witnesses watched the couple stroll past the park, turn a corner, and disappear from sight.

The witnesses reported that just around that corner where the couple had walked was a different person, a stranger staring right back at the witnesses. They did not recognize the person, for the person had no noticeable features. This stranger did not appear to move, except for its steady breathing.

No single witnesses saw the stranger move, but suddenly it was closer to the crowd of onlookers, merely feet away from them.

One of the witnesses said, "We should run away."

Another agreed, "Yes. Let's run away."

They did not go anywhere.

And now, let's check in on the weather.

WEATHER: "Well-Dressed" by Hop Along

If you can hear me, Night Vale, it is because you are one of those still with electricity or whose home is not on fire. Oh. Breaking news, there are a bunch of fires across town. They are spreading from home to home. Fire Chief Ramona Encarnación said that she believes the fires were started by the neglect of common but dangerous things like kitchen ranges, candles, cigarettes, and bloodstones. Encarnación said, "These strangers are appearing at doorways and in windows and inside showers and from behind refrigerators, just staring and breathing and otherwise not moving. Upon seeing these strangers, the residents of those homes became frozen in fear and thus incapable of tending to their flammable items. Never leave a bloodstone unattended, Night Vale," Encarnación cautioned.

Mayor Dana Cardinal finally relented to the sheriff's request to try to round up the strangers. Sheriff Sam responded with a jumping heel click and a "You won't be sorry, Mayor" as they ran out to start making arrests. Sam has long held that the strangers are just troublemakers who've moved here from the collapsed town of Desert Bluffs, our former neighbors.

But upon arriving at several of the burning homes, Sam began to have a change of mind, of belief. These strangers were not from Desert Bluffs at all. These strangers, Sam now believes, are something else. "They're not from here," Sam said. "Not here meaning Night Vale but HERE." Sam then indicated the broadness of the term HERE by swinging their arms slowly to indicate the entirety of the tangible world we all pretend to know and understand.

The Secret Police, instead of arresting or detaining or even getting near the strangers, began to move the petrified residents of each of these homes safely away to an undisclosed location (which I assume means the same thing as a safe location, since the Secret Police are law enforcement professionals). The strangers never moved other than their steady breaths, even when they sometimes appeared dramatically closer than they were before.

"The strangers seem to have no goal other than to threaten our well-being, Night Vale," Sam explained wordlessly, using only a long ribbon and floor dance routine to express the dire situation we are all facing. "My Secret Police and I will work to serve and protect you. Secretly, of course. This is off the record. In the meantime, stay in your homes and lock your doors. If you see a stranger, keep moving. And call us. We're an unlisted number actually, so maybe e-mail," Sam said with a flick of their ribbon and a double somersault.

Night Vale, I think back to the words of Little League coach and ghost Lusia Tereshchenko, "They're no longer coming. They're here, and we cannot stop something that wants nothing." And I think of the image of that young couple and their dog blithely passing the row of fearful hooded figures. No doubt it was Maureen and that boy and that beagle.

Maureen is such a good kid, and that beagle, so, so cute. SO CUTE! But I fear whatever it is she and that boy (and that dog) are involved in.

Heed our sheriff tonight, Night Vale. Stay safe in your home. Get away fast if you see one of them.

Stay tuned next for words ordered intentionally and confidently, saying something, understanding nothing.

And as always, good night, Night Vale. (Maybe lock those windows too.) Good night.

PROVERB: Call me old-fashioned, but I believe there should only be one continent.

EPISODE 87:
"THE TRIAL OF HIRAM McDANIELS"

AUGUST 15, 2016

THERE ARE GOING TO BE SOME SPOILERS TO THIS EPISODE IN THIS INTRO-
duction, so it might make sense to read the episode first. In any case,
I'll cover the nonspoilery stuff first, and then mark clearly where
spoilers begin.

This episode contains the return of a few older Night Vale characters and plots that haven't come up in recent years. In this episode
we see the return, for the first time since Episode 17, of Martin Mc-
Caffry, local representative of the TSA, and his . . . problem. And
the return, seventy-eight episodes after it was destroyed, of the Beatrix Lohman Memorial Meditation Zone. Going through old scripts
to put together these script volumes always reminds me of interesting odds and ends we haven't talked about in a while. Creating the
last round of script books led to these references. Who knows what
making these scripts books will give me!

I don't write poetry much, but occasionally I get the bug, and
when I do, I can always find a way to put it in the show. Often as a
traffic or a word from our sponsors (such as the original word from

our sponsors in Episode 2), but here it shows up as a Children's Fun Fact Science Corner. Nothing, after all, is more scientific than poetry.

There is also a reference to another popular podcast in this episode. If you don't spot it, I recommend listening to every other popular podcast until you notice it. Good hunting!

OKAY, SPOILERS START HERE!

The trial of Hiram McDaniels has mostly been played for a laugh up to this point. But we always knew where it was going. The world of Night Vale is a surreal one. It's sometimes silly and it's sometimes creepy. Rarely is it mundane. Because of that, mundanity has a special power in the writing of Night Vale. It's something we deploy only when we really, really mean it.

The verdict in this trial is mundane. People get convicted and sentenced to death all the time. The method of execution was also chosen to be as divorced from the surrealism of Night Vale as possible.

Even Gold, the unshakably charming head, can't take it. I think the moment that Gold crumbles is the most difficult detail in that scene. There are certain people in our lives we expect to take even the worst news well. When they are shaken, it can destroy us.

So that was the trial of Hiram McDaniels. This is justice, I guess.

—Joseph Fink

> Numbers don't lie. But humans using
> numbers lie all the time.

WELCOME TO NIGHT VALE

The trial of Hiram McDaniels, five-headed dragon, former mayoral candidate, and current presumed criminal, is coming to a close. There are only a few minor legal technicalities to get through, such as testimony from the remaining witnesses, arguments from the lawyers, and deliberation from the jury, and then we'll finally have all that bureaucratic mess out of the way and be able to get to the verdict.

We'll be covering the trial as it continues, so stay tuned here for all of your trial info.

And now for community classifieds.

Item: Big Rico's Pizza is looking for a new cashier. Must have retail experience and be good at not talking if they know what's good for them. No funny business. No secret wheat speakeasies. Why would you even bring that up? Who have you been talking to? To apply, look at yourself in the mirror for a long time, until your face no longer seems to be your own.

Item: Have you seen a tall shadow where no shadow should be cast? Have you seen a person exist in two places at the same time? Have you seen a young girl with an upside-down face? No, you haven't. That would be ridiculous. Grow up. Sincerely, Richard. Also if anyone's seen my wife please let me know.

Item: Lost cat. Blindingly bright, orb shaped, often visible in the sky during daylight hours. If found, please worship.

And finally, item: I haven't forgotten you all. I let you live the first time. The next time you may not be so lucky. Love, the Woman from Italy.

This has been community classifieds.

The Night Vale Parks Department announced that after a multi-year, five-million-dollar repair and renovation project, the Beatrix Lohman Memorial Meditation Zone is once again open for public use. The Meditation Zone, a state-of-the-art meditation facility, was destroyed by a multidimensional sentient pyramid almost four years ago. But the Parks Department used that crisis as an opportunity to update the meditation mats, equipment, and machines. Now you can be hooked up and meditating in no time, and it's almost twice as efficient as before, when measured in gallons per kilowatt.

The rebuilding was funded with a simple tax levied on every school child per school day they attended, and the construction only went three years and four point nine million dollars over budget. We look forward to enjoying the new Beatrix Lohman Memorial Meditation Zone for years to come.

Today the mayor herself, my former intern and current friend, Dana Cardinal, took the witness stand in Hiram's trial, the final witness in the Trial of the Century. She looked at the citizen who had tried to overthrow her beating heart, to sabotage her lungs, to end the administration of life within her body. And, calmly, she met his eyes. And then calmly, she met his eyes. And then she met his eyes calmly. And then, still calm, she met his eyes. She did not even glance at the violet head, the only head who did not participate in the crimes against her.

Her hands were tight in front of her. Her shoulders were back.

She looked tired and she looked determined and heavy with stress and still barreling forward. Judge Azdak asked her to swear to tell the truth, the whole truth, and nothing but.

"You want the whole truth?" Dana said. Everyone got very quiet. That is not a question that is asked often in a town like ours, and it carries a dangerous weight. "I will give you all of it and nothing but," she said.

The defense attorney and the prosecutor, two identical men both named Troy Walsh, objected in unison, although their objections were unclear and consisted of a high-pitched, panicked, "No, stop her." The judge upheld both objections, but Dana ignored all this.

"Being mayor means carrying many secrets," she said. "I am so young to carry so much. Now you will share in my burden."

And she began to tell the truth, all of it, as she knew it. Obviously we can report nothing of what she said. Most of the crowd fled, horrified of what would be done with them if they heard even a fragment of the mayor's testimony. The judge felt obligated to stay, but put on the sound-canceling headphones they assign all judges so none of them will hear anything that might make life too complicated. Only Hiram, already charged, already a criminal, listened with interest, as Dana unfurled the shadows within her.

And then she was done. She said, "Thank you," nodded to the judge, nodded to Hiram, collected her belongings, and walked out of the courtroom.

So the trial is continuing just fine, and we should reach justice, whatever that means, quite soon. Obviously, the transcript for this day of the trial will be burned, along with the court stenographer.

And now for the Children's Fun Fact Science Corner.

Up is up and down is down.
Left is right and right is left.
To the west there are the highest highs

and to the east there are the lows.
The up top is where the bluebirds go
and the witching happens down below.
If you need to cross the street,
mind your shoes and mind your feet,
for there are more to streets
than horns that bleat
or cars that speed
or lights that lead,

there is something stranger yet
that wants to take you, don't forget,
yes there is something stranger still
and if it can, it could
and it would and it will.
Its teeth are sharp, its eyes are sharp,
its voice a dulcet maze,
so walk real quick and step real light
and always look both ways
Look to the left to see your own death
and look to the right to avoid a great fright
and look for what hides under the cars that pass by,

under the trucks that speed,
under the pavement weeds,
under the asphalt and sand,
look for a quick, grasping hand.
Up is up and down is down.
Left is right and right is left.
To the west there are the highest highs
and to the east there are the lows.
The up top is where the bluebirds go
and the witching happens down below.

This has been the Children's Fun Fact Science Corner.

The Night Vale airport announced a trial run of international flights. Previously, there were only the regular flights to LAX, JFK, XTA, Burbank, and, of course, King City. But now, airport administration is unveiling plans to reach more than fifty international destinations, including Mexico, Double Mexico, and Svitz. How these plans can be achieved in a one-terminal airport with no customs facilities and only the capacity to handle two passenger planes at a time has not been answered.

Martin McCaffry, local representative of the TSA, waved away objections to the changes, standing in front of reporters and literally waving his arms in physical dismissal of the questions being raised. He also added an occasional "psssht" and eye roll.

He then gave a statement, "Now that I have provided an official response to any technical questions on this matter, it's time to talk about what's important to this town."

He opened up a box which contained hundreds, if not thousands, of hand-drawn sketches depicting a strange elongated dark figure crawling out of a kitchen refrigerator.

Martin said, "I find one of these on my pillow each morning when I wake up. I don't know who is drawing them or why. Who is doing this to me?"

He collapsed to his knees, his face a perfect portrait of anguish, while above him the bright pink banner saying "CELEBRATING A NEW AIRPORT FOR A NEW NIGHT VALE" flapped loudly in the rising wind, each gust bringing a sharp bark of plastic as Martin, crouched beneath, retreated into a sad, helpless silence.

You know, I haven't traveled out of the country in a long time. I have half a mind to hop on one of those planes and head to Svitz again, or even somewhere new. Maybe Carlos and I could check out a nice resort somewhere tropical. That'd be so fun. Martin is now weeping, and crawling away from the podium, dragging his crumpled-up sketches with him, spit and snot dripping off his face, forming a trail in the dirt below him. A tropical vacation. Could be just what we need!

And finally, a word from our sponsors. Today's show is sponsored by Kleenex brand tissue products. We know that you have a lot of choices when it comes to your nose. For instance, you could choose to simply not have one. Just pop it right off and go on with your day unhindered. Or you could choose to have multiple decorative noses that turn your face into a provocative modern sculpture. But instead you decided to have just the one nose, that half the time doesn't work, and is exactly between your eyes where it sits distractingly in your vision at all times for no reason. Of course your brain tunes that out unless someone calls attention to it, so I guess that's not too bad, but in general you've chosen the barely functioning weird nose you have, and we're sure glad you did. Kleenex brand tissue products. You have a lot of choices in life. We're glad you for some reason chose the faulty body you have.

This has been a word from our sponsors.

Update from the trial.

In a last-minute surprise, there has been a complete turnover in the makeup of the jury. Previously, the jury was made up of seven humans and an AI simulating a five-headed dragon. This was all pretty standard, but now, without warning, announcement, or any decision from the judge, the seven humans were removed from the jury. In their stead were seven strangers. The strangers were unmoving, unblinking. They breathed. Audible, even breaths. The hiss of air through their nostrils. Eyes fixed on nothing.

Judge Azdak said that she does not approve of this change, but also that she's too scared to question it. And anyway she would find it hard to enforce any actions against it since the bailiff too is now a stranger, unmoving, except that every time the judge looks away and looks back again she swears the stranger is slightly closer than she was before.

The defense attorney, on behalf of the four heads he represents, offered strong objections from behind his desk, where he was hiding from the strangers. The prosecuting attorney joined his objections, and also joined him behind the desk.

There was very little comment from the observers in the gallery, as most of them too had been replaced by unmoving, breathing strangers.

"Well, I guess we should get right to deliberations then," shouted the judge through the closed and locked door of her chambers.

"But we haven't even given our closing arguments," said both attorneys simultaneously, sitting back to back so that they could keep their eyes on as many of the strangers as possible.

The judge considered this argument and responded by screaming that one of the strangers was in her chambers and how did he get in there? The Troys did not have an answer to that, and so the deliberations begin.

Listeners, while we wait to hear the verdict to this eventful and historic trial, let us take a quick peek at the weather.

WEATHER: "Cocaine" by Holy Moly

The trial of Hiram McDaniels is over. A verdict has been reached. The jury that consisted of an AI simulation of a five-headed dragon and seven silent, unmoving strangers only deliberated for a few minutes before returning with a verdict of guilty on all charges. The strangers breathed, heavy visible breaths. The AI booped and whistled. It was all very quiet, and polite, and quick.

Hiram's heads responded in ways as differing as their personalities. Green of course roared, and spat out a stream of fire unlike any ever seen from him before, white in its pure heat. Gold nodded gravely, a politician politically accepting bad news. Blue didn't react visibly at all. Gray slumped and curled into his own long neck, a look of supreme dejection on his reptilian features. And Purple sat tall, in satisfaction rather than celebration.

Judge Azdak said, "Well, let's get to sentencing then." And Troy Walsh, lawyer for the defendants, prepared to speak. But the judge went on to say, "There are no arguments to be made. If Hiram is guilty of attacking his mayor, of attacking the very civic structure of our town, then Hiram must be put to death. We have no choice," she concluded.

Even Troy Walsh, the prosecuting attorney, was taken aback by this sudden and severe sentence. He met eyes with his identical legal opposition and made a small shrug. What am I supposed to do here? He signaled through the expressive language of the body. This isn't my problem I guess. It's *a* problem but not *my* problem.

The judge continued. "Sentence to be carried out once all appeals have been received and disposed of. The guilty four heads will be killed with a single bullet each, so as to not harm the lungs, heart, or any other part of the body shared with the violet head, who is not charged by this court."

"But," Violet shouted. "But I am connected to them completely. If my other heads die then I will die too."

Green continued to roar, and for the first time, there was a hard spine of anguish within the pulse of his anger. Gray sobbed, loudly and unashamed. Gold, still nodding at the court with a politician's poker face, surprised himself by throwing up, and in doing so gave up the pretense of geniality. He too began to sob.

"I'm afraid," said Judge Azdak, removing her glasses and cleaning them distractedly with a bit of her robe, "that justice is more important than the life of every innocent who comes through this court. If there is damage to more than the perpetrators, then that is unfortunate but unavoidable. Take him away."

Since the bailiff was an unmoving stranger, the helpful but doomed court stenographer led Hiram away. Violet howled that she couldn't do this, that he was not charged with any crime, but no one intervened. A janitor trundled her cart forward to mop up the vomit left by Gold. The few humans left observing the court seemed at a loss for what to do, and started to disperse in uncertain, uneven groups. The AI did not move, because it was a computer. The strangers in the courtroom did not move either, although they seemed just a little closer to the onlookers than they were before.

And so that's it. That was the trial of Hiram McDaniels. He will be killed. His violet head, innocent, will also die. So that's justice, I guess. I guess we've done it. Good work us, I guess.

Stay tuned next for the awful void of your own doubts and feelings.

Good night. I guess.

PROVERB: "Them's the brakes, kid," said the most annoying driving instructor ever.

EPISODE 88:
"THINGS FALL APART"

AUGUST 15, 2016

GUEST VOICES: ERICA LIVINGSTON (PHONE TREE), CHRISTOPHER LOAR (PHONE TREE), DYLAN MARRON (CARLOS), EMMA FRANKLAND (SHERIFF SAM), KATE JONES (MICHELLE NGUYEN), MAUREEN JOHNSON (INTERN MAUREEN)

LET ME JUST SAY THIS . . . I AM NOT AN ACTRESS. I AM A WRITER. Some days, I am not even a writer. I'm saying it's exciting when I am asked to do something, especially if that something involves acting. So let me pull back the curtain and tell you how I prepared for my performance in this episode.

1. Google *procyon*. Spend five minutes trying to pronounce it. Nail it. Close the browser. Immediately forget how to pronounce it. Repeat until snack time.
2. Wonder who even knows the word *procyon*. Does everyone know it? Have I had a major failing in my education?
3. Consider substituting *trash bandit* to see if anyone notices. They will notice. They are professionals.
4. Google pictures of raccoons. Amazing creatures, rac-

coons. Did you know that they can unlock doors and play the banjo? One of these is true. It's the one with the banjo.

5. Seriously. Who even knows this word? Did they make it up? Consider calling Joseph and Jeffrey to find out which one of them put it in the script. It feels like a Jeffrey but sometimes a Jeffrey is really a Joseph in disguise because in writing, no one sees your face, unless they are looking at you.

6. It's not even that hard to pronounce: *pro-SIGH-on.* Wait. Is that it? I think that's wrong.

7. One time, when I was a kid, my parents said, "Maureen! Come outside! There is a PANDA in our tree!" And I went outside and looked at the panda, but it wasn't a panda, of course. Pandas do not live in suburban Pennsylvania. It was a raccoon. I swapped the words *panda* and *raccoon.* For years and years I had a fond memory of the panda in our tree. Kids are stupid. Anyway.

8. *PRO-see-on?*

9. Pretty sure this was Jeffrey.

10. Having said that, it was Joseph.

11. There are more words in this monologue. It's about a page long. Cannot obsess over *procyon.*

12. *Prok-KEY-on.* Definitely wrong.

13. Now I've forgotten how to say *raccoon.* Words are melting.

14. We have a lot of raccoons in suburban Pennsylvania. Not pandas, as I mentioned. They like to hang out on my family's back porch and poop. They poop quite a lot on our porch. My mom had to buy a bag of dried wolf urine pellets to keep them away. That's a thing you can buy.

15. The raccoons don't even care about the wolf urine pellets. They still treat the birdfeeder like a bucket of popcorn.

They even make eye contact with us through the window as they stick in their little hands and eat the seed.

16. *PRO! see-on.* Just say it with confidence. That's 100 percent of life. Fake it until you make it, et cetera.

17. Wolf-urine-pellet maker isn't a job title you hear often enough.

18. The spellchecker doesn't even know the word *procyon* and you expect more of *me*?

19. I'll mumble.

20. I'll bet Cecil knows how to say *procyon*. I bet he was born with the knowledge. It came preloaded into that magnificent bald head of his. Cecil can say *any word*.

And there you have it. There was more to this episode, I'm sure. I'm sure it was great. They're all gems. All I remember is *procyon*. You try saying it. Anyway, don't think about the word *procyon*. Try not to dwell on it as you read the following. *Don't think about* procyon. *It's not even that important to the story.*

—Maureen Johnson

[*Capital words/phrases marked with* ** *are separately recorded in a monotone voice. The rest is standard pseudo-chipper operator voice.*]

[*sound of phone ringing in earpiece*]

RECORDED VOICE: Citywide utility failures continue to haunt us, but not as much as the strangers who do not appear to move. Welcome to the Night Vale Public Utilities phone line.

If you're calling with a water, power, gas, phone, or surveillance camera malfunction, please press one.

If you just called to chat, pr——

[*beep of keypad 1*]

Night Vale is currently experiencing citywide power outages, as well as polluted water supplies and several gas leaks. It's not our fault but HR says we should apologize for the inconvenience. . . . Sorry I guess. It's not like we're not experiencing the same things though. So, maybe you could reciprocate the sympathies.
CECIL: I'm sorry.
RECORDED VOICE: Thank you. To pay your bill, press one.

To compliment the fine work of the Utilities Department, press two.

To whine about your personal problems, press—
CECIL: [*over this last line*] I am not complimenting the fine work of the Utilities Department.

RECORDED VOICE: I can repeat that last option if you need. To compliment the fine work of the Utilities Department, press two.

[*long pause*]

Okay, fine. To whine about your personal problems, press three. To schedule a Service Technician, press—

[*beep of keypad 4*]

You pressed four. I didn't give you an option four. You just assumed the next number and then cut me off mid-sentence.

CECIL: Oh good god.

RECORDED VOICE: I'm sorry. Is this hard for you? Do you need a hug? Do you need me to sing you a lullaby and feed you? Here comes the airplane spoon to feed the hungry, hungry boy. Vrrrommm. Mmmmm tasty carrots. Feel better now?

CECIL: Wow, the phone tree is getting snippy.

PHONE: Don't be rude. I am a person, not a phone tree. This is my job. To record every possible phrase for every possible person's possible need. I recorded all of it. I'm a real human with a body and needs and a family. And I have a name. I am Maggie Pennebaker. I'm not a disembodied lady voice who'll passively ignore your whiny entitlement.

CECIL: I'm sorry, Maggie. Are we speaking live?

[*pause*]

RECORDED VOICE: You selected Schedule a Service Technician. Please hold.

[*brief pause*]

Our next available service date is between the hours of *ONE* and *FIVE* *PM* on *SEPTEMBER* *FOURTH* *TWO THOUSAND FIVE* in the *COMMON ERA*.

CECIL: That was eleven years ago.

PHONE: To have time explained to you like you were a five-year-old, please hang up now and give up on ever having realistic expectations.

To confirm this appointment, press one.

To speak to a customer service representative, press two.

[*beep of keypad 2*]

PHONE: All operators are currently *SHOULDERING THE IMMENSE BURDEN* of *SOCIETAL DISPLEASURE*. Please continue to hold. Current wait time is *SUPERLONG*.

CECIL: Aggh.

[*hangs up*]

[*phone ringing*]

CARLOS: Hey, Poot.

CECIL: Hey, Bunny. Listen, Carlos, the power is out here at the station. I can't even do my show. I've been trying to get through to the utilities but they're slammed with calls.

CARLOS: Oh, I talked to my friend Maggie who works there. She said her cousin has an extra generator we can borrow.

CECIL: You know Maggie?

CARLOS: Yeah, she used to work with me part-time as a lab assistant. Also, Josie came by with her friends and dropped off some bottled water. Even John Peter stopped by. You know, John P——

CECIL: Yes, John Peters, the farmer. I know.

CARLOS: No, John Peter, remember, the pharmacist? Anyway, he dropped off your prescription this morning.

CECIL: That was nice of him.

CARLOS: Listen, since you don't have to work today, you should come back home. It's bad out there, and if you're going to get killed or possessed by one of the strangers, I'd rather you do it here with me. I'll make us some lunch and we can play Cards in Favor of Humanity.

CECIL: That sounds great, but I still need to get to the bottom of what is going on in this city. Intern Kareem pulled some documents for me that he says I need to read through, and I have some calls I need to make. The invasion by these strangers is a big story, and even if I can't broadcast it, I still need to find some way to report it. I'll call you later.

CARLOS: You're so good at your job.

CECIL: You are too, Carlos. How's your research going?

CARLOS: I've been examining some of the places where the strangers have been spotted. I have a meter that makes squawking sounds sometimes. I'm uncertain if those last two sentences are related. Cecil, be careful. And if you see one of the strangers, just get out of there quickly and call me, okay?

CECIL: We've survived one at the station before, I'll be fine.

CARLOS: Past performance is not an indicator of future results. I love you.

CECIL: Okay. 'Bye.

[*hangs up*]

[*phone ringing*]

SHERIFF SAM: Howdy. Sheriff Sam.

CECIL: Sheriff. Hi, this is Cecil Palmer over at Night Vale Community Radio.

SAM: What I just said was off the record. Don't play it on air.

CECIL: You only said *howdy*.

SAM: Nope. Sure didn't.

CECIL: Sheriff, I'm not even on the air right now. No one is listening to this call except the Secret Police, the City Council, the mayor, and well, some neighborhood espionage clubs but they have our community's best interests at heart.

I'm calling because I wanted to find out what the Secret Police know about the strangers who are showing up all over town. Are the structural failures related to their presence here?

SAM: Now, by strangers, do you mean the foreigners from Desert Bluffs who are taking over our beautiful city, after they managed to run their own city into the dirt? Or are you referring to the people who don't seem to move except for their breathing, who stand and stare at seemingly nothing, who without any noticeable motion suddenly appear much closer and who cause our citizens to stand trancelike until they are taken or killed or subsumed or converted into nonmoving strangers themselves?

CECIL: The latter.

SAM: Cecil, there are two sinkholes opened up on Route 800. The dam along Night Vale Lake broke. Fortunately our lake is just an empty dust hole, but it still broke wide open. Also, I have a caffeine headache even though I don't drink caffeine.

CECIL: That sounds like just a headache, then.

SAM: I don't need the media dictating to me what is or is not a caffeine headache. The point is things are falling apart but not in the fun way, in the awful way.

CECIL: There's a fun way?

SAM: Sure, like during a scheduled earthquake or when the lizard people dig new tunnels below old buildings.

CECIL: Of course. What about the former Desert Bluffs residents who moved to Night Vale? Are the strangers doing the same to them?

SAM: Who cares?

CECIL: I care. The people who know them care. They're humans, Sheriff. And as a reporter, I will report you said that.

SAM: Well, I'm the sheriff of a Secret Police force, so no you won't. You won't do that at all.

[*tense pause*]

I'm just playing with you.

I have a dry sense of humor. You might have missed that. I was delivering a real threat to your life but in a teasing way. For real, you definitely won't report anything I tell you.

Some of those Desert Bluffs people we can't even track. Not all of them stayed here. Some of them moved away. In our regular interrogations and detentions of these noncitizens, we've learned that a lot of them moved to some other place, which they say feels a bit more like home. I don't know anything about that except that I'm happy to get them out of here. They can set up all the Joyous Congregations of the Smiling God that they want some other place.

Just tell your listeners that everything is fixed and everyone is safe. The sheriff saved the day.

CECIL: But you didn't do anything.

SAM: Gotta go, Cecil. Just got some new calligraphy pens I need to break in before the press conference to announce that "All Is Lost."

[*hangs up*]

[*phone rings*]

MICHELLE: Dark Owl Records. Please shut up about music before you embarrass yourself.

CECIL: Michelle, hey, it's Cecil. I hate to bother you but I'm trying to track down Maureen. I heard you two are friends.

MICHELLE: I only talked about Maureen privately into my audio journal. Did you listen to the monologue I recorded?

CECIL: Yes, I played it on the air six weeks ago.

MICHELLE: I didn't want anyone to hear that! That was personal!

CECIL: Michelle, you mailed me a cassette with a note that said, "Here's my monologue to play on your show, Cecil."

MICHELLE: But that was me from more than a month ago. I hate that me. Haven't you ever made mistakes in your youth?

CECIL: Yes. Many. Michelle, you've talked to Maureen recently? How is she?

MICHELLE: She's fine. I mean, she's not that into leading an army or whatever, but it's just a thing she does for a living. I sell records. You talk on the radio. Maureen leads the army of unmoving strangers.

CECIL: She's the leader of the strangers?

MICHELLE: Or whatever. Maureen was sweet and let me see one of the strangers up close. They smell like compost and are all gray and they make you feel cold. They're really beautiful, but they'll devour your soul and turn you into one of them. Maureen says it's super-painful when they do that, and the transformation is forever. That's why they can only stand and breathe and not really move because they're in so much pain for so long, trapped in immortal bodies. It was cool. Kind of cool. I mean, I don't know. Will you hate me if I like something?

CECIL: Michelle, how did you get up close to one without being devoured?

MICHELLE: Maureen said she'd keep me safe from them because we're each other's only friend. Maureen's a kind person. She does like country music, but I think friendship is sometimes about compromise. If it means getting to be around her, I'm perfectly happy covering my ears and humming the Bob's Burgers theme.

CECIL: What about the boy in the hoodie who hangs out with Maureen?

MICHELLE: Chad? Chad's okay, I guess. He's just Maureen's boss though. She has to hang around him a bunch and watch his evil dog. It's just work, you know.

CECIL: Michelle, I—

MICHELLE: Cecil. Music sometimes calms me. You wanna hear a song I really like?

CECIL: Sure.

MICHELLE: Okay, here you go.

WEATHER: "Palestine" by Sam Baker, featuring Carrie Elkin

CECIL: That was a wonderful song, Michelle.

MICHELLE: Are you still talking about that song I started playing five minutes ago? I've moved on from that. Glad you like oldies so much. Anyway, Maureen's new phone number is Old Town 5–7614.

CECIL: Thanks, Michelle.

[*hangs up*]

[*phone rings; Maureen's answering machine*]

MAUREEN: Hi, this is Maureen. I'm probably at work or asleep or somewhere else. Somewhere listening to the sound of the moon slowly trying to peel off our oceans with its gravity. Pulling, its weak chalky little speck of a body grabbing this blue giant and tearing away at its watery skin. A futile fight, a spinning battle of large and small. And in the sky you can hear the whirling of the battling siblings. Or maybe I just don't want to take your call. Or maybe I'm dead. Or maybe you're dead and this is the voice mail you get when you die. "Hi, Maureen here. Sorry you're dead. For some reason I'm the one person you wanted to call the moment you left behind your short life, and I'm not even here to take it. So sorry newly dead person. Make sure you leave a phone number where I can reach you, because I certainly don't know how to call dead people on the phone." Or maybe I lost my phone and it's in my car or under a pillow or I left it in a movie theater or a raccoon ate it. Maybe there's a raccoon somewhere in the brush or in a trash can behind a house, walking with a limp because it just ate a phone, a rectangle of glass and metal and electronics that's a quarter the length of the raccoon's body, and now that phone is inside the raccoon's guts stretching its tiny tummy impossibly long, pressing against the masked procyon's little heart and lungs as it walks tenderly to one

side to alleviate the discomfort of such an intrusive foreign object to hold within. The raccoon—and this is kind of cute, kind of sad, to think about—walks diagonally all the while digitally emitting a little [*deedle-oo-doo deedle-oo-doo deedle-oo-doo-dee*] ringtone all muffled from within its quivering torso and questioning its eat-everything-it-can-find dogma and thinking perhaps to just limit that life philosophy to trash cans. Of course I bet people throw away phones all the time, so that's probably not a big help, although in my case I'm positive I didn't do that because my job is too important to just throw my phone away. Too, too important. Too many evil beings to manage. Too fragile a portal into another dimension—a dimension which is probably hell—I.D.K. I'm not a religious studies major, although if I were, I bet I would have graduated by now. I mean so much can go wrong if I lost my phone. Like no one could get hold of me to help fix it, which is not to say I know how to fix an interdimensional portal between hell and this world, but just that I could be a person to be like, "Oh no. I'm so sorry to hear the portal is malfunctioning. Let me panic a little bit and make some phone calls to feel like we're all doing something about it," and that would be helpful because sympathy is critical to good teamwork, and if you don't care about your job, you're not going to make anything of yourself. I am. I am making something of myself. Just sculpting away. Here's a clump of Maureen. Let's work it a bit with these hands. Yeah, this is looking great. This is a really nice Maureen here. All ready to be put in a fire and cooled and painted and set upon an alabaster pedestal in the foyer. So leave me a message and I'll get back to you.

[*beep*]

CECIL: Maureen. I finally figured it out. Chad Boenger. That boy I've seen you with. He used to intern here, just like you. He went to report a story on that used sporting goods store that we thought was a front for the World Government and never came back out. I guess it was something much worse he found in that shady old building. Now the two of you have a really successful start-up. I'm proud of our internship program here at the station.

I'm also proud of you for becoming a professional. You're leading an army, Maureen. That's very impressive, much more so than filing papers, fetching me lunch, and updating my erotic fan fiction blog.

Sounds like a great job with good benefits. It's a tough job market for young people these days. Lots of changing technologies making old jobs like print journalism, cardiology, and computer programming obsolete. Plus, all these new people moving here from Desert Bluffs. Kudos to you, Maureen.

Here's my question though, and it's an important one.

So, Carlos, my boyfriend. Earlier when I talked to him, I forgot to say "I love you" at the end of the call. I was preoccupied. No big deal. My love was implicit in the way we talked to each other. Love needn't be verbalized when it exists in intuition and physical contact. He knows I love him, but part of me wonders what if one of those rare times I forget to hug him good-bye or fail to say "I love you" turns out to be the last time I have that chance. Lots can go wrong in an indifferent universe.

I'll see him in a couple of hours, right? I'll see Carlos later. Right, Maureen?

Please call me back. I want to talk more about what you and Chad are doing to my town. I—

[*clicking*]

I'm getting another call from an unknown number. I'm hoping this is the sheriff. Call me back.

[*clicks over*]

Hello?

[*very faint breathing*]

Hello?

[*very faint breathing*]

Who is this?

[*distant dog bark*]

[*click*]

PROVERB: Wanna feel old? People born in 2014 have already graduated college, don't know what a trombone is, and are all named after gourds.

EPISODE 89:
"WHO'S A GOOD BOY? PART 1"

AUGUST 15, 2016

I LOVE BEAGLES.

Let me back up. I love dogs. But of all dogs, I love hounds best. It's their dumb floppy ears, you know? And of all hounds, I love beagles best.

When I was a small child, I used to hang out with my neighbor's beagle, Romeo, in their driveway. He would be tied up outside while my neighbor was in his garage, and the neighbor was nice enough to let me just come over and sit with his dog, because his dog was a beagle and therefore my favorite thing in the whole world.

One time I hugged Romeo too hard and he lightly bit my face to get me to let go. I once got bit by a beagle because I hugged it too hard.

I wonder if most of the plot for this year was pretty much written so that we could name the last episode of the year "Who's a Good Boy?" Probably, yes it was.

We were doing an event in Jersey City with Maureen Johnson to promote the first *Welcome to Night Vale* novel, and I turned to

Maureen and said, "I have this idea where Satan brings an army to attack Night Vale and you end up as Satan's right-hand woman. Does that sound good?" and she was very into the idea. A lot of Night Vale ideas start with one of us saying, "Man, wouldn't it be interesting if . . . ," and then we go from there.

There was a clue we put in very early on this year that the thing that Chad had summoned was Satan, but I don't think anyone caught it. Maybe no one ever will. If you want to try to find it, here's a hint: It was during one of the episodes of our show. (Okay, since you went ahead and paid for this book to get the real dirt, I'll tell you it was in Episode 81. No more hints.)

Incorporating some traditional horror elements into the Night Vale story this year was a lot of fun. We don't often swing completely creepy, but sometimes it's nice to take away all humor and let the horror stand on its own. This was also the year that I started writing my other podcast, *Alice Isn't Dead*, which often goes into straightforward horror. Doing that definitely gave me a taste for it, and emboldened me to create episodes of Night Vale that were more scary with less humor to balance. Sometimes you want nervous laughter, but sometimes you want to go for blood.

Who's a good boy? Who is it?

—Joseph Fink

Who's a good boy? Who's the good
boy? Who is it? Who is it?

WELCOME TO NIGHT VALE

All over town, the question, painted on walls. Written in the sky by our flying aces. Tapped out in Morse code from within the walls of our homes.

"Who's a good boy?"

The radio station is . . . unavailable, as so much of the town is currently . . . unavailable. Down for maintenance. Wiped off the map. However you want to say it.

The strangers who do not move, but who seem closer every time you look, they have torn our town apart. They do not seem to have an agenda, no plan, just destruction. They only seek to rend, to shatter.

Carlos has locked himself in the lab with his team of scientists, working without sleep to find a solution to this crisis, as they have found solutions to so many crises before. He wanted me to stay there with him, since within the proximity of science is of course the safest place to be in any natural or unnatural disaster. But I am a reporter. I can't not report. My town needs me to witness. And so I will walk through my city. And I will witness.

I sent my sister, Abby, and her family to the lab, so they could keep my niece safe.

"Keep them safe," I said to my brother-in-law, Steve.

"Ah geez," he said. "With Abby around, I can't imagine a bad thing that could happen."

He really loves my sister. If I am to spend this time witnessing, maybe I should start there. Maybe I should finally allow myself to see the depth of his love for my sister and their daughter. Ugh, and then he tried to hug me and he smelled like onions and I shouted, "Oh no, we better get you barricaded in there Steve, I think I see some strangers not moving," while I slammed the lab door on him.

The wreckage of Night Vale is complete. It is even worse than Valentine's Day, 2013, when much of the town was reduced to rubble and candy hearts.

I passed by the Desert Flower Bowling Alley and Arcade Fun Complex, site of so many great and terrible memories. Old Woman Josie throwing the ceremonial first pitch of the Bowling Tournament. City Council and Station Management finding horrifying love on the skating rink. And other memories, too, that I don't like to talk or think about.

Now the complex was boarded up, under siege from the strangers. There were three of them in its parking lot. None of them were moving. The only car in the lot was upside down and on fire.

Dark Owl Records was somehow untouched. It was the only building in blocks without smashed windows, and it somehow still had electricity.

Michelle Nguyen and former intern Maureen were leaning casually outside, smoking candy cigarettes. This took a lot of relighting as candy cigarettes do not burn well at all.

"Maureen! Michelle!" I said. "You're okay!"

They both rolled their eyes.

"Michelle, how did you keep Dark Owl from being destroyed along with everything else?"

She glanced at Maureen.

"Um . . .," she said.

"Well," Maureen said, "say someone was leading an army or whatever. Then they could command that army to not attack a specific person or place. Or whatever. So maybe that's what happened. Anyway, if that's what happened, then that person wouldn't be leading that army anymore."

"You quit your internship?"

"I didn't like my boss. Especially since I found out what . . . who he is. I didn't have all the details before. Feels like I was misled. That's a familiar feeling, Cecil," she said, narrowing her eyes at me. "At least you were just clueless."

"What?" I said.

"Never mind."

"Maureen and I have, like, a plan," said Michelle. "It's very secret. But we're teaming up to save Night Vale."

"I'm so glad you two have become such good friends," I said.

They looked at each other for a long moment.

"We don't want to, like, put a label on this," said Michelle. "Not everything has to be named."

"Yeah," said Maureen. "So anyway we have a secret plan. Plus Chad is now panicking about what the thing he summoned has ended up doing, so he's been trying to figure out how to reverse the ritual."

"LOL," said Michelle.

"LOL," agreed Maureen, putting the lighter to the end of her cigarette, and letting off a cloud of smoke that smelled like overcooked caramel.

Let's have a look now at the community calendar.

All events this week are canceled. This week is also canceled. You might be canceled too.

This has been the community calendar.

I found Lusia, the ghost that haunts the haunted baseball diamond, looking sadly at the nearby Shambling Orphan Housing Development. The development somehow has been hit even harder than the rest of Night Vale. There was almost nothing left to show that life had once existed there.

"Ah, Cecil," she said. "It is all happening as I was afraid it would."

"Do you know how we can stop them?" I asked.

"No, I have no ideas. Only the fear. A writhing, biting thing within me." She slapped her spectral chest with her spectral hand, making a deep resonant pop. "In here, Cecil."

She narrowed her eyes and pointed.

"There. The beast."

I saw, a few blocks away, a beagle puppy cross the street.

"The beast?"

"He is so adorable, yes? Just the cutest. So cute that you would do anything for his little face, for his dumb floppy ears, yes? That is how he controls you. That is how he controls everyone. He is so cute you would just do anything for him, and you will. You will do everything for him, things you never dreamed you would be capable of doing. Ghastly things."

"Who's a good boy?" I said.

"Who indeed," she said.

I called Carlos to see how far along he was in saving the day. He said that he wasn't very far along at all and it was frustrating to him. He said he's been letting brightly colored liquid bubble in beakers and has been writing numbers all over chalkboards and it hasn't helped anything at all. He even drew a structural formula for cyclohexane, but it also didn't help.

"It's like," he said, "this is somehow a problem that can't be solved with science. But there are no problems that can't be solved with science. Science fixes everything and is always on the side of good. I just . . . I can't figure out what these strangers want. They don't seem to want anything."

"You sound very upset," I told Carlos. "You know that it's not good for you to get worked up like this. Take a break. Play some Bloodborne. That'll relax you."

"Okay, yeah, I guess," he said. But I knew he didn't mean it. He was going to keep trying to save Night Vale, and I loved him for it even as I wished he wouldn't be so hard on himself.

And now a word from our sponsors. It is possible the world is ending. If you cannot hide, then you must run. If you cannot run, then you must die. This message brought to you by Clorox Bleach.

Two blocks past Mission Grove Park I saw the house of Frances Donaldson, the manager of the Antiques Mall. The door was off its hinges. The mailbox had been killed and skinned. For reasons I couldn't explain to myself, I crossed that ruined front yard and entered the house. I needed to see. I needed to report on this disaster.

Three feet into the door, I looked up to see a stranger before me. Her shoulders went up and down, a deep, constant breathing. Otherwise she did not move. At this distance, I could see the pupils of her eyes, unfocused, frozen on a point in the room several feet above my head. Her hair was greasy, and it stuck to her face. Her skin had faded into gray, like a person dying, or a person carved from stone. She stood in the ruined living room, surrounded by a pattern of destruction that splashed out from her, the echo of a flurry of movement even as she was perfectly still.

I was distracted by the mess, and when I looked back she was much closer to me. I could feel her breath. It was room temperature, unchanged by her body. Air in, air out, but no transformation.

"Hello, Cecil," she said.

Her mouth did not move. Her voice came not from her but from a glass of water on a side table that had somehow been spared the destruction. The water vibrated slightly with the voice.

"Hello?" I said to the glass. "What do you want?"

The lamp hanging above me laughed. There was no joy to it,

just a replication of the sound of laughter. It went on and on, slowly petering out to a quiet choking and then nothing.

"What do I want?" asked the glass of water. "I want nothing."

"Nothing at all?"

"Nothing."

The lamp snickered. My left shoe joined in, and I jumped back. But the stranger was even closer than before.

"We want nothing at all. Everywhere there is something. All of these things. Like this glass."

The glass of water shattered.

"One less thing," said my left shoe. "Soon there will be no things. We will take away your government, your laws, your infrastructure. All of your possessions. All of you. What we want is nothing."

"But why?"

"A why is a thing," the lamp said sternly. "We destroy whys. We destroy explanations."

I recognized the stranger. Behind the slack stillness, there was a human face. It was Frances herself, in the wreckage of her own home.

"Frances. What happened to you?"

At the sound of her name, her eyes focused in for a moment, and flicked down toward me, before drifting back up to the ceiling.

"I was made strange," the lamp said. "So strange that I became a stranger. There is a cavern."

I merely looked at the lamp, confused.

"There is a cavern, Cecil. I was taken there. The ground is covered in mud. You walk through the mud, in the darkness, because you think there must be something else. But there is never anything else. For years, you walk through the mud."

My shoe chimed in, "Sometimes you feel as though there might be other lost people, also searching through the mud. Maybe you can even hear the soft swish of them in the black, but your hands never meet, and you cannot speak out. You are alone. Sometimes the mud goes over your head, and sometimes it is just a slight damp beneath your feet."

The lamp spoke again, "Years go by. You feel yourself hollowed out by time. Everything that was you slips away. There is a great power that replaces you with his desires. He is your leader. And you want what he wants. And he wants nothing."

"When did you leave the mud and come back to Night Vale?"

"Leave?" This time Frances herself spoke. Her vocal cords cracked with lack of use. Her eyes focused on me again. Her parched lips clung to each other as she spoke.

"Cecil, I'm still in the mud. I'm still in the mud, Cecil. I'm still in the mud. I'm still in the mud."

She said this over and over, quickly losing control of volume and articulation. Tears rolled down her face from her unblinking eyes. I turned and ran. Behind me, her cracked voice, more and more distant. "I'm still in the mud. I'm still in the mud."

I had a vision of the beagle, loping adorably through a burning building, his big stupid ears flapping as humans screamed and pleaded around him. He watched them burn, and replied only, "Woof. "Woof," he said, as Night Vale fell.

I am passing Louie Blasko on the street right now. He is frantically working the pumps of his pipe organ, tipping his hat at me while keeping time with a simple gamelan setup.

He is holding out his hat for spare change.

"Louie, I'm sorry," I am saying to him. "But . . ." And here I am gesturing around at the decimated street.

"Just say *weather*," he is telling me.

I am not responding.

"Say the word *weather*," he is hissing.

"Weather?"

WEATHER: "Plunder" by the Felice Brothers

"What was that about?" I asked Louie. But he was gone. In his place there was a stranger. Unmoving. Breathing. I hurried on, and did not look back.

A black sedan drove slowly through the streets, the first functioning vehicle I had seen among the carnage.

I waved it down and two men got out. One was not tall and the other was not short.

"We had nothing to do with this," said the man who was not tall.

The man who was not short nodded vigorously.

"Do you know what happened?" I asked.

The man who was not tall stood between me and the man who was not short and said, "Don't talk to him. He's new," though I had directed the question at both of them.

The man who was not short said, "The question isn't 'what happened.'"

"What is the question?" I said.

"Don't talk to him, he's new," the man who was not tall said. "Anyway, you know what the question is."

He leaned in close to me. I could smell anise on his breath.

"Who is a good boy?" he whispered.

"Do you have a pen I could borrow?" said the man who was not short.

"Sure," I said, handing him the one from my reporter's notebook.

"Thanks," he said. He opened the trunk of the sedan, tossed the pen into it, slammed it shut, and got back into the passenger seat.

"Don't talk to him, he's new," said the other man, and then he, too, got into the sedan and the strange pair drove away.

Finally I reached City Hall. It had been ravaged. There was no sign of City Council. Likely they have fled, as they often do during danger to our town. Or, I'm supposed to say, taken a sudden and fortuitous vacation. But I am not on the radio. I do not have to say what I am supposed to say. I wonder if Station Management is even in town. I suspect that they may have taken the same sudden and fortuitous vacation as City Council, their many strange and endless appendages entwined on some beach somewhere.

Deputy Mayor Trish Hidge came running out of the building, holding a desk lamp in one hand. She ran by me, wild with panic, huffing. She was barefoot.

Huff huff huff.

Or no. That was not her at all. A wet, rapid breathing. Waiting for me at the door to City Hall. What she had been fleeing from. The beagle puppy.

Huff huff huff.

He padded forward. He was adorable. Or was he? I had thought he was a cute beagle puppy, but there was something off about him. A sneer in his lips. A strange bend to his legs. His body was misshapen. He was not cute at all.

Breath came in and out of his mouth, which was gray and squishy within.

Huff huff huff.

The beagle rose onto his hind legs, higher and higher, until he was standing fully upright, his spine elongated and straightened.

I felt something rising in my throat. I did not want to open my mouth for fear of an organ or bile or hot black tar pouring out. But that was not what was pushing its way out of my mouth. It was words. The words sputtered out of my lips, against my will.

"Who's a good boy?" I said.

"I am the good boy, Cecil," the beagle said. "You wanted to witness, so witness. I am the good boy, and I rule over the dark, wet caverns of hell."

Huff huff huff.

He cocked his little beagle head. He stood so much taller than I thought a dog could stand. His breath was thick and wet and labored.

"I want nothing, Cecil. Nothing at all. And I will have it."

Huff huff huff. Huff huff huff.

PROVERB: Remember to compliment-sandwich when critiquing. Example: That's an okay shirt you have on. Everything you wrote was bad. You're wearing a shirt.

EPISODE 90:
"WHO'S A GOOD BOY? PART 2"

AUGUST 15, 2016

JOSEPH AND I TALK A LOT ABOUT FLYING. WE BOTH DEAL WITH FLIGHT anxieties while having to fly a lot for our job.

In talking about why flying is scarier than driving despite being overwhelmingly safer, I said, "I suppose it's about control. You can control a car but not a plane." Joseph countered that flying removes all illusion that we have control over our lives. There's an important distinction in his point. Illusion of control. Not actual control.

We deal with existentialism a lot on Night Vale, especially the bleak point that we're all gonna die and it could happen at any moment. Despite a random and indifferent universe, we make up stories about why we die. Sometimes there are strong correlations of control: They were a reckless driver. She really loved BASE jumping. He liked trying to hug badgers. Sometimes not: Wrong place at the wrong time. Unlucky I guess.

We make up stories about why we live too. He was so determined to beat cancer. She was chosen by God. They are the luckiest person I know.

In this two-part episode, we're playing around with that very notion that we can prolong life/avoid death. The strangers want nothing, need nothing, and ultimately are controlled by nothing. The town rallies. People take action. They pray. They fight. They sic their floating cat on the enemy.

Night Vale suffers from an illusion of control. The strangers cannot be fought off or bought off or prayed away. As the Faceless Old Woman says, Night Vale's efforts are all just noise.

But another way to say that previous paragraph is that Night Vale needs stories to survive. There are conflicting stories. Who's the hero? Tamika? Melony? The Erika? The spiritual coming-together? Maybe these stories are all self-deception, meaningless in the face of an indifferent universe. But these narratives help hide their lack of control.

If we cannot explain why something bad happens or convince ourselves we can eventually stop it, then what's the point of any of this? [*points at all of human life*]

I vote. I try to eat healthy. I read. I speak my mind about causes I find important. I knock on wood when watching sporting events. I don't drink and drive. I listen to Beyoncé during every airplane takeoff and landing.

My candidate won. I haven't gotten heart disease. No senile dementia for me. Social justice has made progress. The Red Sox won a bunch of titles. I won't be killed in a drunk driving accident. I have never died in a plane crash.

Are these illusions of control? Yes, most definitely. But they are narratives to help me cope with fatalism, to cope with the indifferent universe, to make me think that what I am doing makes a difference. I make up truths to feel sane.

Stories cannot protect us from the void, but they can protect us from staring too long into it.

—Jeffrey Cranor

You wanna go outside? Outside? You
wanna go outside? You do? You do? I bet
you want to go outside. I bet you do.

WELCOME TO NIGHT VALE

Huff huff huff.

The beagle puppy stood fully upright on his hind legs, breathing
heavily. I inched back from the dog.

Here's where I want to tell you I drew a glowing sword and
he drew a sword made of fire. I want to tell you our mighty blades
clashed above our heads as our elbows and faces met. I think it'd be a
really cool thing to say that I then pushed him back with a kick to the
chest and swung my blade down upon him and as he tried to deflect
it with his own, my sword shattered his, causing him to burst open
with white light and doves, and order returned for good to Night Vale.

But what I'm going to tell you is I don't own a sword. Doves
aren't real. And the dog had destroyed everything we are without a
single conventional weapon. Plus, I tripped while trying to run away.

The beagle was standing over me.

Huff huff huff.

There was a boom that dimmed my hearing, and the dog was
jolted backward violently. Sam, our sheriff, stood behind me, a shot-
gun in their hand.

"C'mon," Sam said as they grabbed my shoulder and pulled me up.

I turned back to see the carnage, but the beagle was standing again, exactly where he was the moment before, perhaps a little closer actually. His adorable puppy mouth distended horribly with each labored breath.

Huff huff huff.

"Don't look at it," Sam said as they pushed me into City Hall and through a door marked "FORBIDDEN." Sam slammed the door shut and bolted the lock.

We were in the City Council's chambers. The council was there. They had not fled their city after all. They all spoke in unison, their black robes undulating like a storm-tossed ocean. The only details of the council's hood-shrouded faces I could discern were their reddish-brown teeth.

"We have reopened the Dog Park," the City Council shouted. It sounded like an accusation. "Sam plans to lure the strangers into the Dog Park and lock them away there."

"How do you get them to go into the Dog Park?" I asked.

The council was silent for a long time, finally muttering, "Well, their leader is a beagle. So . . ." And then trailing off.

Sam interjected, "We get every person left in Night Vale in front of that Dog Park. If they want nothing, they'll have to go there to create it."

I was thinking about what nothing meant. About beings that don't exist. And who better to fight off a lord of hell than . . .

"Sounds good," I said. "Is there a way out of here that doesn't go through that beagle? I need to visit a friend of mine."

Let's have a look now at traffic.

There's a metal grate about eleven feet off the ground. It's large enough for most human bodies to fit through. There are eight ten-millimeter hexagonal bolts holding it in place. Sitting atop a person's shoulders who's sitting atop another person's shoulders and then using a simple torque wrench, it is not difficult to remove these bolts and pull oneself through into the ductwork.

The duct eventually ends at a similar large grate.

Then there is a twelve-foot drop to the ground behind City Hall, next to a dumpster. A car driven by Mayor Dana Cardinal is there. Then that car drives to Old Woman Josie's house out by the used car lot.

This has been traffic.

"Can I speak to Erika?" I said to Old Woman Josie.

"Which Erika?" she asked.

"All of them. I need to speak with the angels."

Old Woman Josie winced.

A couple miles off, I heard the Angel Acknowledged Siren go off down by the firehouse, but I was certain law enforcement was dealing with bigger problems than a radio host who happened to acknowledge an angel or two.

There are way more than two, though. A bright black light filled Old Woman Josie's living room, illuminating at least a dozen tall winged beings. Dana and I shaded our eyes. My body tingled. I swore I could hear a cello and smell confectioners' sugar. Dana and I explained the sheriff's plan to lure the strangers to the Dog Park.

"How do you lure something that wants nothing?" one of the Erikas asked.

"Technically wanting nothing is actually wanting something," one of the Erikas explained

"We're not having this argument with you again, Erika," another Erika shouted.

"We just need to do something," I said. "If what they want is nothing, then we must make sure that we are always doing something. Can you help us?"

The black light grew painfully bright. I took that as a yes.

Let's have a look now at today's horoscopes.

The stars are silent. They have been absent from the sky for weeks now. They refuse to tell us anything. Perhaps the silence is for our own protection.

This has been horoscopes.

On the drive back to town with Dana.

"I know he tried to kill you," I said carefully. "I know he's on Death Row now for his crimes, but what if . . . What if we made a deal—."

Dana interrupted. "I'm not offering Hiram a deal."

We drove past the dark and empty radio station. I thought about Khoshekh, our station cat, who hovers four feet off the ground in what used to be the men's restroom. All of our restrooms are unisex now, which is great because everyone can visit Khoshekh. He'd been much happier with the extra attention, buzzing and licking visitors with his chest tongues.

But when I had last checked in on him before we lost all power to the radio station, he was gone. His kittens were also gone. No sign of a fight. Just gone. I missed him. I missed the radio station.

All over town, no electricity or gas, barely any drinkable water. I could smell distant smoke. The sky was completely gray even though there was not a single cloud.

Dana said: "I'll talk to Hiram, Cecil. I'll find out if he knows anything about the strangers and if he could be of some help. But I'm not cutting a deal with him."

We pulled up to a mob of about fifty people. In the front was the sheriff, hand in hand with a woman in long yellow robes and a wide, rectangular hat. I recognized the medallion on the front of her chest. She was one of the leaders from the Joyous Congregation of the Smiling God, the church that most of Desert Bluffs and a few Night Vale residents belonged to.

In the crowd I saw John Peters, you know, the farmer? And also John Peter, remember, the pharmacist? I saw Tamika Flynn and her teenage militia. In Tamika's left hand was Sarah Sultan, who is a fist-sized river rock and current president of Night Vale Community College. Around them were many faces I didn't know. Former Desert Bluffs residents. I could see it in their eyes.

Dana and I got out of the car and joined them, a prayer march against a common enemy. How strange humankind is that two cities—Night Vale and Desert Bluffs—could hate each other so much and then hold hands so tightly in mutual hatred of something else.

We marched toward the center of town, chanting prayers. I have never been a believer in the Smiling God, so some of the chants were new to me, but a lot of them were similar to recitations, verses, and prayers common across most religions. Basic stuff like "Please God, Destroy Our Enemies. Amen"; some really long gurgling sounds; and one chant that sounded identical to an old prayer I was taught in Torah school where everyone just shouts "DE-FENSE!" while clapping in rhythm.

Our crowd grew. We saw strangers on the street, not moving, just breathing and watching. We were nearing a thousand, our mob, feeling invincible, united to save our town, a town we all loved and believed in no matter how long each of us had lived here.

Carlos joined, along with my sister, Abby, her husband, Steve; and my young niece, Janice. I was worried for their safety out here, surrounded by the strangers. But I was also worried for their safety at home, hiding from the strangers. I was worried for their safety, always and everywhere.

Our huge crowd stopped near the Dog Park. There were hooded figures in the Dog Park. The gates were open. They are rarely open.

We looked to the strangers. Their numbers had grown as well. An equal motionless mob to our heaving, praying one. Being at the front of the crowd, I could feel the steady breath of the stranger directly in front of me.

They weren't dead. They weren't undead. They were nothing.

I was afraid of dying, of becoming one of them, of existing only in the dark, wet cavern. Frances's voice in my head, *I'm still in the mud. I'm still in the mud.* And also her voice from right in front of me, suddenly at the front of the crowd of strangers, eyes wild as though struggling against the complete stillness of the rest of her body, screaming, "I'm still in the mud. I'm still in the mud."

The crowd of strangers parted—although none of us saw them move—revealing the beagle puppy on his hind legs, his front paws dangling crookedly against his chest.

Huff huff huff.

The breathing wasn't coming from the dog, but from behind me. I turned to see Sheriff Sam, their jaw hanging limp and open. The dog's breath came from their mouth.

Huff huff huff.

"Who's a good boy?" said the voice coming from Sam. "Who's a good boy?"

Huff huff huff.

"Am I the good boy?" said a different voice from right next to me. My brother-in-law, Steve, his eyes locked to mine, confused. "Am I the good boy?" he said.

I cried out "No!" and held him tight. Janice, Abby, and Carlos all put their arms around him too. Trying to hold him in place, keep him from being taken to the cavern. Helping him to resist the pull of a dark and muddy hell, dragging at him from within.

We heard a sound above us. Like wings. Many wings. We looked up and saw all of the Erikas circling above.

"There are angels," said Janice, in awe. No one corrected her.

There was also the sound of a different kind of wing, not angelic. Reptilian.

We saw the five heads of Hiram McDaniels, four of them with prison tracking collars. Fire spewed from Hiram's mouth, and for a moment the gray cloudless sky shone blue. And I finally noticed, in

the heart of all this fear and tempest, how calm the weather was. No, not calm. The weather was. It was—

WEATHER: "The Queer Gospel" by Erin McKeown

Night Vale, we have power once again. We have electricity and water. I'm back on the air, and many of you are back in your homes.

The strangers and the dogs are gone. Defeated, question mark.

Frances, Sam, Steve, those who were taken or who were about to be taken, all humans once again. But here's where we run into the problem of my narrative. Because I don't know what caused it to happen.

Our crowd had chanted and prayed. I'm not a religious person mostly, but I do think we had an impact driving away that Thing summoned from the dark wet caverns of hell. And even if it wasn't the bloodstones or the Joyous Congregation's Smiling God, or any other kind of god, the mere spiritual coming together of so many people may have been enough to rid the town of this hound and his army.

But then, Intern Kareem reported that Khoshekh is back in the station restroom. Khoshekh was badly scratched up, as though he had been in a great battle, and Kareem noted that inside Khoshekh's second row of teeth was a small piece of fur-covered flesh. Kareem thought it was a piece of a dog's ear. Is Khoshekh our hero?

Janice says Tamika Flynn drove away the strangers with her militia of book-loving children. Abby and Steve told Janice she's still too young to join a militia. Tamika is running drills out in the desert and will not comment on what happened.

Old Woman Josie claimed the angels used their powers of heavenly good to push back the brazen evil of the beagle. Who else can destroy a creature of hell other than angels? Maybe that's true, if you believe in angels, which you are not allowed to do.

Melony Pennington, celebrated computer programmer, managed to get the power utilities back on, and claims that, with the help of young prodigy Megan Wallaby, she wrote a deadly computer virus to bring down the strangers. I'm not really an expert on programming, but I feel like you need a computer to catch a computer virus.

What? Oh. Kareem is telling me you don't anymore. Computer viruses are totally airborne. Wow. Technology.

Sheriff Sam and the City Council claimed their plan to lure the strangers to the Dog Park worked perfectly and the strangers were rounded up and locked away.

Sam also added, "Now that the situation is under control, the Dog Park is no longer open." And then they folded an origami sea urchin, elaborate thin spines and everything. "Yeah, no, it's off-limits once again," Sam said.

Michelle and Maureen, over at Dark Owl Records, claimed they were playing a copy of Beyoncé's newest album, the follow-up to Lemonade. An album no one else has heard. According to Michelle, the strangers wanted to hear that album quite badly and this human desire filled in the hollow that the years in the mud had carved in them, turning them back into nonstrangers. Into friends. Michelle and Maureen claim to be the real heroes, or whatever.

I asked Michelle if I could hear the album. She said no because Beyoncé asked her to stop playing it.

"Beyoncé called you?" I asked, astonished that Michelle knew such a famous musician.

"Well, her lawyers called," Michelle said. "They were really angry and also confused and scared because Beyoncé hasn't actually written or recorded the album yet."

Chad, my former intern who summoned the beagle in order to destroy the World Government, says that he thinks the reversal of his summoning worked. He is no hero, he says, but perhaps he is not a villain either.

"He's pretty okay, I guess," Maureen said. "At least I got my internship credit."

And then there was Hiram McDaniels's brave fighting against the strangers. If anything was more powerful than our coming together as a town, it was the brute force of an eighteen-foot-tall dragon with five heads. He fought valiantly for a town he had once threatened, a town who had recently condemned him to death. And we all saw his bravery, and we all knew that he must be pardoned. "Pardon him!" we cried.

He was not pardoned. They locked him back up. He is still scheduled for execution.

So perhaps Hiram was the hero.

But there is one more theory. One more possible story.

Just before coming on the air, I felt a presence behind me. It was the Faceless Old Woman Who Secretly Lives in Your Home.

"We didn't drive them away, Cecil, " she said. "We didn't win. They chose to leave."

I argued that surely it was because we, or someone, forced them.

"They don't need a reason," she said. "They never did. They left and they may return. It won't be for any reason but it could be at any time. They want and need nothing, Cecil. The computer programming and Dog Park and Beyoncé album. It's all noise."

She added, "They left because they decided to leave. And if they return, it will be because they decided to return. And it will be unrelated to anything we do."

Night Vale, we live with the illusion of safety, that we can use caution and care in order to preserve our lives. The strangers came and we don't know why. And then they went, and we don't know why. We are always in danger. It was just that while they were here, we were made aware of the danger. They simply revealed to us that personal control is an illusion. We live and die, and we never get to learn any reasons for that.

In any case, the strangers are gone, and we can go back to living the lie of reason and control once again. It is a very, very comfortable lie.

Stay tuned next for a deep sigh. Deep. Deep. No, deeper than that.

Good night, Night Vale. Good night.

[*after the credits*]

KEVIN: Hi, friend. It's Kevin. So many of my old pals from Desert Bluffs came to live here in the desert otherworld with me. We've built quite a little city with roads and a school and a radio station! I'm back on the air, Cecil! We even built our new little town to look just like our old little town. In fact, we just decided to call this new place Desert Bluffs Too. *Too* as in *also*, not the number two. Although we debated that. But we thought it was too charming. We need to build to that level of charming. Someday we will. Someday we'll be so charming, it will hurt.

PROVERB: You can tell a lot about someone by coming into our office and confessing everything you know about them.

"THE INVESTIGATORS"

PERFORMED MARCH 26, 2015 AT THE KESWICK THEATRE, GLENSIDE, PENNSYLVANIA

Cast

Cecil Baldwin—CECIL PALMER

Meg Bashwiner—DEB

Mark Gagliardi—JOHN PETERS

Jeffrey Cranor—SECRET POLICE SPOKESMAN

Mara Wilson—FACELESS OLD WOMAN

"THE INVESTIGATORS" WAS THE SHOW THAT CEMENTED NIGHT VALE AS a live touring podcast.

The community calendar bit was the piece that we decided to do on *The Late Show* with Stephen Colbert because it was funny, it was self-contained, and we'd done it live so many times. We performed eighty shows of "The Investigators"—approximately sixty-two thousand people saw it live in six different countries—and that was all the rehearsal I needed for my late-night talk show debut. Side note: You never realize just how indie-cult you are until Oprah is in the dressing room right upstairs (and no, you are NOT allowed to go talk to her).

I have been touring professionally since I was twenty-two years old. My first national tour was right out of college, a group called the National Players, the oldest classical touring company in the nation. For nine months we drove a box truck, a van, and a sedan all over the lower forty-eight, playing Shakespeare and Molière in community and university theaters. So the task of taking "The Investigators" on the road for three months sounded like a dream. I think, however, some of the others on the Night Vale crew may have described the experience a bit differently.

The live show of "The Investigators" is over two hours long with anywhere from four to seven guest spots.

I think the LA live show was like two hours and twenty minutes and the only time I got to sit down was for two minutes during the weather. While I was pulling faces onstage, everyone else was in the greenroom, drinking Jim Beam and eating LA guacamole. I wouldn't have it any other way though. Building my performance in "The Investigators" over those eighty plus performances was one of the greatest joys of my career. The moment you walk onstage, all you have to do is trust that you've created a package where each note you hit is solid in voice, in body, in psychology, in emotion, in tone. And by then, you're already on the ride, and there's no stopping, so why not just enjoy yourself!

When people say they hate audience participation, I can only agree with them. Audience participation as we know it is torture, or at best ritualized bullying usually hiding behind a two-drink minimum. What was fun about Night Vale was the way we transformed "audience participation" into something positive and organic. We had the audience interact with each other—a random other third party, who is equally bewildered with the whole thing. By the end of the show, theoretically, if they follow their cues, those audience members take some of the bonhomie that the fans have for Cecil Palmer (or dare I say Cecil Baldwin) and plant it in another member of the audience. It was just a show, but the interactions that they shared with another person were real. Sustained eye contact is a real interaction. Waving hello to someone is a real interaction. And then, those two people will undoubtedly see each other in the lobby, buying a T-shirt or waiting for their parents to pick them up. Maybe they exchange info or look each other up on Twitter or Tumblr. And somehow, what began as an artificial relationship has transferred into a real one. It's magical, creating human connection from nothing but a willingness to be present, an openness to play, and a trust in the folks onstage to take you on the journey.

—Cecil Baldwin

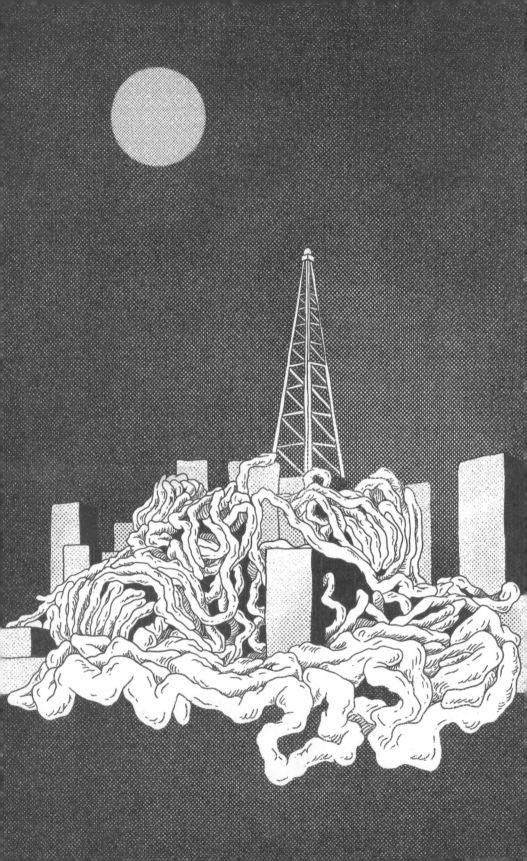

The writing is on the wall. It's not written in English. It's not really even written. Clawed, more like. The claw marks are on the wall.

WELCOME TO NIGHT VALE

Listeners, be warned. There is a murderer in our midst.

Oh, wow, sorry that was megadramatic of me. Let me start off with some pleasantries. Hi. I'm Cecil. Welcome to my show on Night Vale Community Radio. Got some news and stuff coming up later. How are things going with you?

I can't hear you.

I can't hear you.

I really can't hear you because I'm sitting in a radio studio by myself but I hope you were yelling your heads off out there in your homes and offices and cars and witching caves.

Now that the small talk is out of the way, a quick bit of news: Be warned, citizens. There is a murderer in our midst. Last night, at the corner of Sausalito and Somerset, a body was found. Police suspect foul play.

Specifically, they suspect murder, but they don't want to get you all upset, and foul play sounds less alarming, more fun.

A Sheriff's Secret Police spokesperson said, "Murder is just so final, you know. So scary. We like foul play. It's like people were having fun, like a game, but a little rougher. But murder is . . . just so harsh.

"But yeah, anyway, someone died pretty violently from foul play. It's really gross, but don't worry. The first rule of any murder investigation is to immediately clean up the murder scene and make sure it's tidy," the spokesperson said.

As is the usual murder investigation procedure, the Sheriff's Secret Police is ordering every single citizen of Night Vale to gather in the Rec Center for a mandatory night of Murder Mystery Dinner Theatre so they can determine the killer's identity. There will be catering by Big Rico's Pizza, and the Moonlite All-Nite Diner will be providing Invisible Pie for those citizens who do not eat visible food.

More on this soon, but first, a word from our sponsors. Today's sponsor is Dasani. Here on their behalf is, of course, a sentient patch of haze, and her name is Deb. Deb?

DEB: Doncha know it, Cecil. Okay, listeners. I'm here to tell you about Dasani brand water beverage. And I certainly do hope you consider Dasani brand water beverage over all other water beverage opportunities that are available to you.

I know that you humans, insignificant meat-filled wisps that you are, are thinking: What difference could the water beverage opportunity I select possibly make?

And I'm sure you're right. You're very smart, I'm sure. I'm sure that all other water beverage opportunities haven't been poisoned by unknown malicious parties, leaving Dasani brand water beverage the only safe selection. Why would that even happen? That would be illegal, immoral, and great for our sales.

Marketing a particular brand of water beverage is certainly difficult. You know what else is difficult? Death by poison. Hard, slow, and painful. Yes, if all other water beverage opportunities were poisoned, why then, your choice to select Dasani brand water beverage would be very important indeed.

CECIL: Deb. Please tell me the truth. Did you poison our water?

DEB: Oh, Cecil, not to my definitive out loud knowledge. But who even knows?

CECIL: I feel like you know.

DEB: Then maybe just follow that feeling. See where it takes you. Maybe it'll take you to Dasani brand water beverage. Maybe it'll take you to a slow oblivion. The important thing is that nothing you do could possibly affect me. As the good book says, "Human life is just a means to an end."

CECIL: The good book?

DEB: *The Sentient Haze's Guide to World Domination.* It's actually a great book. Dasani brand water beverage: "Can't Live Without Unpoisoned Water."

CECIL: Listeners, I know you're at a dinner theater, but perhaps avoid drinking anything with your food until we have this situation sorted out.

DEB: It'll be fine.

CECIL: Still though. And thank you, Deb.

And now a public service announcement. The Night Vale Psychological Association reminds you to take a few moments each day for relaxing your brain. Never tried meditative exercises? They suggest the following:

First, close your eyes. Breathe. Think about your breaths. In. Out.

Next, picture a beach. Picture gentle waves, and then wet sand, and then dry sand, and then dune grass, flittering in a soft wind, and then a house.

Picture a house. A really big house. Bigger even than that. Square footage I'm thinking at least 3,000. Picture, let's say, a 3,500-square-foot house. Bedroomwise, let's say three, and bathrooms let's go two and a half.

And we're relaxing. And we're breathing.

And we're picturing a 3,500-square-foot Craftsman-style house. With a wraparound porch and porch swing. We are picturing our best selves living our best lives, we are picturing a calm ocean, we are picturing a media room with a back projection screen and reclining movie seats. Let's really relax now, let's feel very calm, and let's put a massage function on those movie seats.

We should now be feeling warmth prickling throughout our bodies, and we allow ourselves to follow that warmth. We're picturing peace. We're picturing love. Love of every kind. We're also picturing a wine cellar. We're picturing a better wine cellar than that. No! We're picturing a modern, humidity-stabilized, temperature-controlled wine cellar. Come on, work with me on this. And peace.

We're picturing peace.

This is really coming together. We're all doing a great job, picturing this house with a strong foundation, like our spiritual foundations, grounded and stable. With a good roof, like our minds, sheltering and waterproof and recently redone by a certified contractor. With a walk-in closet off the master bedroom, like our hearts, finished with recessed lighting and a rotating shoe rack.

Picture the house. Build this house in your mind. Have it overlooking a tropical beach but still close to markets and nightlife. Have you pictured this house?

Great. You can open your eyes now. Thanks everyone. You've just built the Night Vale Psychological Association a luxury beach house in your subconscious. We've already put it up on Airbnb, but we hope to have a few weekends a year to use it ourselves.

Every time you fall asleep you will see strangers gathering in this house, living in your dreams. Keep doing your relaxation exercises, we don't want our dreamworld beach house spoiled by your weird mother issues. Thanks a lot.

This message was brought to you by the Night Vale Psychological Association.

A spokesperson from the Sheriff's Secret Police has just handed me a note explaining I am not required to attend the Murder Mystery Dinner Theatre, as I was here in my booth broadcasting during the time of the murder. But it is mandatory for all other citizens of Night Vale.

After much debate over how to stage such an enormous theatrical endeavor, the Secret Police have settled on a very traditional Murder Mystery Dinner Theatre, in which the audience just stares at each other in suspicious silence for a long time until the mystery sort of solves itself.

And indeed, everyone in the theater was already looking around for a stranger who might be the murderer. Everyone. All of them were looking around for a suspect. They did not look at someone they knew personally or that they came to the show with. Those are people they foolishly trust. No, they sought out the eyes of a complete stranger, and then they made eye contact, and they locked in.

They glowered suspiciously at each other and only each other. "That person could be a murderer," they thought, and then they pointed at the person they were making eye contact with. They pointed at each other and said aloud, "You could be a murderer."

And they were each of them right. That person could be a murderer. Keeping their finger pointed, they narrowed their eyes. They widened their eyes. They crossed their eyes. Then they uncrossed their eyes because it made it hard to see this person they suspected.

They each slowly lowered their pointing fingers. And they each said to the other, "I have my eye on you, suspect," and then they looked away, hearts aglow at a job well-done. They would remember the face of that stranger because they knew it would be important throughout the evening.

We're getting word that there may have been an eyewitness to the murder, which is one of the top three witness types behind foot witness and kidney witness. We have the witness on the phone right now. It is John Peters, you know, the farmer?

JOHN: Yep, that's me.

CECIL: Now John.

JOHN: Yep, that's me.

CECIL: You're saying that you saw the murder take place.

JOHN: Absolutely.

CECIL: Tell us all about it. What did you see?

JOHN: Well, I was out in my fields this morning. I'm a farmer, you know.

CECIL: Oh, I did not know that.

JOHN: Really? I feel like most people . . .

CECIL: Yes, I know you're a farmer.

JOHN: Okay, great. Well, I was out in my fields this morning, growing imaginary corn, and I saw some movement at the edge of my vision. Right in between that point where seeing becomes not seeing. I turned. And I saw, I saw a great silver craft, disk shaped, with portholes at regular intervals.

CECIL: Wait a second.

JOHN: There were beings inside, of astonishing structure, and they were looking out of the windows at me. I felt the hairs on the back of my neck. I felt them with my hand because I had put my hand on the back of my neck in surprise. Those hairs are so soft. You ever just think about those hairs back there, Cecil?

CECIL: Yes. Constantly, but what does this have to do . . .

JOHN: The craft landed, and the beings came out. They were of astonishing structure, and one of them, their leader, said, "Behold. My name is Klangor. We have arrived on your earth from someplace distant. We have much to show you."

CECIL: John. Did you or did you not see a murder?

JOHN: These beings (they were of astonishing structure), they took me into their craft and showed me times and places far and along from this here and ago.

Did you know that the universe is not, in fact, a single, everexpanding four-dimensional sphere of light and matter? No, Cecil, the universe, I have learned, is merely a particle composed entirely of itself and comprising a greater version of itself, a recursive function of its own body, repeated like identical cells forming the shape of that which each cell physically expresses. I think of Benoit Mandelbrot's famous set of equations, each iteration a repeated pattern, psychedelic and vast. Our universe is not made of matter, nor space, nor time, Cecil. it is made of possibilities.

CECIL: So you saw nothing useful or interesting at all.

JOHN: And then the beings placed me, childlike, back down upon my earth, and their craft sprang up into the air, leaving a strange imaginary shape in my imaginary cornfield. I held up my hand in farewell, and through the windows, I could see them hold up . . . well whatever it was at the end of their limbs . . . they were of

astonishing structure, and then they were gone. I do not believe I
will ever be the same again. I do not believe I am the same now.

CECIL: Oh, John. I should have known you were a farmer, not a witness. This is why witnessing should be left to the professionals. Paid
witnesses who will witness whatever crime you want for a nominal
fee. That is how witnessing should be done, not by amateur citizens
who might see incorrect things or repeat forbidden truths.

JOHN: I just really wanted to tell that story. Sorry I couldn't be of
any help with the murder. Ever since this morning, I've been too
busy weeping in awe and transcendent grief to witness anything
at all.

CECIL: It's okay, John, but next time please only call if you have
something interesting to tell us. Good-bye, John.

JOHN: Thanks, Cecil.

CECIL: Let's have a look now at the community calendar:

Wednesday evening, Night Vale's most popular restaurant,
Tourniquet, will be hosting a special Chef's Table Dinner. This exclusive event costs five hundred dollars, and is limited to only thir-
teen attendees. Diners will enjoy a special tasting menu personally
curated and prepared by chef LeSean Mason. The five-course menu
will center around quail.

Chef Mason rediscovered the joy of quail meat and would like
to share this joy with Night Vale. Sous-chef Earl Harlan will recite
instructions for gutting and cleaning, while each diner will be given
a live quail and a brick.

The Chef's Table Dinner begins at 7:30 P.M., at which time all
diners from last year's event will finally be released from the kitchen,
back to their old lives.

This Thursday night, the Night Vale Tourism Board will be holding an opening night party to celebrate the new artwork on display
at the Night Vale Visitors Center along Radon Canyon.

The theme of this gallery collection is "PAIN: Internal, External, and Beyond!" and will feature several works by local artists, expressing a wide array of popular art techniques, from post-modern monochromatics to outdoor rock sculptures, and even some interactive exhibits like "PUT YOUR FOOT IN HERE" and "HURTS DON'T IT?" and "STOP HITTING YOURSELF! STOP HITTING YOURSELF! WHY DO YOU KEEP HITTING YOURSELF?"

Say, did you know that it is completely possible for the human body to survive unprotected in space for several seconds? It's true. And this information will be superuseful for you this Thursday evening around 8:00 P.M.

Friday at noon, the eastbound lanes of Route 800 will be closed between exits 17 and 19. All traffic will be rerouted onto side streets. Highway crews will be posting street signs with ALL ROADS NO-WHERE and EVERY PATH DEATH and also some frowny faces to help you with your morning commute.

Saturday afternoon, the Night Vale PTA is hosting its Third Annual Youth Arts Fair in the front parking lot of Night Vale Elementary School. The fair focuses on creativity, fun, and personal expression for kids. But the PTA is warning all attendees that there will be clowns at the fair. Clown Local 189 requires the hire of at least two dozen union members, but for the sake of easily-frightened children, these clowns will not be allowed into the actual fair. They will simply stand inside the elementary school, watching through the darkened windows. The clowns will be just barely discernable in the shadows, and thus not at all a distraction for the children who will only be able to see faint shadows of curly wigs and round noses and sharp yellow teeth from behind the breath-frosted glass of the rooms the children must sit in day after day. Also, just so the kids feel totally safe, Slenderman will be there. Principal Angela Slenderman will stand in the back of the fair silently watching the children.

Sunday afternoon, the Night Vale Community Players will be hosting auditions for their next show, which is called *Oklahoma!* It's an old musical about people from a fictional U.S. state that must fight off an attack from ballet-dancing farmers that ride a herd of elephants with corn husks for eyes. The controversial musical has been lauded and derided by theater critics for its graphic and gory death scenes.

Auditions are from 2:00 P.M. to 2:05 P.M. A postcard announcing the exact location of the auditions will be sent the day before, so make sure you wait silently in the shrubbery for the mail carrier.

Tuesday is a lie. Calendars are propaganda. Days and times are just artificial walls built to divide us.

An update from the Rec Center . . . Everyone in town is still participating in the Murder Mystery Dinner Theatre, and the evening is certainly providing a lot of theater, dinner, mystery, and, unfortunately, murder.

It seems that whoever is the culprit in this case is working to expand the number of cases that they are a culprit in. They have taken advantage of the fact that all citizens are required to be at this dinner theater production, and are slinking about in the shadows, picking people off one by one.

Janice Rio, from down the street, said that Bernie Simpson had been right next to her, and then the next thing she knew. Bam. Bernie Simpson was right next to her. Then, after telling me that, Janice paused for a long time, as though expecting a reaction, and then she said, "Oh, sorry, I forgot to say that Bernie was a ghost the second time. That's an important part. Yeah, he was a ghost. He winked and said, 'Hey, Janice. Looks like I've been murdered.' He laughed and laughed and said, 'They got me. I'm dead now.' He just wouldn't stop laughing. It was very off-putting and I had to switch seats," Janice said.

Who is this fiend and where will they strike next? It could be anyone. It could be anywhere.

It is like that wonderful children's book classic, in which the reader is playfully warned again and again that there is a monster at the end of the book, but of course when the reader gets to the end it turns out that there is indeed a monster at the end of the book, just as they were warned, and many of our children are eaten after reading it. What a beautiful book.

Citizens, please be safe. Please. I'd be very upset if you weren't safe, so just . . . please.

In light of the current emergency, the Sheriff's Secret Police has sent a spokesperson to the radio station to provide information and answer any questions that might be raised about the current "dangerous murderer on the loose in the room you're all in" situation.

The spokesperson has tunneled their way into my booth using their long digging claws and has just pushed their soft wet snout out from the soil toward the microphone, so let's say hello to the secret spokesperson.

SPOKESPERSON: [*seeming unprepared to speak*] Ah! Hello. Yes. What?

CECIL: You are here to speak to us about this dangerous situation.

SPOKESPERSON: Sure, sure. What? Right. Citizens, we are completely in charge, nothing to fear.

CECIL: That's great news . . .

SPOKESPERSON: [*interrupting*] Ah! Sorry, just thought of something frightening.

CECIL: That's quite all right.

SPOKESPERSON: Oh god!

CECIL: Did you just . . .

SPOKESPERSON: No sorry, I remembered how I thought of something frightening. Now I'm thinking of remembering it. Truly fear devours. Anyway, the investigation is moving forward. We've got our best officers on it. And all the rest of the officers who aren't on it are busy worrying that they apparently aren't the best officers. Are they the worst? This will eat away at them at night. They will toss and turn. So everything is under control. I wouldn't worry. I'm great at not worrying. You all might worry though. I guess it depends on how well you handle the stress of being in great danger.

CECIL: How close are the Secret Police to identifying a major suspect?

SPOKESPERSON: Oh man. Woo. Well that's entitlement if I ever heard it.

CECIL: Entitlement?

SPOKESPERSON: We're doing everything we can to stop this murderer, like having a dinner theater and announcing that there is a murderer and running through neighborhoods crying, "We're done for! We're all done for!" And now you're all like, "Name a suspect. Make an arrest. Keep us safe." You're all fine. Probably. Listen, you're either already dead or probably you're safe for this exact moment.

CECIL: It doesn't sound like we're safe.

SPOKESPERSON: I understand your concern, Cecil.

[*beat*]

CECIL: And . . .

SPOKESPERSON: I dunno. I understand it. It seems valid. Good concern. I'm going to go back to the Secret Police hover office in the clouds until it gets less dangerous around here.

CECIL: You're just going to hide.

SPOKESPERSON: [*nodding*] No.

CECIL: You just nodded though.

SPOKESPERSON: [*nods*] Doesn't sound like something I'd do. All right citizens, we're out of here. Hope it all works out okay. Just write any messages you have for us on paper planes, and throw them at that one low hanging cloud that has windows and a ladder going up to it, and someone from the Secret Police will come to your aid as soon as there are no murderers around and it is safe to do so.

CECIL: Hey, wait . . .

SPOKESPERSON: No need to thank me, Cecil. But obviously I would appreciate it. It's always nice to be thanked.

CECIL: I'm not going to thank you.

SPOKESPERSON: I'll just give you like a moment more in case you change your mind. A thank-you would be nice. Okay, no, I get it, no need to thank me if you're a jerk. Good-bye.

CECIL: Sensing that they would not be safe relying on the protection of others, the citizens in the Rec Center were getting nervous. They were shifting. Some of them were shifty. One of them was a murderer but we don't know which one.

And so the citizens began to act in their own protection. They each looked back to the same stranger they had suspected before, each of them looking at the same person, except for those who had refused to look at someone before and so now found themselves partnerless. Those people took this opportunity to jump on board by looking around until they found a similarly reluctant stranger, and then those people became paired strangers and everyone had a stranger and everyone was looking at that stranger. Great.

And these two strangers were pointing at each other again. And, in their deepest, coolest voice, they said, "I don't trust you." They tried, successfully or not, to raise one eyebrow. And then they said, "But we're in danger, kid." If they were going to solve this, they would need to work together. They would need to solve this as partners. But they didn't have to trust or like each other. No way.

In fact one of them was already holding up a fist and the other one was pointing a finger at the ceiling, and immediately they did not know which of them should be doing which since the description was not clear on that issue. And just as they wordlessly had settled that, it turned out that one of them was shaking their head while the other was nodding and again there was confusion between them about who was doing which. See how much their personalities clashed. See how uneasy their working relationship. What a comically odd pairing, what an unexpected duo. They were a classic trope, those two.

But there was a murder to solve, and so they would reluctantly partner up all the same. Then they looked away from each other once again. Watch out murderer, these two are on the case.

Also on the case are some middle schoolers as is standard these days when Night Vale is in danger. Yes, a brave group of child vigilantes and avid readers, led by Tamika Flynn, a courageous fourteen-year-old, and one of the few children to face down a librarian during the Summer Reading Program and survive.

Tamika's army donned capes and bulletproof vests made from copies of Thomas Pynchon's *Against the Day*, keeping them safe from any murderer. And keeping any murderer very unsafe from them.

They did not trust the Murder Mystery Dinner Theatre to solve this case. "We must be ever vigilant, Night Vale," Tamika shouted from atop the ancient Pepsi machine at the Rec Center. "This murderer will keep on murdering until there isn't anyone left to murder and then they won't be a murderer anymore. Actually, that would solve the problem. Huh," Tamika considered aloud but then raised her fist anyway to bloodthirsty shouts from her followers.

I have to agree with Tamika. I'm a bit disappointed that the Sheriff's Secret Police is staging a traditional "audience members staring at each other suspiciously and then deciding to solve the case on their own" stuff that we all know from every Murder Mystery Dinner Theatre we've ever been to. It'd be nice if they were putting on one of those great mystery tales from the masters of the craft, full of intrigue and plot twists and long lost twin brothers and fake mustaches, like *The Fault in Our Stars* or *The Time Traveler's Wife* or James Joyce's classic spy caper *Araby*.

I mean, I just love the helicopter chase at the end of *The Time*

Traveler's Wife. And that awesome line she says right before she arrests the main bad guy, "This one's for my husband. He's a time traveler." It's classic!

In any case, Tamika concluded her rallying speech. "What chance does one murderer stand against the power of books," she cried out to her adoring, vengeance-minded supporters. "Heavy books," she shouted. "Heavy, heavy books dropped on their head. I'm going to drop so many books on this criminal's head as soon as we catch them," she added.

"Dump them right on there. Bam. Bunch of books," and the crowd cheered mightily.

So while the Secret Police get bogged down in the bureaucracy of standard police procedure, this highly motivated and heavily armed group of teenagers are crushing evil under complete hardback editions of all seven volumes of Marcel Proust's monumental novel *Ramona Quimby, Age 8.*

Truly the American Justice System is the greatest in the world.

Oh dear, listeners. We're getting word that there has been a nearly fatal incident back at the Rec Center. And many suspect that this was no mere accident. The fifteen-gallon tub full of old socket wrenches that was balanced precariously atop a few two-by-six planks next to the Rec Center basketball courts fell over, nearly crushing the pair of strangers who recently came begrudgingly together to help solve a terrible murder.

The two strangers had been getting in each other's way, challenging each other's authority. Thinking things like, "You are getting in my way, buddy" and "Nuh-uh. You are," and displaying their hurt feelings using the shapes of their mouths, worried that at any moment—in fact, in just a few moments—they might have to look the other in the eye and say words out loud again.

And all along, above them, the tub full of wrenches teetered. Eye contact can be uncomfortable, yes, but way less uncomfortable than the weight of heavy metal objects falling upon thin human skulls. The tub teetered. The narrow planks beneath it groaned. Groaned, and then gave. A snap. The strangers winced, both of them. Because the socket wrenches began their fall, a heavy scattering toward the pair's unprotected heads.

The partners stopped wincing, and they looked at each other and simultaneously shouted, "DUCK!" And they were right. A duck had flown in through a nearby window and knocked the tub of wrenches harmlessly out of the way.

They nodded while smiling. They said, "You have duck telepathy too?" Then they laughed together. It was a completely natural, unforced laugh. A long, healthy, true laugh. And then they turned away from each other, back to the job of solving crimes. But each of them thought, "I'm starting to have a begrudging respect for your skills, kid."

Sadly, that tub full of wrenches had been teetering twelve feet off the ground on those thin pine boards since the Rec Center was built five years ago, so it's a real shame to lose this important architectural feature of a historic building.

CECIL: Listeners, I can see a slight movement in my periphery. I can feel a gentle, chilly touch along my neck. Also, my coffee mug has moved from where it was. Just a moment ago my mug was next to my left hand, and now it is upside down, on my right side, and crawling away on spiny white legs.

FACELESS OLD WOMAN: Hello, Cecil. It's me. It's the Faceless Old Woman Who Secretly Lives in Your Home.

CECIL: I thought that was you. You know, it's really hard having these conversations when I can't ever quite see you.

FOW: Cecil, there's a murderer on the loose, and everyone's going to die.

CECIL: I doubt the murderer is going to kill everyone.

FOW: Oh, no. Sorry for the confusion. Those were two separate thoughts. One, there's a murderer on the loose. Period. End of thought. Next, everyone's going to die. End of second thought.

CECIL: Oh, that's a relief. Hey, so you secretly live in every person's home? Right, Faceless Old Woman? You must know who the murderer is!

FOW: Oh, I absolutely know who the murderer is.

CECIL: Great! You can help us track down and find this criminal.

FOW: Sure, I'll tell you what I know. The murderer has eaten hundreds of flies in their sleep. The murderer has several shirts with buttons, but I have removed some of those buttons with an old knife I found in Pamela Winchell's mailbox. The murderer sometimes stares at birds. Sometimes the birds stare back. Bird-watching goes both ways. Did you know birds talk? Not through something so manipulative and corroded by history as words and sentences, but though the clear, clean language of hunger and horror and boredom and rote reproductive desires. A chattering of starlings told me once, and I quote, "Tree." Then they said, "We're in a tree." They repeated that over and over, and it was the most interesting story I had ever heard.

CECIL: Do the birds know who the murderer is?

FOW: I was in Tristan Cortez's house the other night, and he couldn't find his remote. He just kept shouting, "STOP IT, YOU'RE THE WORST," at his television.

CECIL: Faceless Old Woman, it would be superhelpful if we could learn—

FOW: And I started to feel sad for him because it was that *Property Brothers* episode where they keep taking out walls while lecturing the home buyers on the importance of an open floor concept. They remove every single interior wall, and then the outer walls of the home, and then the surrounding trees and vehicles and other homes and adjacent buildings until everything is gone and all is void. And the closing credits of the episode are just jumbles of letters drifting aimlessly on screen to the whispers of "open floor concept, open floor concept."

CECIL: But—

FOW: They really jumped the shark with that episode. So out of pity, I revealed to Tristan where I hid his remote.

CECIL: Faceless Old Woman—

FOW: It was just behind his right eye. It took him a while to get it out but he finally did it because I gave him Pamela's old knife. And now his remote is all sticky, and also he has to get a new rug and couch.

CECIL: So Tristan is the murderer? I'm confused.

FOW: We're all murderers, Cecil. Where do you think meat comes from?

CECIL: Well, meat comes—

FOW: It sure doesn't come from animals.

[*pause*]

CECIL: Wait. Where does our meat come from?

FOW: I didn't finish my story. In conclusion, I know who the murderer is. Everything will be fine. I'll keep a close watch on the situation. I won't stop anything from happening, but I will watch it happen closely.

CECIL: Faceless Old Wom—— And she's gone.

An update on last week's power outages. The Night Vale Electric Utility announced today that there may be more power outages in coming weeks, this time due to sadness.

"We've been sad this week," said the utility company. They continued, "Not for any reason. Sometimes we get sad. Why do we need a reason? Last week we were feeling vengeful, so thus power outages. This week, we're sad, and we're going to continue expressing ourselves through the medium of power outages."

Power outages, of course, were certified by the Supreme Court as a protected form of free speech in the 1973 case of Hayworth

Electrical Company versus the Hayworth Hospital. The court stated
that reasonable causes for a power outage include: celebration of a
special someone's birthday; expression of undirected anger at an
intransigent political system; and periods of just feeling sad for no
reason.

The Night Vale Electric Utility also reminds you that power outages are no excuse not to pay your electric bill.

Electricity, after all, is a privilege, not a right. Failure to pay electric bills may result in localized lighting storms, shrouded figures
standing silently in the background of familiar TV shows, and gout.

The Murder Mystery Dinner Theatre is still in full swing, but
frankly, give or take a falling tub of socket wrenches, there seems
to be not much of a murder mystery left to solve. The murderer
hasn't murdered anyone in a while. I mean, sure, a bunch of murders
happened today, but those were several minutes ago, maybe even
a whole hour, and it just feels like, I don't know, why go digging
through old dirt?

Plus I'm not sure we could even charge anyone with those
crimes. I mean the Statue of Limitations . . . you know, that statue
of our own limitations we carved last year, et cetera. Et cetera. It just
feels like we might be done here.

Sorry to disappoint anyone who was looking for the whole mystery side of things to be res—— What was that?

I heard a noise. I heard a noise beyond my own voice and the
small nest of owls kept in the corner like in any normal radio studio.
But there shouldn't be anyone here. Everyone has to be at the Rec
Center. It's the law. No one breaks the law. No one except . . . oh
no . . . lawbreakers.

Listeners, I think the murderer might be in the studio with me.
They have taken advantage of the fact that all citizens are at the Rec
Center to creep over to the radio station, where I am all alone.

I see movement in the dim of the control booth. Hello? Are you here to feed the owls? No answer. Carlos? Could that be you? Nothing. Just my breath in and out.

Even as all of you are hearing my voice right now, I am alone. Or worse, I am not.

Is that a footstep behind me? Yes. There is a footstep behind me and another and another. It is a person walking toward me. I dare not turn my head. I cannot move. The murderer is here for me. A shadow across my desk. The shadow reaches for me. The murderer is here, and I am narrating my own demise. There is only one thing to do. I must act quickly. I must take you to the weather.

WEATHER: "Maker of My Sorrow" by Eliza Rickman

Hello, Night Vale. It is a relief to say those words aloud, alive, to you once again.

Just after introducing the weather, I felt movement. I heard footsteps. I saw my life flash before my eyes and its imminent ending made them water.

And then, the murderer attacked. I tried to scream, but managed only faint gargles to no one, except one person. The person least likely to provide me aid.

Fortunately, I had the copy of Lois Lowry's novel *The Giver*, which Tamika Flynn had loaned to me recently. It was the limited edition that comes without cover or pages or words and is made entirely of wood and metal and is in the shape of a hammer. It's a hammer. Tamika loaned me a hammer earlier.

Unfortunately, the hammer was just out of my reach. I stretched out a hand, struggling, heaving, grasping for that classic of contemporary children's fiction so I could crack the head of my attacker.

And that is when I heard a noise. I thought it was my death rattle, or perhaps my death chime, or the even rarer death trombone. But it was a shout. Two shouts. Two people.

I felt warmth. I felt air gasp into my chest. I felt the hands upon me loosen. And I saw the two people who had saved me, and then they brought me here to the Rec Center. Here now with you.

Not just all of you. Specifically you.

[*points*]

You, the murderer. Yes, you're the murderer, stand up.

Everyone in the crowd, all of you citizens, gasped and pointed at the murderer. The crowd all shook their heads, not in anger, but disappointment.

And I asked the murderer, "Why?"

And the murderer said an answer . . . but their answer was ultimately meaningless against the gravity of their actions, and anyway I talked over it.

We all knew that the murderer must be punished the way all murderers are punished in Night Vale. The punishment was coming. Here it came. The crowd, oh I couldn't watch, the punishment was so severe, the crowd said to the murderer, in unison, "Please do not ever murder again."

And the murderer shrugged their shoulders and said, "Sure."

And they applauded the former criminal for reforming their evil ways. They wildly applauded this newly formed good citizen. And the new nonmurderer sat back down happy to know that everything was okay. And the rest of Night Vale let the tension relax from their shoulders, secure in the knowledge that this person would definitely never murder again.

But of course, I had not forgotten the two strangers, those two heroes, that odd couple, that unlikely duo. Those two that had saved my life at the radio station. They knew they had overcome their distrustful start, their discordant partnership, and had learned to lean on each other.

While all of Night Vale sat huddled in the Rec Center, shivering and hiding and dreading murderers and actors and live theater, these two put their seemingly incompatible minds to work.

One of them had noticed the murders had stopped and realized that the murderer had left to find others to murder. But who was left to murder in town? The other one realized it must be Cecil. For Cecil was by himself at the radio station. He alone was alone. And they both, without even having to exchange a word, with only a knowing glance, rushed to the radio station and saved my life.

These two—once strangers, now not—looked at each other one last time. The case was solved. The danger was over. No one else would die this day. Or if they did, it would be because their body simply stopped, just had an error and toppled over, not because of something as mundane as murder.

I want to reemphasize here that the strangers were looking at each other, unwavering in their eye contact. They had been through so much, and had seen each other through all of it. What luck they had in picking a counterpart so competent and trustworthy, so completely not a murderer. They winked at each other. Big winks. Or maybe they didn't. Maybe, for just one moment, they didn't follow any instructions at all, and they just looked at each other as one human being looks at another, just themselves, with whatever face they had, with whatever feelings, with whatever moment is this moment, no expectations. Just their honest selves, for better or worse.

And then they smiled and gave a thumbs up. Bigger smiles. Bigger. More teeth. An unnatural amount of teeth. They looked back at the stage, still smiling.

Because these two, you two, had made it. They had done it. These ex-strangers. These friends. These great, these true, these investigators. You.

As Shakespeare's famous detective character Veronica Mars once said, "All the world's a stage, and all the men and women are frightened people blackmailed into acting upon it."

The evening turns to night. Soon all of the citizens of Night Vale will disperse back to their homes and hovels and hideaways and witching caves. But for this one evening we all came together. And what are human beings except a coming together? What are we for except to lean into each other? To balance precariously against those around us, a delicate but provocative sculpture.

The Night Vale Murder Mystery Dinner Theatre is over, sure. But what happened within it will always have happened. We lived together, this night, and we always will have.

Harm can come from anything or anyone at any moment, whether a stranger or a loved one or one of those intersections that has poisonous snakes instead of traffic lights. But still we reach out the hand. Still we allow our eyes to meet. Still we hope for the best and try to be the best in return. Because if not, then what else. Because if not, then nothing. A human life is just this. A moment of eye contact in a crowd.

Stay tuned next for tomorrow, by any means necessary.

Good night to every listener here.

And good night, Night Vale. Good night.

ABOUT THE AUTHORS

JOSEPH FINK created the *Welcome to Night Vale* and *Alice Isn't Dead* podcasts. He lives with his wife in New York.

JEFFREY CRANOR cowrites the *Welcome to Night Vale* and *Within the Wires* podcasts. He also cocreates theater and dance pieces with choreographer/wife Jillian Sweeney. They live in New York.

ABOUT THE CONTRIBUTORS

CECIL BALDWIN is the narrator of the hit podcast *Welcome to Night Vale*. He is an alumnus of the New York Neo-Futurists, performing in their late-night show *Too Much Light Makes the Baby Go Blind*, as well as Drama Desk–nominated *The Complete and Condensed Stage Directions of Eugene O'Neill, Vol. 2*. Cecil has performed at the Shakespeare Theatre DC, Studio Theatre (including the world premiere production of Neil Labute's *Autobahn*), the Kennedy Center, the National Players, LaMaMa E.T.C., Emerging Artists Theatre, and the Upright Citizens Brigade. Film/TV credits include Braden in *The Outs* (Vimeo), the voice of Tad Strange in *Gravity Falls* (Disney XD), The Fool in *Lear* (with Paul Sorvino), and *Billie Joe Bob*. Cecil has been featured on podcasts such as *Ask Me Another* (NPR), *Selected Shorts* (PRI), *Shipwreck*, *Big Data*, and *Our Fair City*.

KEVIN R. FREE is a multidisciplinary artist whose work as an actor, writer, director, and producer has been showcased and developed in many places, including *The Moth Radio Hour*, Project Y Theater, Flux Theater Ensemble, the Queerly Festival (of which he is now the curator), and the Fire This Time Festival, where he served as producing

artistic director, winning an Obie for his work in 2015. Recent direct-
ing credits include *Lady Day at Emerson's Bar & Grill* and *The Last
Five Years* (both at Portland Stage) and *Topdog/Underdog* (University
of Arkansas). New York City directing includes the Fire This Time Season 10 World Premiere 10-minute Play Festival; Okello Kelo Sam's
Forged in Fire; Renita L. Martin's *Blue Fire in the Water* (Fresh Fruit
Festival); *The First Time, Standing Up: Bathroom Talk and Other Stuff
We Learn from Dad*, and *Poor Posturing,* all by Tracey Conyer Lee;
Michelle T. Johnson's *Wiccans in the 'Hood*; and *Legislative Acts,* a
sketch comedy show performed by New York City legislators. His full-
length plays include *Night of the Living N-Word!!* (Overall Excellence
in Playwriting, FringeNYC 2016); *A Raisin in the Salad: Black Plays
for White People* (New Black Fest Fellowship 2012; Eugene O'Neill
Semi-Finalist 2013); *Face Value* (Henry Street Settlement Playwrights'
Project Grant, 2000); and *The Crisis of the Negro Intellectual, or Triple
Consciousness.* His webseries, "Gemma & The Bear!," was an Official
Selection of the New York Television Festival in 2016; and his latest
webseries, "Beckys through History," received a creative engagement
grant from Lower Manhattan Cultural Center in 2018 (more at www
.MyCarl.org). He has worked as an actor across the United States and
internationally, most recently appearing in New York City as Michael
Curtiz in Reid and Sara Farrington's Drama Desk–nominated *Cas-
blancaBox* (HERE)—and as the Narrator of Lisa Clair's *The Making of
King Kong* (Target Margin Theater). He is an accomplished voice actor
as well as having recorded more than three hundred audiobooks, and
is the voice of Kevin from Desert Bluffs on *Welcome to Night Vale.*
Twitter: @kevinrfree; www.kevinrfree.com.

MARK GAGLIARDI is an actor and podcaster. He is best known for his
narrations on the Comedy Central series *Drunk History* and for the
long-running stage show and podcast *The Thrilling Adventure Hour.*
He grew up in Tennessee, trained at the Theatre School in Chicago,

moved to Los Angeles, worked at theme parks, and currently performs on stages and televisions.

JESSICA HAYWORTH is an illustrator and fine artist. She has produced a variety of illustrated works for the *Welcome to Night Vale* podcast since 2013, including posters for the touring live show. Her other works include the graphic novels *Monster* and *I Will Kill You with My Bare Hands*, as well as various solo and group exhibitions. She received her MFA from Cranbrook Academy of Art and lives and works in Detroit.

MAUREEN JOHNSON is the *New York Times* and *USA Today* bestselling author of many YA novels, including *13 Little Blue Envelopes*, *Suite Scarlett*, the Shades of London series, and *Truly Devious*. She has also done collaborative works, such as *Let It Snow* (with John Green and Lauren Myracle) and *The Bane Chronicles*, *Tales from the Shadowhunter Academy*, and *Ghosts of the Shadow Market* (with Cassandra Clare), and *How I Resist*, a collection to benefit the ACLU. Maureen lives in New York, and online on Twitter (or at www.maureen johnsonbooks.com).

KATE JONES is a writer, performer, and wedding officiant from Howell, New Jersey. She is an alum of the New York Neo-Futurists and Degenerate Fox (UK). She plays Michelle Nguyen on *Welcome to Night Vale* and currently lives in Switzerland, where she can often be found performing stand-up comedy, whether or not there is an audience. www.katekatekate.com or @QTPiK8.

ZACK PARSONS is a Chicago-based humorist and author of nonfiction (*My Tank is Fight!*) and fiction (*Liminal States*). In addition to *Welcome to Night Vale*, he has worked with Joseph Fink on the website Something Awful and can also be found writing for his own site, The Bad Guys Win (thebadguyswin.com). You can call him a weird idiot on Twitter at @sexyfacts4u.

JONNY SUN is the author and illustrator of *everyone's a aliebn when ur a aliebn too* (HarperPerennial, 2017) and the *New York Times* bestselling illustrator of *Gmorning, Gnight!* by Lin-Manuel Miranda (Penguin Random House, 2018). He is currently a writer for the Netflix Original Series *BoJack Horseman*, and is writing the animated feature *Paper Lanterns*, based on an original idea of his, for 20th Century Fox and Chernin Productions. Tweeting as @jonnysun, he was named one of *Time* magazine's 25 Most Influential People on the Internet of 2017. As a doctoral candidate at MIT, an affiliate at the Berkman Klein Center for Internet and Society at Harvard, and a creative researcher at the Harvard metaLAB, he studies social media, virtual place, and online community. As a playwright, Jonathan's work has been performed at the Yale School of Drama, Factory Theater in Toronto, Hart House Theater, and Theater Lab in Toronto. As an artist and illustrator, his work has been exhibited at MIT, the Yale School of Architecture, New Haven ArtSpace, and the University of Toronto. He previously studied as an architect (M.Arch., Yale) and engineer (B.A.Sc., University of Toronto). He is the creator of @tinycarebot and the cocreator of the MIT Humor Series. His comedic work has appeared in *Time*, *BuzzFeed*, *Playboy*, *GQ*, and *McSweeney's*. Recently, he was profiled on NPR and in the *New York Times*, and was named to the Forbes 30 Under 30 Class of 2019.

ACKNOWLEDGMENTS

THANKS TO THE CAST AND CREW OF *WELCOME TO NIGHT VALE*: MEG Bashwiner, Jon Bernstein, Desiree Burch, Nathalie Candel, Adam Cecil, Aliee Chan, Dessa Darling, Felicia Day, Emma Frankland, Kevin R. Free, Mark Gagliardi, Glen David Gold, Angelique Grandone, Marc Evan Jackson, Maureen Johnson, Kate Jones, Ashley Lierman, Erica Livingston, Christopher Loar, Hal Lublin, Dylan Marron, Jasika Nicole, Lauren O'Niell, Zack Parsons, Flor De Liz Perez, Teresa Piscioneri, Jackson Publick, Molly Quinn, Em Reaves, Retta, Symphony Sanders, Annie Savage, Lauren Sharpe, James Urbaniak, Bettina Warshaw, Wil Wheaton, Brie Williams, Mara Wilson, and, of course, the voice of *Night Vale* himself, Cecil Baldwin.

Also and always: Jillian Sweeney; Kathy and Ron Fink; Ellen Flood; Leann Sweeney; Jack and Lydia Bashwiner; the Pows; the Zambaranos; Rob Wilson; Kate Leth; Jessica Hayworth; Holly and Jeffrey Rowland; Andrew Morgan; Eleanor McGuinness; Hank Green; John Green; Griffin, Travis, and Justin McElroy; Cory Doctorow; John Darnielle; Aby Wolf; Jason Webley; Danny Schmidt; Carrie Elkin; Eliza Rickman; Mary Epworth; Will Twynham; Erin McKeown; Mal Blum; the New York Neo-Futurists; Janina Matthewson; Christy Gressman; Adam Cecil; Julian Koster; Gennifer Hutchison; Kassie Evashevski; Chris Parnell; Amy Suh; the Booksmith in San Francisco; and, of course, the delightful *Night Vale* fans.

Our agent, Jodi Reamer; our editor, Amy Baker; and all the good people at Harper Perennial.

BOOKS BY JOSEPH FINK & JEFFREY CRANOR

MOSTLY VOID, PARTIALLY STARS
WELCOME TO NIGHT VALE EPISODES, VOLUME 1

Mostly Void, Partially Stars introduces us to Night Vale, a town in the American Southwest where every conspiracy theory is true, and to the strange but friendly people who live there.

THE GREAT GLOWING COILS OF THE UNIVERSE
WELCOME TO NIGHT VALE EPISODES, VOLUME 2

In *The Great Glowing Coils of the Universe* we witness a totalitarian takeover of Night Vale that threatens to forever change the town and everyone living in it.

WELCOME TO NIGHT VALE
A NOVEL

"The book is charming and absurd—think *This American Life* meets *Alice in Wonderland*."
—*Washington Post*

From the creators of the wildly popular *Welcome to Night Vale* podcast comes an imaginative mystery of appearances and disappearances that is also a poignant look at the ways in which we all struggle to find ourselves...no matter where we live.

IT DEVOURS!
A NOVEL

"A confident supernatural comedy from writers who can turn from laughter to tears on a dime." — *Kirkus Reviews*

From the authors of the *New York Times* bestselling novel *Welcome to Night Vale* and the creators of the #1 international podcast of the same name, comes a mystery exploring the intersections of faith and science, the growing relationship between two young people who want desperately to trust each other, and the terrifying, toothy power of the Smiling God.

ALICE ISN'T DEAD
A NOVEL

"*Alice Isn't Dead* remains an intriguing complement, imbued with newfound soul—and romance. Alice has always known suspense, but as a novel it finds true love."
—*Entertainment Weekly*

From the *New York Times* bestselling co-author of *It Devours!* and *Welcome to Night Vale* comes a fast-paced thriller about a truck driver searching across America for the wife she had long assumed to be dead.